"... calls to mind the forensic mysteries of Aaron Elkins and Patricia Cornwell ... with her own brand of spice as a pert and brainy scholar in the forensic analysis of bones"

—*Chicago Sun Times*

"... combines smart people, fun people, and dangerous people in a novel hard to put down."

—*Dallas Morning News*

"... ingenious plot, intriguing character, and a mystery as well hidden as rubies on a beach."

—*Booklist*

"... uses archaeology as a general setting that promises well for future books."

—*Mystery Review*

"What Lindsay is to forensic anthropology, Kay Scarpetta is to forensic pathology with one significant difference. Lindsay is a warmer character than Ms. Cornwell's famous protagonist."

—Harriet Klausner, *Internet Reviews*

"… an excellent murder mystery."

—Midwest Book Review

"… as chock-full of engrossing anthropological detail as a newly discovered burial mound."

—The Tennessean

"… intelligent, riveting and dynamic plots"

—Romantic Times

"Chamberlain is a fascinating, offbeat, and always beievable sleuth; settings and supporting characters are equally realistic and intriguing, and the story satisfies both as a mystery and as an entree into the fascinating world of bones and what they tell us about human behavior. Add Connor's dark humor, and you have a multidimensional mystery that deserves comparison with the best of Patricia Cornwell. Expect to hear more from Lindsay Chamberlain."

—Booklist

A RUMOR OF
BONES

A LINDSAY CHAMBERLAIN MYSTERY

Beverly Connor

CUMBERLAND HOUSE
Nashville, Tennessee

To my husband,
Charles Connor

OTHER LINDSAY CHAMBERLAIN TITLES

Questionable Remains
Dressed to Die
Skeleton Crew
Airtight Case

Acknowledgments

SEVERAL PEOPLE HAVE assisted me in making this book possible and making it a better book as well. First, my husband, Charles Connor, who read and reread my manuscript, made valuable suggestions (many of which have made it into this book), and generally put up with me during the process.

Many thanks to Harriette Austin, my creative writing teacher and mentor, and to Judy Iakovou, Jim Howell, Diane Trap, Alice Gay, Takis Iakovou, Dannah Prather, Valerie Towler, Julia Cochrane, and members of Harriette's writing workshop who read the various drafts and made frank and invaluable comments on the manuscript.

A special thanks to my agent, Bob Robison, for having so much faith in me.

And finally, I want to acknowledge and thank my parents, Edna P. Heth and Charles W. Heth, for raising me to love books and to like the kinds of things that I like.

Thanks to all of you.

Crew's Quarters

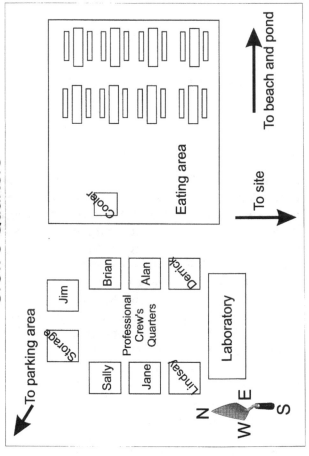

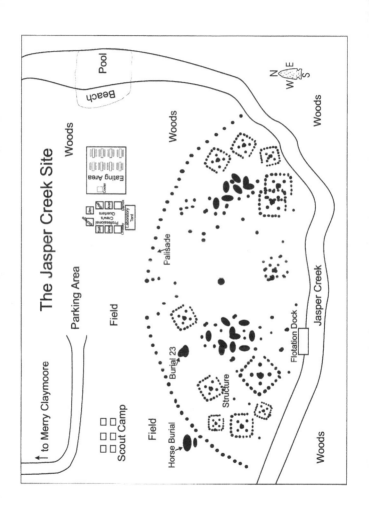

The Jasper Creek Site

A RUMOR OF
BONES

*Here and there there are scattered white objects which glisten
in the sun, and stand out against the dull deposit of alkali.
Approach, and examine them! They are bones: some large
and coarse, others smaller and more delicate.*
—Sir Arthur Conan Doyle
A Study in Scarlet

The valley ... was full of bones ... and lo, they were very dry.
—Ezekiel 37:1-2

Chapter 1

THE MIST ROSE from the uncovered graves like a
spirit. Soon the sun would rise above the horizon and
burn off the haze, and the site would be alive with the
activity of archaeologists. But now, in the predawn
hours, it was a mystic place—silent, stranded between
the past and present. This was the time of day when
Lindsay loved the site best. She could almost breathe
in the past.

Now, in the dim light, she could almost see the tall
wooden palisade constructed from rough-hewn trees
surrounding the village. Inside, she saw square wattle
and daub houses with thatched roofs built around a
plaza. Smoke rose from a central chimney hole in the
middle of the broad, cone-shaped roofs and drifted
southward with the breeze. Lindsay saw racks holding skins being tanned, others holding meat and fish
being smoked and dried.

She saw people—beautiful, dark-haired, dark-eyed, elegantly-boned people. In a house she could see one woman grinding corn on a metatae, another picking up discarded flaked chert debris and cutting up squash, pokeweed, chenopodium, and scaling fresh fish. Another woman was stamping designs onto freshly made pots. Children ran in, grabbed nuts and muscadines from a clay bowl, and ran out laughing. A man was sitting close to the hearth, chipping away at a piece of black flint, making points for his arrows.

Outside the house, older children were playing a game, throwing spears at smooth stone disks that other children rolled in front of them. They all looked up as a hunting party came walking into the palisade pulling a travois laden with freshly killed deer and wild turkey. The hunters had also killed a bear, and the people ran to them to hear the story of the hunt. Beyond the palisade was a field of corn. Not large, but enough to feed the village. A small group of women tended the field under the protective eyes of two braves.

Lindsay looked beyond the village and fields. She could see the conquistadors riding in the distance, hot and heavy in their armor, brandishing their weapons. Would they find the village? Lindsay couldn't see that. They hadn't yet.

Faint sounds of a vehicle brought Lindsay's thoughts back to the present, and the village dissolved back to the smooth, tan, shovel-shaved two acres of ground marked with the dark stains and littered with unearthed artifacts of past habitation. She looked over to the dirt road leading to the site and squinted, trying to make out the vans that brought the field crew from town, but she saw only a dim cloud of dust. Suddenly, Derrick came into view.

"Time tripping again, are we, Lindsay? What do you see?"

She smiled at him. "Caught me. I was looking at the conquistadors riding in the distance. We haven't found any European artifacts yet, have we?"

"Nope," replied Derrick. "Not a one." He looked out over the site and squinted as if trying to see Lindsay's vision of conquistadors.

"I haven't seen any battle wounds on any of the burials," Lindsay said, "but I haven't examined them thoroughly. If they see the village, maybe they will be friendly, maybe they won't be carrying disease." She sighed. "What's up for you today? Tearing up any new ground?"

"Don't know. I guess it depends who won today's battle—Frank's deliberate approach, or Ned's bat-out-of-hell methodology."

The morning light was coming fast. She could now make out the stakes and string that formed a grid over the places on the ground they had identified as structures.

"It must be hard, caught between them as you and your crew are."

Derrick shifted the shovel to his shoulder. "I just do what Frank tells me. He's the principal investigator."

"You know, if you …"

Derrick put a finger on her lips. "I sense a lecture coming on, something about me finishing my degree. I'll get around to it sooner or later." He smiled, winked, and walked over toward his crew, who were looking for artifacts in the back-dirt pile.

Lindsay shifted her attention to the five graves from which she had just removed the protective black plastic coverings, squatting beside the nearest. The dim light barely revealed the skeleton flexed in a tight fetal position. She looked up at the sky. These would have to be finished today, for the weatherman had predicted rain.

The vans came rattling into the graveled parking area and stopped under the trees. Lindsay and the rest of the professional archaeology crew, except for Frank, lived at the site. It was a Spartan lifestyle, living in tents and bathing under a homemade shower, but Lindsay enjoyed it. Kind of like the Swiss Family Robinson, she thought. The field school students were another matter. They were archaeology students from the University of Georgia, and they were working at the site to earn college credit. Their numbers varied from fifteen to twenty throughout the summer. It was impractical to house and feed that many students at the site, so they were housed in a large, old Victorian structure in Merry Claymoore that Frank had rented for them.

For the duration of the dig, Frank had rented a small house for himself next door to the field students — close enough to keep an eye on them, but far enough for his own privacy. Ned Meyers actually supervised the male students at the house, and Michelle Peterson supervised the females upstairs.

Ned jumped out of the driver's side of the first van as it rolled to a stop and charged across the site in chunky, short strides, swinging his arms like a power walker. His round, whiskered face was already red from the effort. Lindsay didn't bother wondering what had set him off this time; he approached everything like a mad bull.

He went directly to Derrick and his crew. "All right, we are going to open up Section Three today," he announced before he had reached his destination.

"Is that what Frank wants to do?" Derrick replied.

Ned's words, delivered in short staccato bursts, contrasted with Derrick's slower drawl. "Frank is not here, and I am in charge in his absence."

"Where is Frank?" Derrick asked.

"He was detained by the sheriff. I don't know how long he'll be."

"But he's coming?" Derrick leaned on his shovel, relaxed and immovable.

"Sooner or later." Ned waved an arm over the site as if to indicate the amount of work to be done. "But we can't wait on him to start."

"No, but we can finish up here in a couple of days. We only lack smoothing the area beyond Structure 4 and mapping the artifacts so we can take them up, and I'm sure Frank will be here soon. He's probably talking to the sheriff about those pothunters we ran off the other night."

Ned squared himself in front of Derrick, battle ready, a bantam rooster against the taller, broader Derrick. "Dammit, I'm in charge. Do what I tell you."

"It's supposed to rain. We don't want to open up new ground today."

"It is not going to rain." Ned lifted his chin, daring Derrick to disagree.

"We are wasting time." Derrick turned to Brian. "You and Jim finish up behind structure 4. Alan and I will map." He turned back to Ned. "The Boy Scouts are coming in a few days. You'll have all the crew you need to uncover Section 3."

"We need to have a serious meeting during lunch about your insubordination," Ned angrily muttered at him. He turned and walked away, studying his clipboard.

"Insubordination?" Brian asked.

"Forget it," Derrick said. "Let's get to work."

Lindsay and her burial crew watched the scene calmly as they divvied paint brushes, dental picks, and tongue depressors: tools they used in excavating the fragile bones of the burials. "Do we have to go through this every day?" Sally whispered to Lindsay. "What is Ned's problem?"

Lindsay smiled at Sally and shrugged. "A need for control, I suppose. We're fortunate he isn't interested in burials." She turned to Jane. "We have to get these burials finished and out before it rains. Do you think you, Sally, and Carrie can do it?"

"Five burials? I don't know. Maybe. They're all nearly finished, aren't they?"

"Yes. Just to be sure, get some of the field students to help. When you finish, ask Derrick or Michelle if they need any help."

Tall, willowy Michelle walked up to them, grinning. "Well, there's a hard decision. Do they work with gorgeous Derrick, moving all that heavy dirt, or with me, digging out grid squares in a structure. Personally, I'd work with Derrick."

They all grinned.

"You know," said Jane, "we do seem to have an unusual number of great looking guys this season. Brian, Jim, and Alan aren't too bad either."

They all looked toward the objects of their admiration, who were already taking off their shirts in preparation for the hot summer sun that would be beating down on them too soon. Brian and Jim began the task of shaving the uncovered ground surface smooth with sharpened square-bladed shovels. Derrick and Alan sorted the mapping equipment.

"All right, girls," said Lindsay after a moment. "Let's finish the burials. There is plenty of time to gawk during lunch. Seriously, Michelle, do you need any help?"

"I'm not shorthanded. I have most of the field students, and we're going at a pretty good clip."

"Okay, then," Lindsay said to her crew. "When you finish here, help Derrick finish up his section. Maybe that'll make Ned happy."

Lindsay was preparing to help Jane finish burial 21 when she looked up and saw Frank walking toward her. His forehead was creased into a frown.

"Ned said you were meeting with the sheriff," she greeted him. "Was it about the pothunters?"

Frank shook his head. "More serious than that. I have a favor to ask." He paused. "A hunter found a human skeleton just outside of town."

"Are they sure it's human?" Lindsay asked.

"Yes. It looks like it may be the remains of a local child who's been missing for over a year. The coroner is out of town, and the parents are waiting in the sheriff's office. I told Sheriff Duggan you have experience with this kind of thing and I would send you. See what you can do. Marsha will be here soon to take you."

Lindsay's fingers tightened on the trowel she carried in her right hand. "You should've asked me first."

The furrows in Frank's brow deepened. He ran a hand through his dark hair. "I didn't think you'd mind. Lindsay, some of the townspeople don't like

us being here. If we're helpful, it will be easier on all
of us."

"We?"

"You know this is something you can do in your
sleep. Just ID the bones and come on back."

Lindsay looked down at her T-shirt, cut-offs,
bare legs, and work boots and sighed. "All right, I'll
change clothes and get my things."

She didn't tell Frank how hard it had been for her
the last time she had to identify the bones of children, standing in a California vineyard while diggers
uncovered those bones lying forlornly in shallow
graves with their little red or white tennis shoes and
tiny, tattered clothes. He didn't understand what it
was like, looking into the faces of parents, their eyes
conveying the hope that their baby was not here but
somewhere else—alive somewhere else—and yet at
the same time longing for their ordeal to be over. So if
this was their child, they could finally know and take
him home and bury him.

She particularly remembered one mother whose
eyes were permanently swollen from months of
crying. She insisted on showing Lindsay a picture
of her son. She seemed afraid that Lindsay wouldn't
understand that the bones she identified as his had
belonged to a living person, a loved person, her
son. Lindsay had looked at the studio picture of an
eight-year-old boy dressed in a suit, smiling into the
camera—healthy and well cared for—and wished she
had had some comfort for the mother.

Lindsay walked to her tent to change clothes and
then to face more grief-stricken parents and pitiful
little bones.

In fresh blue jeans and a white cotton blouse, her long brown hair combed and fastened into a pony tail, Lindsay slid a backpack containing her tools over her shoulder and waited while Marsha Latimore's white Lincoln pulled up in the parking lot.

Marsha was wealthy and well-connected in Merry Claymoore. The less-than-well-dressed excavation crews often invited small town suspicion. As a member of the garden club and president of the local historical society, Marsha was useful, or so Frank seemed to think, in keeping them on the good side of the townspeople. Lindsay put her pack in the back seat, climbed into the passenger side, and closed the car door a little too hard. She glanced over at Marsha and briefly noted the pale yellow sundress trimmed in daisies. Lindsay wondered how much hair spray it took to keep Marsha's helmet of bleached blonde hair so perfectly still.

"Thank you for doing this, Lindsay," said Marsha. Her manicured hands gripped the steering wheel so tightly her knuckles turned white as she wheeled the Lincoln around in the parking lot and headed back to town. A frown creased her perfectly made-up face.

"This is a real sad case," she said. "Sarah and Mike Pruitt's little girl, Peggy, disappeared a year and a half ago. She'd just turned six ... I'd helped Sarah with her birthday party. We had a clown, and Sarah's cousin performed some of his magic tricks ... it was real nice. All the children had such a good time."

Lindsay wanted to say something comforting, but everything she thought of sounded trivial. After a moment, she asked, "Do they have dental records or x-rays?"

"I don't know."

"I need a good picture of her. If they have one made by a studio, that would be good."

"I'm sure they do. Sarah's cousin Mickey has the portrait studio in town."

They rode in silence for over a mile before Marsha ventured conversation again.

"Frank told me there was some trouble at the site the other night."

"Pothunters, most likely."

"Pothunters?"

"They're collectors who vandalize burials looking for Indian artifacts, mainly clay pots or nice point caches. Pots in burials are usually found intact, so they are valuable to collectors."

"That's terrible."

"Every site I have ever worked on has had trouble with them. These were a little unique, however. They wore Halloween masks."

"Halloween masks?"

"Yes, apparently, they docked a boat and came up through the woods. Jane and I saw them first. They ran when we yelled for Derrick and Brian. We all chased them, but they got away in their boat. I don't think they'll be back."

"Weren't you scared?"

"A little, but like I said, pothunters are a common problem."

"Yes, but the masks. They might have been...well something different from collectors."

"Maybe, but they ran away in a hurry. Derrick can look very formidable when he wants to."

"Derrick is a handsome young man."

"Most women think so."

"Do you know him well?"

"We've been friends for a long time. We went to graduate school together," Lindsay replied, wondering what Marsha was fishing for.

"I understand you've known Frank a long time, too."

Ah, thought Lindsay, of course. My relationship with Frank. "Yes. We have worked other sites together." Lindsay left it at that, and silence settled uncomfortably between them.

They passed an ornate entranceway with lion-topped pillars and heavy wrought iron gates emblazoned with a large flowery T. Marsha nodded her head toward the gates.

"That's Tylerwynd. Isabel Tyler is what passes for the town matriarch. She thinks she still lives in the past when her family owned the town and everyone worked for them. Sarah Pruitt, the mother of the missing girl, is Isabel's husband's niece. He's dead now, and Isabel has disinherited Sarah. I suppose Isabel doesn't want her own children to share the family inheritance with any of her husband's family."

"Sounds like a disagreeable woman."

"She is. She's certainly a strange woman."

They arrived at the sheriff's department, and Marsha led Lindsay through the reception area. A young-looking couple sat huddled together, holding each other's hands. They looked up expectantly at Lindsay and Marsha. Another man, about the same age as the couple, stood behind them with his hands on both their shoulders.

The sheriff stood and held out his hand to Lindsay.

"I'm Sheriff Greg Duggan. Marsha tells me you're a forensics expert." He looked skeptical. "Somehow I pictured you as a much older person."

Lindsay took his hand. She had met him before when he came out to visit the site, but apparently he didn't remember her, probably because she had been covered with mud.

The sheriff was a large man with wavy graying blond hair and even, white teeth. He looked good humored, but Lindsay had overheard some of the locals in a diner say that he could be a son-of-a-bitch.

"Yes, sir, I am. My name is Lindsay Chamberlain."

"This is Sarah and Mike Pruitt and Sarah's cousin, Mickey Lawson." The sheriff performed the introductions.

They did not offer their hands but nodded their heads, as if any unnecessary movement was beyond them. Sarah had a large envelope in her lap and timidly handed it to Lindsay. Tears brimmed in her blue eyes, which held the familiar painful expression of hope and dread. Lindsay took the envelope and steeled herself as she opened it. She took out photographs of a smiling, dimpled, blonde, curly-headed little girl.

"When were these taken?" asked Lindsay.

"About a month before she … before she got lost," answered Mike Pruitt.

"How long will it take?" Sarah Pruitt asked.

"I don't know," said Lindsay kindly. "Possibly not long. Has she ever had dental work?"

Sarah shook her head, sobbing softly. "She didn't have any cavities. We were so proud of how she took care of her teeth."

"Did she ever have any broken bones, or x-rays taken for any reason?"

Sarah Pruitt shook her head. "No."

"Okay, thank you, Mrs. Pruitt." Lindsay directed her attention to Mickey Lawson. "I understand you are a photographer."

He nodded his head solemnly. "Yes, ma'am, I took those pictures you're holding there."

"Do you keep records of camera distance, negative size, focal length, and such?"

"Yes, so if a shot is particularly good, I'll know how to reproduce it."

Lindsay smiled. "Good. Can you get me that information for this picture?" She showed him a full-face portrait of Peggy.

"Yes, this is a standard shot. I'll have to look in my files to make sure, but I think I can give you the information you want. I'll go back to my studio now and get it."

"Thank you." Lindsay looked up at the sheriff, and he took her cue.

"This way," he said, escorting her through a doorway. Marsha stayed with the Pruitts.

The sheriff showed Lindsay to a back room lined with locked gun cabinets. A couple of worn couches, a dilapidated coffee table, and an old television created a lounge in one corner. In another corner stood two long tables, chairs, and a chalkboard. On one of the tables sat a white plastic tub. Lindsay could see the shadow of bones through its thin sides. No one was in the room except a stout deputy, standing erect by the table as if guarding the bones. He smiled broadly as they approached.

"This is Deputy Andy Littleton," the sheriff said.

"Howdy do, ma'am." He inclined his head.

"Hello. These are the bones then?"

"Yes, ma'am. I gathered them up myself. I was real careful with them."

Lindsay smiled at him as she slipped on a pair of latex gloves and pulled the tub toward her. She began placing the bones on the table in their anatomical positions. Most were still articulated with thin leathery strips of ligament. A waxy odor rose to her nostrils. Even this was information to her. Lindsay expected the odor to be stronger from bones only a year and a half old.

"Did she have her dog with her when she disappeared?"

The deputy looked puzzled.

"Not that I know of," answered the sheriff.

"This is the front leg bone of a dog," said Lindsay, holding up the bone. The deputy looked a little embarrassed, as if he had done something wrong, but she smiled at him. "Bones can get mixed up in the ground—erosion, animal activity, all kinds of reasons."

She set the bone aside, took out the skull, and examined it. Then she looked at the photograph.

"These are not the bones of the Pruitt girl."

The sheriff, who until now had appeared to be gaining confidence in Lindsay's expert handling of the bones, looked surprised.

"How can you tell from just looking at the photograph?"

Lindsay pointed to the picture. "Peggy has a pronounced dimple in her chin, almost a cleft, which means she would probably have a dimple in the underlying bone. Notice that the chin on the skull is smooth and pointed, not like Peggy's at all. Her chin is a little squared. Also, look at the teeth. You can see both the upper and lower teeth in her smile. Notice how they fit together. Now look at the teeth in the skull." Lindsay held the skull and lower mandible so they could see the bite articulated. "This child had an overbite. Also, the lower incisors are slightly crooked and are beginning to overlap. Peggy's are straight. This child will have a small heart shaped face with a small pointed chin and a slight overbite."

"Okay, you've convinced me," said the sheriff.

"These bones have been in the ground a lot longer than 18 months. In that short period of time, I would expect more skin and sinew to still be attached. Of course, that depends on how oxygenated the soil is..." Lindsay hesitated a moment, not sure if she wanted to proceed or just go and leave this to someone else. Finally, she said, "I would still like to make all the measurements on the bones."

"Sure," the sheriff agreed, touching the little skull with his fingertips. "We still have to find out who this was."

Lindsay told the Pruitts, and they grasped each other's hands and thanked her through teary smiles, as if they had been given a miracle. The sheriff saw them out, and Lindsay went back to the bones.

When she completed examining the bones, she took a deep breath, wondering if she should have left after telling the Pruitts this was not their daughter. The coroner would return eventually, and he could deal with these little bones. Her eyes stung with tears that threatened, but did not spill over.

The back room of the sheriff's department was quiet. Earlier, some of the deputies and secretaries had come in and watched her work with the bones. Occasionally, they asked questions, but soon grew bored watching the tedious measurements on each bone, and left. She took the stack of papers that comprised the report with its accompanying data and evened the edges by gently bouncing the pages on the table, just as the sheriff came through the door carrying two cups of coffee.

"I should have brought you something sooner," he said. His broad smile was a welcome relief.

"That's all right," she answered, taking the cup from his hand and smiling at him. "I've finished the report."

He looked at her for a moment. Lindsay realized he had noticed her teary eyes, and it embarrassed her. He said nothing, however, and merely pulled up a chair as he picked up the pages, sipping his coffee as he read the report. "Says here, sex is undetermined."

"You can't really sex the skeletal remains of children."

"Undetermined cause of death," he read.

"I didn't find anything that would suggest a cause." She paused. "But there is something I need to show you." She set her coffee down, rose from her chair, and beckoned to him. The sheriff walked over and stood beside her.

"The bones of children are more elastic," she began, "because they are still growing. In many ways they are harder to break. However, they are also delicate. Look at this." She picked up the pelvic bones. "This region is the pubis bone. It is the front part of the pelvic girdle. The two halves of the pubis bone have been pulled apart. You can see the damage mostly in the stretched tendons." Lindsay pointed to the left femur. "This is the upper leg bone. This rounded area joins the pelvis in this cup-shaped area. Look at the damage to the iliofemoral ligaments that attach the two. I believe they have been stretched and torn, as if the leg has been pulled away from the socket. And no clothes were found on the body. All traces of clothing would not have disappeared this soon."

"Oh, God," exclaimed the sheriff.

"I'm showing you this specifically because it suggests some of the things that happened, and if you find the skeleton of Peggy Pruitt, it may show the same pattern of damage. Both children are roughly the same age. Two children of the same age missing —it may be a pattern."

"Don't mention this to anyone," he said.

"I won't."

The sheriff sat back down in the chair and rubbed his eyes with his fingers. "This is bad business." He picked up the report again and thumbed through it. "You signed it, Lindsay R. Chamberlain, Ph.D."

"Yes."

"You have some kind of doctor's degree in this?"

"Yes. I've also appeared as an expert witness in court before."

The sheriff looked satisfied with that.

Lindsay and the sheriff were leaving when a short, plump-faced fiftyish man dressed in a white suit came in and walked toward them holding out his hand to Lindsay. He had a full head of dark hair that she observed was a toupee.

"This is Seymour Plackert," said the sheriff. "He's an attorney in town."

"And you are Lindsay Chambers, one of the archaeologists," he informed them. He barely looked at Lindsay as he took her hand, gave it a brief shake, and let go.

"Lindsay Chamberlain," she said.

"Yes, well…" He turned to the sheriff. "Mrs. Tyler asked me to drop by. This," he gestured briefly at the tub of bones, "might have been her grand-niece. She thought I should come by and talk to you."

"It's not Peggy."

"Yes, but we want to be sure, you understand."

"We are," the sheriff answered.

"Well, it was mighty nice of the archaeologists to send someone out to help, but you understand her identification needs to be verified by an expert."

Lindsay opened her mouth to say something, but closed it again after seeing the hard set of the sheriff's face.

"Dr. Chamberlain is a court recognized expert. I have read her report, and she has explained how she ruled out the bones as Peggy's. I'm satisfied. Now if there is nothing else I can do for you, I need to finish with Dr. Chamberlain."

"No, nothing else. I'll tell Mrs. Tyler your position."

He nodded curtly at Lindsay and left the room.

The sheriff watched Plackert leave, then turned to Lindsay. "I don't like lawyers. Never did." He smiled. "I'll take you back to the site."

For most of the way back, they didn't speak. The sheriff seemed irritated and preoccupied, and Lindsay didn't want to get involved in any town politics.

Finally, before he turned off onto the dirt road that led to the site, she broke the silence. "This may sound unusual, but since the crime scene is old, it's a good idea."

"What?" he asked, looking over at her briefly.

"Let me have part of the site crew excavate the place where the bones were found." She saw skepticism in his face, "Look, we can find trade beads a millimeter in size. We can find fish bones so tiny they look like hairs. The crew can do a thorough excavation in the immediate area around the child's grave — sift and float all the dirt, the whole works, and do a surface survey of a larger area. We have the methodology for the kind of thoroughness needed for the task, and we have a good eye for finding anomalies. It is what we do."

The sheriff said nothing until he pulled into the makeshift parking lot at the site. "I suppose it is really the same thing, isn't it? Archaeology and crime investigation?"

"Yes. All we're doing here at the site is looking for clues."

"Have you had any more problems with masked vandals?" he asked.

"No."

"I'll have the deputies put this place on their night route."

"Thanks. We appreciate that."

"Thank you for the analysis. I'll be in touch."

He mouths a sentence as curs mouth a bone.
—Charles Churchill
The Rosciad

Chapter 2

LINDSAY HOPPED OUT of the sheriff's car and walked straight to her tent, one among six that formed two opposite sides of a square where the professional site crew was housed. The third side was a long tent that functioned as a laboratory and storage area for artifacts. The fourth side was another storage tent and another crew member's tent. Lindsay dropped her backpack inside the doorway of her tent and went to find Jane, whom she had left in charge of the burials.

It was three o'clock, and the blistering sun was reflecting off the ground in waves of heat. The digging had stopped for the day, and only a few supervisors milled around discussing what was to be done the next day. Jane was nowhere to be seen, and the site was covered with different-sized squares of protective black plastic anchored with stones. Derrick came out of a group of trees bordering the site, wiping his face with a damp T-shirt. His long brown hair hung dark and limp on his bare shoulders.

It had been a hot day at the dig. Derrick had a sly smile on his face, and his soft brown eyes appeared to twinkle. He was known for his elaborate practical jokes, and Lindsay wondered what he was up to.

"Who's going to get it this time?" she asked as he approached.

Derrick feigned a look of innocence and asked her what she meant. "Never mind. I suppose I'll find out soon enough. Have you seen Jane?"

"We heard you were taken by the local gendarmes. We thought they might keep you overnight, so Jane is off raising bail."

"Really. Where is she?... Sorry, I didn't mean to be short."

"Were you short?" Derrick said kindly. "I didn't notice. Jane is in town. She said to tell you all the open burials have been photographed and packed and are in the lab."

"Thanks."

"Found three more today," he said, pointing to a patch of black plastic. They walked to an area adjacent to the open excavations. Derrick kneeled and lifted the plastic, revealing a large dark stain in the smooth soil in the shape of a lopsided heart with a rounded point. "Looks like one burial intrudes into the other," he said, "I don't know which is older. Jane gave them numbers: 22 and 23."

"Okay. Heard the weather report?"

"Clear. Looks like the rain may have passed us by. I guess ole Ned was right about the weather."

Derrick supervised the digging crew, whose job was to remove the overburden from the site floor, then shave it clean, revealing patterns left by the ancient inhabi-

tants. He was also in charge of mapping. It was the ser-
vices of Derrick and his crew that Lindsay may have
committed to the sheriff. She must have had a guilty
expression, because Derrick gave her a quizzical smile.

"And just what are you up to?"

"You said there were three new burials?" she
asked, diverting his attention. She wanted to speak to
Frank before she discussed digging the crime scene
with Derrick.

"The other burial is near the new structure." He
placed the plastic over the burials and pointed across
the site.

"Where is Frank?"

Derrick frowned. "Arguing with Ned."

"Doesn't Ned ever get tired of arguing?"

"I think he probably gets more tired when nobody
pays attention to him. He's going on like Chicken Little
about the dam."

"Even if they were to start on the dam today, we
would still have time to finish a thorough investigation before the place is flooded, wouldn't we?"

"Yes. But you know Ned. Just because he spent
his summers surface collecting around here, he thinks
he's got some psychic link with the place."

"You'd think he would appreciate Frank's thoroughness."

Derrick shook his head. "Ned's really just upset
because Frank has top billing here."

Lindsay frowned and gazed out over the site. She
spotted a lone crew member digging just outside the
main boundaries of the site. He looked down at his
work, cursed, and went to another spot, where he
started digging again.

"What is Thomas doing?" she asked.

Derrick grinned. "Thomas wanted to dig something really significant, so Frank and I gave him a piece of ground just outside the palisade to work on his own. We thought we could watch him and make sure he didn't screw up too much. He uncovered some parallel rows of stains, and he thinks they were the posts of a long house."

"A long house? Here? You're kidding."

"No, I'm not kidding. He's cross-sectioning the holes. I think he's finding that they were rows of trees and not post-holes. He curses every time the cross-section shows up the tree roots."

Lindsay smiled for the first time since she got back, then sobered. "I need to talk to Frank. Point me in his direction, and maybe I can rescue him from Ned."

"They're down at the flotation dock."

Lindsay walked to the large covered dock extending into the river that bordered one edge of the site. As she got closer, she heard Frank's raised voice.

"Dammit, Ned, what is wrong with you? Do you know how much we would miss if we take your approach?"

"Why don't you listen to me?" Ned yelled back. "I'm not saying we just sample artifact clusters. I'm saying we combine sampling techniques. The way you are going about it, they will flood the place before you finish, and how much will we miss then?"

"According to the schedule ..."

"Damn the schedule! I'm telling you, Frank, if you would listen, they are going to advance the schedule."

"They have not told me ..."

"I'm telling you, dammit. I'm telling you ... why

do I bother, you are so pig headed. You think you know every damn thing!"

Frank spotted Lindsay and turned away from Ned. "How did it go?" he asked with that earnest expression in his hazel eyes that often made Lindsay's heart beat faster.

"Marsha didn't come by?" she asked.

"No."

"The remains didn't belong to the Pruitt child."

"Could you tell anything about the death from the bones?"

She shook her head, telling him nothing about her finds. Instead, she took a deep breath and told him about the suggestion she made to the sheriff about using Derrick's crew to excavate the crime scene.

"You did what!" Ned's voice was so loud Lindsay was sure it carried over the site. "I don't believe this. I don't believe this. We are never going to get this site dug. If you two can't focus your attention on this site, you should just turn it over to me."

"Ned," said Lindsay, "These people need our help. The crime scene is small. It won't take that long."

"Then why don't you do it?" Ned retorted.

"That's enough, Ned," said Frank.

"No, it's not enough. We have a tight schedule."

Frank's voice was very calm, but Lindsay could see him clinching his jaw.

"The schedule is under control. I don't want to discuss this anymore."

"This is an important site," said Ned, unwilling to let go.

"We all agree," said Frank.

"I believe it is a very important site," Ned repeated.

"I know your theories about this site, and I believe they have merit. We will get the site excavated. Now let's drop this."

Ned hesitated a moment, torn between continuing the argument or accepting the bone of professional recognition that Frank had thrown him. Finally, he left the flotation dock with a nod.

"You are a good diplomat," she said to Frank.

"I have my moments. However, about loaning the crew, you should have talked to me first."

"It was kind of in the emotion of the moment. Are you going to fire me?" she teased.

"Oh, come on. I suppose I deserve this, after volunteering you."

"That's true," Lindsay said.

"I'll talk to Derrick about excavating the crime scene, and we'll come up with a plan."

"Good. Well, since I'm not being fired, I'll make plans for opening up the new burials."

Frank frowned. He seemed to hesitate before speaking. "I had a strange call from the Archaeology Department head about Coosa Valley Power Company's part of the excavation contract. He said one of the directors of the company tried to cancel the contract. He said they wanted to withdraw permission for us to be on the land and for us to get off the site. Impossible, of course, but curious."

"That's odd. I wonder what that is about."

Frank shook his head. "Historical recovery is written into the law, and we have a contract." Frank ran a hand through his hair. "You know, between that and Ned…"

"Do you want me to talk to Ned, maybe smooth things over?" Lindsay asked.

"He's not your problem. I'll handle it." Frank smiled. "Maybe I'll drown him in the river."

Lindsay returned his smile. "By the way, the sheriff is sending a patrol by here at night to watch for pothunters."

Frank nodded, "Good, maybe that's one worry off my shoulders."

Lindsay stood with Jane over the dark stain in the earth that was designated as burials 22 and 23. She took her trowel and drew a line around one lobe and the rounded point of the heart-shaped stain, making an oval. "This one is the first; we'll label it number 22." Again, she drew an oval with her trowel, this time around the other lobe of the "heart" and inside the boundaries of the first oval. "This one intrudes inside the first; we'll call it 23. Twenty-three will probably be on top, but you may have to dig them both simultaneously. Get Sally to help."

"Couldn't it be the other way around?" Jane asked. "Couldn't 23 be the first and 22 the intrusion? How can you tell which is first?"

"I can't, but this one, 22, has an east/west orientation, which is the predominant burial direction so far at this site. Twenty-three is northwest/southeast, an uncommon direction here. I'm assuming one anomaly goes with another, and that the burial with the less common direction is the intrusion."

"Makes sense to me," Jane agreed.

"I may be completely wrong. We'll find out shortly."

Lindsay left Jane and was headed toward Burial 24 when she saw Frank and Deputy Littleton walking across the site in her direction. A sick feeling rose in her stomach.

"Howdy, Dr. Chamberlain," greeted the deputy.

"Call me Lindsay, please," she said.

He smiled and nodded. "Sure thing."

"Can you go into town with the deputy?" asked Frank. "There's another couple who have a missing daughter. They think the bones may be hers."

Lindsay sighed with resignation. "All right. I've put Jane and Sally on burials 22 and 23. I'll hold off on 24."

Frank nodded his agreement and headed toward the flotation dock. Lindsay turned to Andy Littleton. "What do you know about this couple?"

"They're from the next county. Their little girl, Amy Lynn Hastings, went missing about three years ago. She was about the same age as little Peggy when she disappeared."

"I need to get my tools. It won't take a second. I'll meet you at your car."

The sheriff was behind his desk when Lindsay and the deputy arrived. It looked like a replay of the previous day with the Pruitts. A man and woman sat clinging to each other, looking scared and full of dread. The man and the sheriff rose as she entered, and the sheriff introduced Lindsay to Anne and Guy Hastings.

Sheriff Duggan handed her a large envelope. "These are some x-rays taken of Amy about six months before she disappeared."

"She fell from a tree," explained Anne Hastings. "She had no broken bones, but we had her x-rayed anyway, just in case. They were taken of her shoulder and right arm and her head."

"They will help a great deal," said Lindsay.

"And this is a photograph of her." The expression in the sheriff's eyes was intense, like a communication, as he handed Lindsay the envelope, so she opened it and pulled out the picture. It was a little blonde pixie-looking girl with a heart-shaped face, a small, pointed chin, and a slight overbite. Lindsay felt her stomach lurch as she looked at the mother, who was asking her a question.

"How long will it take?"

"Several hours," she said. "Can you tell me something about her disappearance? What month did she disappear, for instance?"

"It was the end of summer, the 25th of August. We had gone camping at Olika. She had Pepper with her."

"Pepper?" asked Lindsay.

"Her dog, a cocker spaniel. They both disappeared." Anne began to cry softly.

"All that's in the police report," said her husband. "Can't you read it there?"

"Of course." Lindsay had heard what she wanted to know.

"I can tell you what she was wearing," Anne offered.

"I'll read the report," Lindsay smiled at her. She did not want to tell her that the remains were not found with clothes. Anne Hastings nodded, but her husband was not fooled by Lindsay's evasion. He understood and put his arm around his wife, while avoiding her eyes.

"Look," Lindsay said, "the garden club built a beautiful park a block from here. It is a peaceful place to wait."

"I'll send the deputy to find you wherever you are," said the sheriff.

They agreed, and Guy Hastings led his wife out of the sheriff's department.

"There's a good chance it's her," the sheriff commented as he led Lindsay to the back room.

"It certainly doesn't look good."

"You said it would take several hours?"

"If I don't find anything that definitely rules out an identification, like with Peggy Pruitt, it will take a while. It takes a lot more information to say the bones do belong to a specific person."

The tub of bones was on the table, as before. Lindsay sighed, put on her gloves, and began laying the bones out again.

"I don't suppose you have a light table I can use for the x-rays?" she asked.

"We don't, but I sent Ricky out … Here he and Ray come now." Two deputies came in carrying a glass-top drafting table between them.

"This will do fine," said Lindsay as the deputies scrambled around unwinding the cord and plugging it in. Lindsay turned on the light and set the x-rays on the glass top. On the table she arranged her calipers, magnifying lenses, and report forms. She sat at the light table and began the meticulous measurements of the images on the x-rays.

After several hours, Lindsay walked around the room to stretch. She had made all the measurements and observations at least three times.

"Are you finished?" She looked up to see the sheriff. "The Hastings came back an hour ago."

"Yes. I'm finished." She handed him a page. The

measurements for both the bones and the x-rays were listed next to the description of what was measured. He glanced at each entry—identical all down the list.

"It is her, then," he said.

"Yes. The report is here." She handed it to the sheriff.

The sheriff shook his head. "I'll tell the parents. Andy'll take you back to the site. Thanks. I'm sorry you had to come back to do this."

As before, the main crew had left by the time Lindsay got back to the site. She did not feel like talking to anyone, so she went to her tent, turned on her radio to a classical station, took off her shoes, and lay down on her bed with a mystery novel she had been trying to find time to read.

"Lindsay?"

She looked up from her reading and saw Frank's silhouette outside her tent.

"Yes."

"Are you all right?"

"I'm just tired."

Frank stepped into her tent. "It was that couple's little girl then?"

"Yes."

"I'm sorry," he said, sitting down at the foot of her bed.

"It had to be somebody's child," she said.

"Let me buy you dinner," he offered.

"I'm not really hungry. How did things go today?"

He picked up one of her bare feet and began to knead the sole. "Fine. No problems. That feel good?"

"Yes. Is this a new service to keep the crew in shape?"

"No. This is just for you." He put down her foot and picked up the other one and massaged it. His hands were warm. "Lindsay, you need to eat. Come with me. I found a great place to get chicken fingers and margaritas. I'll buy."

"Chicken fingers and margaritas. You know my weakness." She reclaimed her foot and swung her legs to the floor. "I need to talk to Derrick about excavating the crime scene first."

"I've already talked to him."

"How did he take it?"

"Well, he actually seemed interested."

"Good. Let me clean up. I'll meet you in about 20 minutes."

"Sure, take your time."

The shower was a wooden outdoor structure that the supervising crew had built for themselves. Lindsay stepped in and pulled the cord, drenching herself with cool water from the reservoir. It washed away more than the day's accumulation of sweat and dust, and Lindsay stepped out feeling that her sad mood had been rinsed away as well.

Frank took her to a restaurant were she had a margarita with beer-battered fried chicken fingers and spuds. "I guess I was hungry after all," she said, wiping her mouth with a napkin.

"I'll say," Frank told her in mock seriousness. "I was afraid you would eat mine, too. How do you keep such a slender figure and eat like a horse?"

"You work us to death." Lindsay smiled at him.

"I have to, so I can keep Ned off my back." When

he smiled, he had a boyish face, which was enhanced by the lock of black hair that kept falling over his eyes. "I thought we could go to a movie," he said.

"A movie? Sounds like you have the evening all planned."

"You can use a diversion. I know it was hard to examine those bones, then have to meet the parents. I should have been more sensitive."

"That little girl was really hurt before she died. She must have been terrified. I don't understand how people can do such things. What kind of society are we that we're producing so many monsters?"

"I don't know," Frank said.

"The bastard even killed her little dog. Probably in front of her."

Frank reached out and took Lindsay's hand. "Try to clear your mind of it now. Your part is over. Come on, I'm taking you to a nice little light-hearted movie."

At first glance the town of Merry Claymoore looked as if it had stayed in the fifties. Brick stores, crammed together so close they looked like one long building, made up the business district. A single main street, called Main Street, ran through the center of town. Diagonal parking spaces and parking meters lined the two-laned street.

Even a second look didn't indicate that Merry Claymoore was approaching the millennium. The hardware store still carried wash basins, old-fashioned looking stove pipes, water pitchers, and an assortment of faded cardboard packaging containing miscellaneous tools that the proprietors had not given up on eventually selling. Even the dress shops and shoe store seemed to cater to a clientele that preferred older styles.

The drug store beside the hardware store was perhaps the favorite spot of the site crew. It had a soda fountain with ice cream sundaes, malts, cherry cokes, and an assortment of pies and served BLTs and egg sandwiches.

Downtown also boasted Mickey Lawson's portrait studio, a flower shop, an antique store, and several vacant buildings. The only business reflecting the current decade was the video store with movie posters plastering its tall glass windows. Most of the people who lived in Merry Claymoore shopped in the new mall fifteen miles away near the town of Cullins.

The theater was strategically situated beside the drug store. Lindsay read the marquee: *Young Frankenstein.*

"You're kidding? Isn't this an old movie?"

"1974. Directed by Mel Brooks, starring Gene Wilder and Peter Boyle. It's absolutely hilarious. Have you seen it?"

"No."

"Great. The Cinema Plex at the mall gets all the new movies. This theater shows only oldies. This month they're doing nothing but Mel Brooks. They have a huge screen, plush seats, carpeting, everything but usherettes in those little red uniforms with gold braids. You'll love it." He took her hand and led her up to the ticket booth.

Lindsay laughed at Frank's enthusiasm and tried to push all thoughts of Amy Lynn Hastings from her mind and enjoy her date. Occasionally, in the darkened theater, she glanced at Frank's profile as he laughed out loud and wondered what had happened with their first try at romance.

Coming out of the movie, they met Jane and Alan, from the site.

"Hey, didn't see you guys in the theater," Jane said.

"Great movie. Marty Feldman made a great Igor," said Alan.

As they walked to their cars, Alan and Frank did a fair imitation of "Putting on the Ritz." When Lindsay and Jane finished laughing, Lindsay asked Jane about the excavations.

"How did 22 and 23 go today?"

"I'm half finished with each of them. You were right. Twenty-three intrudes into 22. Twenty-three is a lot more shallow, too. Twenty-two is flexed, and the bones are in bad condition. Twenty-three is extended. Those bones are in great condition. I wish they were all like that. I don't see how there could be such a difference in burials that close together."

"Depends on how the water drains through the soil and such," said Lindsay. "Could be that the bones in the other half of 23 are in as bad condition as 22."

"I'll know tomorrow," said Jane.

"Come on," complained Alan. "No site business tonight. We're still out on the town, what there is of it. So far, besides the movie, the biggest attractions are watching some local amateur magician at the summer school fair and cruising McDonald's. Want to go have a Big Mac and fries with us?"

"No, you guys enjoy yourselves, I think we'll head on back," said Lindsay, waving them on.

"Come have a glass of wine at my place." Frank took Lindsay's hand in his.

"Just one. Then I'd like to turn in."

"I can work with that."

• • •

"I'm sorry I got you involved in identifying those bones," Frank said as they entered his house.

"It's all right. I'm not a hothouse rose, you know."

"I know. You're tough when you want to be."

"How are you doing with Thomas?" asked Lindsay. "Derrick told me about the area you let him have."

"He's not so bad. A little over enthusiastic at times. He could make a halfway good archaeologist. Ned hates him."

"Well, to be honest, you did sort of promise Thomas's father to give him significant assignments. I can kind of understand Ned's disapproval." They sat down on the sofa.

"So can I. Assigning Thomas to a feature now and then is a small price to pay for the funding his father contributes. I'm not compromising the dig in any way. Thomas still has to do his share of shovel shaving." Frank squeezed her hand. "I'm glad you are here."

He rose and took a bottle of wine from an old sideboard standing against the wall and poured two glasses, handing one to Lindsay. She smiled when she saw that it was really one of the plastic variety that could be bought at any grocery store.

Frank grinned, too. "I couldn't bring my good crystal around this rowdy bunch," he said. "Let's forget about archaeology for the rest of the evening."

The sudden loud knock on the door brought a curse to his lips.

He walked over and jerked open the door. Hurricane Thomas blew in, carrying an armload of books. "I have this great idea," he said, ignoring Lindsay, the low lights, and the wine glasses.

Lindsay rose and smiled at Frank. "I'll take your car back to the site. You can come in the van with the crew." She left Frank glaring at Thomas.

There was no moon, so as Lindsay drove away from the lights of Merry Claymoore, the night became so dark and clear that the sky was thick with stars. Lindsay could see the slash of the Milky Way across the night sky. She rolled down her window and let the cool night air blow on her face. It was a pleasant end to a nice evening. Only one other car was on the road. She didn't really notice it until it was close behind her, shining its bright lights into her car. Lindsay tapped on her brakes, warning it to back off. It dropped back for a moment, then sped up again, following close to her bumper. She slowed down, hoping it would pass. The car slowed, too, maintaining the close distance. Lindsay reached down and took the car phone out of its cradle. The turn-off to the site was just ahead. She put down the phone and gripped the wheel, then sped up until she came to the dirt road that led to the site and turned off, creating a cloud of dust in her wake. The car drove on by, staying on the paved road. Lindsay breathed a sigh of relief.

"Jerk!" she muttered to herself as she headed up the road to the site.

good frend for jesus sake forbeare
to digg the dust enclosed heare
blese be ye man yt spares thes stones
and curst be he yt moves my bones
—epitaph on Shakespeare's tomb at Stratford

Chapter 3

OH, DAMN," exclaimed Lindsay, sitting back on her haunches and staring down into Burial 23.

"Oh, no. What'd I do?" asked Jane.

"I don't believe this."

"What?"

"Jane, don't tell anyone about this. Do you understand?"

"Tell what? What are you talking about?"

"If anyone comes over here, gently send them away and don't say anything."

"Don't say what?"

"I'll be right back."

Lindsay looked around the site for Frank and finally spotted him in Structure 4, turning a large rock over in his hands. She hurried over to the edge of the structure, leaving Jane staring down into the pit.

"I need to speak to you."

He replaced the stone, rose, and, carefully stepping

over artifacts, followed her to the edge of the site.

"This is about Burial 23," she said in a low voice. "It has a gold filling in its lower second molar."

"Good God, Lindsay! How do you do these things?"

"Me? It's not my fault."

"I suppose we can't cover it back up."

"I think it's classified as a dead body. We have to report it to the sheriff."

"Good thing you're so friendly with him."

"I'll help Jane finish and get Derrick to photograph the bones. Derrick and I can take them up, but we'll have to talk to the sheriff and coroner first."

"How long has it been in the ground? Can you tell?"

"Not yet. Jane has only uncovered the upper half. I'll have to wait until the bones are out of the ground. When did gold fillings come into dentistry?"

Frank shrugged. "I don't know. Well, we sure didn't need this. And Ned will pitch a fit when he gets back from whatever thing he had to do today. Damn!" He hesitated a moment, then finally nodded. "Okay, I suppose there's no choice. Go ahead and call the sheriff. We'll get Derrick to take the photographs after everyone has left the site this afternoon. I hope this doesn't get around. We'll have every sightseer and ghoul in the county out here stomping around. Derrick!" he called.

Derrick left the transit and walked over to them. His hair was damp and pulled back in a pony tail. Sweat made little trails through the dust covering his body, and he wiped it from his brow with his forearm.

"Damn! It's hot today. We could use a little rain. What's up?" Frank told him, and he winked at Lindsay. "Way to go."

"Honestly, you guys, the way you talk you'd think I killed someone, undressed their bones, and buried them. You don't happen to know when gold fillings came into use, do you?" she asked Derrick.

Derrick thought for a moment, then to Lindsay's surprise said, "The Italians used gold leaf for fillings in the 1400s."

"You're kidding," Lindsay and Frank exclaimed. "That early?"

"Amalgams with gold as a component didn't come until much later," Derrick explained. "You don't think the guy's a European, do you? Now that would be interesting."

"I guess we had better have a look," said Frank.

The three of them casually walked over to the burial. Jane greeted them with a wide grin.

"I found what you were talking about."

"Don't talk too loud," cautioned Frank.

They stared down into the grave. The bones, similar in color to the soil, stood out in relief. The skeleton lay on its back with its jaws open wide as though the person had gone to the grave screaming in protest.

Derrick took a dental pick from Jane, lay on his stomach and leaned into the pit. Lindsay lay beside him, took a brush, and cleaned dirt away from the molar. Derrick carefully cleared around the filling with the pick, then gently scraped it.

Lindsay and Derrick turned their heads toward each other, their faces so close Lindsay could feel his breath as he spoke.

"We need to find a better place to meet," he said, grinning.

Lindsay couldn't help but smile at him. "I agree."

Frank was squatting next to the grave. "What about it?" he asked. "Or are you two going to just stare at each other?"

Derrick didn't move. "This looks like an amalgam to me. That would make it much more recent," he said.

"I agree," said Lindsay, who looked at Derrick a moment longer before she turned her attention back to the skeleton. "Here is some residual cartilage on the head of the right humerus," she pointed out. "Can't be too old."

Both pushed themselves up and dusted themselves off.

"Keep this quiet, Derrick," said Frank. "You, too, Jane."

"No problem," Jane replied.

"I'll get the photographic equipment ready," Derrick said.

He trotted off to the laboratory tent, and Lindsay walked to the parking area to use the phone in Frank's car. The sheriff drove up just as she arrived.

"Hello, Sheriff Duggan. I was just about to call you."

"I thought I would take you up on that offer of the use of your crew."

"Okay. I'll take you to Frank, but first I have to tell you something. We came upon a burial that is much more recent than the others. An adult with a gold filling." The sheriff's mouth fell open, and for a minute Lindsay thought he was going to ask her how she got into things like that. She took him over to the grave, and he looked down at the half-buried anachronistic bones Jane was carefully excavating.

"Why is its mouth opened like that?" asked the sheriff.

"That's not uncommon," explained Lindsay. "Dirt is very active. It is constantly being moved around by the percolation of water, changing temperatures, the burrowing of insects and small animals. And when the flesh and ligaments are gone, the jaws move freely and the dirt action often forces the jaws apart. It creates the appearance of a scream."

"Well, it looks rather startling. How old do you think it is?" he asked.

"I don't know. I can't examine it until it is fully excavated, but I'd guess between 25 and a 100 years." Lindsay explained to him what she wanted to do with it.

"Sounds fine. If it's that old, there is no hurry. This case with the little Hastings girl is more urgent."

"Sheriff, would you mind keeping this quiet? We'll get all kinds of curious people out here walking all over the site if news gets around."

"No, I don't mind. If the papers get ahold of it, they will insist I do something about it, and right now my plate is full."

Lindsay smiled. "I'll take you to Frank."

As they walked across the site, Lindsay showed him various stains on the ground she thought were burials.

"How can you tell?" he asked.

"The shape and size, mainly. You get accustomed to what to look for."

"How did you know the Indian village was here?" asked the sheriff.

"Ned surface collected here for years. That is one way you know there is something under the soil,"

Lindsay explained. "Debris filters up to the surface."

The sheriff nodded, and she continued. "Over the years the flooding of the river and runoff from higher ground covered the area. The really heavy work is in removing the dirt overburden to get to the site floor. Once that's done, we shave the area smooth with sharp-edged shovels, which lets us see the markings that reveal where houses, burials, and other kinds of structures were when the village was here."

"What's this here?"

He pointed to a fifteen-by-fifteen-foot area bounded by an outline of round stains. It was filled with rocks, broken clay pots, and bones scattered about. Overlying the area was a grid of string supported by wooden stakes a foot apart. Workers were carefully digging out one square at a time, putting the dirt in labeled bags.

"Structure 4. It was a house."

"How do you know?"

"See all those roundish stains about six inches to a foot in diameter? Those are postholes. When a post rots in the ground, it's similar to having been burned and it leaves a dark stain. Sometimes we even find a small core of wood."

"Don't trees do the same thing?"

"Yes. That's why we cross-section some of them. The cross-section of a posthole is bullet shaped. The cross-section of a tree shows dark stains of the roots leading from the trunk."

The sheriff nodded.

"If you notice, the posthole pattern makes a square with rounded corners."

"Yeah, I see that."

"They built the houses in that shape. After putting up the posts, they wove sticks and grass between them and covered it all with clay. We call the process wattle and daub. They usually made a timber and thatched roof. As we excavate, we'll find domestic artifacts—potsherds, stone tools, stuff that indicates it was a dwelling."

Lindsay pointed to an excavation beyond Structure 4. "That structure over there was burned. All that black charcoal-looking stuff on the floor is the remains of the roof timbers. If we're lucky, the house burned accidentally, and all the domestic artifacts are there under the timbers where they were in use. That gives a lot of information."

"Not too lucky for the people who owned the house. Just who were these people?" the sheriff asked.

"That's a good question. The site is not far outside the area that archaeologists have defined as the Chiefdom of Coosa, dating to the sixteenth century. We're finding some of the same type of artifacts, and the settlement pattern is the same. But we're finding other types of artifacts, too. Frank thinks this is a different component of the Coosa chiefdom. Ned, however, thinks they are a different group that traded with the chiefdom but were not part of them. He thinks they were part of a more isolated group."

"I see," said the sheriff, who apparently had been satisfied with simply a name and a date. "That'd be Ned Meyers?"

Lindsay nodded.

"I remember him when he was a little kid. Spent his summers with his grandparents, the Hardwicks. Quiet little kid, always going around looking for arrowheads."

"Yes, that's him."

Frank came over and held out his hand, and the sheriff grabbed it. "Lindsay giving you a tour of the site?"

"Yeah, interesting." They walked away from the crew before the sheriff spoke again. "Lindsay tells me that your crew can make a thorough examination of the place where we found the bones of the little Hastings girl."

"Yes."

"How long would it take?"

"Perhaps a week or two. Probably a little longer."

"Can they start tomorrow morning?"

"Sure thing. Did Lindsay tell you about her find?" asked Frank.

"Yeah. She really has a knack, doesn't she."

Lindsay opened her mouth to protest, then closed it again.

That evening, Lindsay visited Derrick's tent across from hers and found him packing his equipment. "I hope you aren't too angry with me," she said.

Derrick grinned. "I guess you owe me."

Lindsay grinned back. "I guess I'm in trouble."

"Actually, I think it'll be interesting."

"I'm glad you see it that way." She sat down on the end of his bed and watched him pack.

"Did you seriously think I would be mad at you?" he asked.

Lindsay looked into Derrick's gentle brown eyes. "Not really. I just hate involving anyone else in this."

"Maybe it would be easier for you if you had someone else, like me, working with you."

"You're probably right."

"Does the sheriff have any idea who the bones in 23 belong to?" Derrick asked.

"No. He didn't get too excited about it, considering its age. That's good for us. Maybe it won't make the papers," Lindsay replied.

"You think whoever buried the body knew Indians were buried here and thought a graveyard would be a good place to hide a body, or was it a coincidence?"

"I don't know. I haven't seen any evidence of grave robbing. I'm not sure anyone knew there were burials here until we arrived."

"Funny thing, though, isn't it, a recent grave dug right into an ancient burial like that?" Derrick finished packing the smaller equipment and zipped up his bag.

"I've certainly never seen it before. Derrick, I appreciate your helping with the Hastings child."

"Well, then," said Derrick, smiling, "I'll have to think how you're going to repay me." Lindsay grabbed up his pillow, throwing it at him as she left his tent.

She started toward her own tent, but her curiosity about Burial 23 sent her to the laboratory instead. The bones of the anomalous burial were stored inside a cabinet away from other artifacts. Lindsay set the box of bones out on a table. The skull, sitting in a separate smaller box, was wrapped in cotton swathing. She gently picked it up, unwrapped it, and rotated the skull in her hand. An object fell to the table and rolled toward the edge. Lindsay grabbed it before it fell to the floor.

It was a bullet. She set the skull down and examined the bullet, weighing it in the palm of her hand. It was small, about the size of her fingernail, and the tip was smashed. Lindsay wondered if a ballistics expert could get any information from an examination of it. The gun from which it was fired probably had disappeared long ago, lost the way artifacts are lost, migrating from one place to another, mislaid, destroyed, hidden. She dropped the bullet into a plastic vial, wrote B23 on the lid, and put it in the box with the bones.

Lindsay picked up the skull again and looked for evidence of where the bullet had entered. A nick in the orbit indicated the bullet had entered the left eye. The skull still contained loose debris from the burial. She gently cleaned it out with a brush and examined the inside of the skull with a small flashlight. The bullet had impacted high on the occipital. Lindsay took a pencil and aligned it with the two marks on the skull left by the bullet. This person was shot straight on in the face by someone approximately the same height. This person ... Lindsay realized that she hadn't even sexed the individual yet.

She began setting the bones out on the table in their anatomical positions. She noted that the killer had taken the clothes as well, for no scrap of material, button, shoe, or anything had been found in the burial. Perhaps so that if the body was dug up, the clothes wouldn't identify it.

The yellow-brown bones had no odor except of fresh earth. She picked up a femur. It had been made hard from minerals leaching into the bones. That pushed the age of the bones past 50 years. The hard brown cartilage on several of the joints made it not over a hundred. Lindsay guessed around 60, but she would need to see an analysis of the soil to be sure. A cursory examination of the long bones revealed prominent muscle attachments. The person had been strong, possibly athletic, and had been right handed.

She picked up the parts of the pelvis. The skeleton was obviously that of a woman. The wide, shallow pelvis girdle had every female indicator. At first the skull had fooled her. The brow ridge and jaw line were a little more prominent than normally found in females.

Her attention returned to the skull. The extended nasal bones and relatively thin nasal cavity indicated that Burial 23 had a long, slender nose. With her sharp face, prominent features, and high cheekbones, she must have been a striking woman. The skull had a rare prominent metopic suture from the nasal cavity up the frontal bone to the top of the head. This rarity most often occurred in Caucasians. Lindsay turned the skull over. The relatively triangular palate was another indicator that the skeleton was Caucasian.

Lindsay made a quick measurement of the femur and guessed the woman's height to be about 5'10". She would do more thorough measurements later. She then examined the long bones to see if the shafts were fused to their epiphysis. The humeri and the femurs were fused. She looked at the clavicle—the proximal end had not yet fused. Nor had the shoulder blade or the pelvis. Okay, she thought, between 18 and 21. She looked at the teeth. The third molars were not yet in, but that only meant that the skeleton was probably not over 25. Lindsay looked at the pubic symphysis. There was no scarring that occurs during childbirth, and the surface was that of someone 18 or 19 years old. She picked up the fourth rib and examined the sternal end, which indicated the age to be between 16 and 19. She's over 17, Lindsay thought, judging by other indicators. Eighteen or nineteen is the best I can do.

Lindsay had seen no sign of disease in her examination of any of the bones. Nor did she find any breaks. She perused the smaller bones and stopped short at the fourth metacarpal of the left hand. There was a nick on the surface not unlike the nick in the eye socket. The woman had held her hand, palm outward, in front of her face when she was shot.

Burial 23 was a healthy white woman, 18 or 19 years old. She stood five feet, ten inches—tall for a woman about 60 years ago—at the time of her death. It had been a crime of hate, so Lindsay imagined. You would have to hate someone to look her in the eye and kill her. The woman had been talking to someone. She had thrown up her left hand in defense as the killer had raised a gun and shot her in the face. She had known her attacker. Lindsay smiled to herself. Frank always told her that even if Homer hadn't written about it, she could have described the Trojan War if anyone had ever uncovered a wooden hoof.

Lindsay took some graph paper and a pencil and began to draw the skull, but stopped halfway through the drawing. She wanted to reconstruct the face. An examination of the supply cabinet yielded the things she needed to make a mold of the skull. She piled everything on the table and began working.

When she finished, Lindsay sat back and inspected her work. Facing her was a plaster replica of the skull.

Not bad, she thought. She looked at her watch. It was late, 3:00 A.M. She would get only an hour's sleep.

"Great," she told the skull. "I'm going to be dead on my feet at the site, and it's your fault. Maybe I can sneak a nap during lunch."

She took the plaster skull to her tent and put it in a box under the table. Tomorrow she would call a friend at the university and ask him to send her the kit she would need to reconstruct the face.

Lindsay didn't nap during lunch. Instead, she picked up some of Derrick's duties. Careful not to make any serious mistake with the measurements, she double checked as she recorded the numbers she saw on the rod through the scope. It was her bad luck that Frank had assigned her to a task that required concentration.

"What's this I hear about Burial 23?"

Lindsay turned to face Ned, who was glowering at her. His Burnside-style mustache and sideburns had been neatly trimmed, giving him the appearance of a Civil War general in jeans and T-shirt.

"You been for a shave and hair cut?" she asked.

"Don't change the subject."

"What have you heard?" she asked.

"Frank told me that you found someone in the ground who wasn't supposed to be there."

Lindsay almost laughed. "That's right, and I told her so, too."

Ned did not smile. "You know what I mean."

"I'm in the process of analyzing the bones."

"Why didn't you just cover it back up?"

"That would've been illegal. Ned, why are you in such a hurry?"

"I just want the site dug."

"Everything seems to be going fine. I really don't understand—"

Frank walked up next to them. "Ned, the scouts will be here in a couple of days. Do you want to take half of them and open up another section?"

"Yes, but I need some professional crew as well."

"We are almost finished up here, then—"

"Tell Lindsay to cover up any more bodies she finds." He marched away.

Lindsay shook her head as she and Frank watched him recruit some of the field school students to help him mark off Section 4 to prepare for digging. They could hear the students protest being pulled off the structure they were working on.

"How about dinner?" Frank asked Lindsay.

"I'm exhausted." Lindsay rubbed her eyelids with her finger tips.

"What? From this little mapping?" asked Frank.

"I stayed up all night last night."

"Doing what?"

"Just working with the bones."

Frank frowned. "Pack up the transit. You've done enough work for one day. If I had known you had been up all night, I wouldn't have piled all that extra work on you."

"I was on my own time. I was working on Burial 23."

"All night? Doing what?"

"Making a cast of the skull. I'm going to reconstruct her face."

Frank eyed her for a moment. "Why?" he asked.

"Someone shot her and dumped her in the middle

of nowhere and left her there for 60 years. I want to at least know what she looked like."

"She was shot?" said Frank

"Yes. I found a bullet in the cranium."

She thought he might remind her not to take time away from the site on a task that was not really their responsibility. But what he said was, "I'd like you to spend some of your free time with me." He pushed a wayward strand of hair behind her ear. "I'll go get us a pizza. You might find you're hungry after all."

Frank walked to his car. Lindsay stood for a long time watching him drive out of sight.

"Damn!" Michelle came hurrying up to Lindsay. "He got away before I could catch him. Do you know Ned came and commandeered some of my crew? He didn't even ask. At least he could have taken that damn Jeremy."

"Jeremy? Isn't he that smart-mouthed kid?" asked Lindsay as she motioned for the student holding the survey rod to pack it in. "What's he up to now?"

"Just his usual royal pain-in-the-ass routine. Always sarcastic. I have to watch him all the time, or he'll mess up something in the structure."

"Have you mentioned him to Frank."

"Yeah, but Frank thinks Jeremy's just being a normal student. You know, immature and irresponsible. Frank says he will straighten up when he understands what he is supposed to do. At the house he keeps trying to sneak upstairs to the girls' section. I've asked Ned to make him stay downstairs, but Ned won't even talk to him. I don't know why Frank let Ned supervise the male students in the house. He is hardly ever there."

"You want me to talk to Frank?"

"I'd like you to take Jeremy off my hands. Next time you open up burials, let him sift the fill. He can't screw up much there."

"Sure."

Lindsay packed and stored the transit, then went to her tent. She stretched out on her bed and was asleep when Frank returned with the pizza. He quietly called her name and entered the darkened tent. She raised her head, confused for a moment.

"I think you need sleep more than you need pizza." He kissed her cheek and left.

The next day was hectic. Thomas pestered her to let him do a burial, so she put him and Sally on Burial 24. The sheriff and Derrick arrived about the time that Thomas went ballistic with excitement. Frank and Lindsay were standing in a structure, discussing a cache of animal bones when Thomas jumped up and shouted, "It's an atlatl!"

"What now?" groaned Frank.

Lindsay walked to the burial. "What you got?" She directed her question to Sally, who grinned up at her.

"His ribs are covered with copper gorgets."

Lindsay peered at the mass of green oxidized copper overlaying the bones. "See, the copper preserved the wood," said Thomas. "It is an atlatl."

"I think it's probably the sternum," said Lindsay calmly.

"I doubt there'd be any throwing sticks at this site," said Frank. "Atlatls were much earlier."

"Some isolated places still used them in historic times," Ned answered. "This may be evidence supporting my hypothesis."

"Look at the shape," insisted Thomas. "It looks just like an atlatl.

"You can't see much of the shape. We'll see when it's excavated," said Lindsay.

"Look at this," said Sally, pointing to a cache of fancy arrowheads. "Think we have the chief here?"

Frank was sitting on his haunches, looking into the burial. He gave Sally an annoyed look as if to say, Don't encourage Thomas. "There is no way to know," he said. "The only thing we can say is that he did have a high status."

"Or she," said Sally.

"It will be a he," said Frank.

"It looks like a she. Look at the brow ridge."

"I think when you uncover the pelvis, you'll find it is a he," said Frank.

Lindsay looked up to see the sheriff and Derrick peering into the burial along with everyone else. "Found something special?" he asked.

Lindsay and Frank stood up to greet him. "Looks like we uncovered a VIP," said Frank. "At least he has quite a collection of grave goods."

"And an atlatl," Thomas boasted. "You don't find too many of them because they are made of wood. Being next to the copper preserved it."

Lindsay rolled her eyes upward.

"Atlatl?" asked the sheriff.

"Throwing stick," said Lindsay. "You use it with a spear to give extra leverage when you throw. But this is the breast bone."

"Well, look at this!" shouted Thomas. "Tell me it's not a banner stone." He picked up a smooth stone and handed it to Frank.

"A banner stone is used to weight an atlatl," Derrick explained for the sheriff's benefit.

They looked up at Lindsay and grinned, as if suddenly the great Lindsay could be mistaken, humbled by the likes of Thomas. Derrick, however, winked his "I'm with you, kid" wink at her. The sheriff grinned as if he were witnessing a contest.

Lindsay could see this was becoming a matter of face. "That's most likely the head of a club, not a banner stone."

"Don't some people think that's what a banner stone is really for, to make it double as a war club?" asked Thomas.

"We'll see when it gets uncovered," Frank said, smiling at Lindsay. Turning to the sheriff, he said, "Is this social or business?"

"Business, but it can wait for the outcome of the controversy here. I'd just as soon wait."

"We can't take it up until it's photographed, and the preparation for that will take a while," said Frank. "We can go have a Coke and talk if you want."

"Lindsay better come, too," he said. They walked over to the eating area, which was out of the sun and out of hearing distance.

"Don't you all get so excited that you rip out all the artifacts before they're recorded," Frank shouted back at the crew.

They sat at the table, and Derrick reached into the cooler and pulled out bottles of soda for everyone .

"Ah, this is good," said the sheriff. "It still has ice in it." He allowed everyone to take a few sips of drink before he said anything else. Then he told them, "Derrick found more bones."

Lindsay was silent for a moment, then realized he meant bones of another child. "Oh, no," she whispered.

"I know," said the sheriff. "I'm keeping it quiet until we can identify them. I thought you might go back with me and take a look."

They drank their drinks in silence. Lindsay sipped slowly so she would not finish too soon. After a while Sally shouted and waved for them to come over.

Thomas and Sally had cleaned the dirt from the chest area of the burial. A series of green copper plates covered most of the front of the rib cage. A long bone or wooden looking object lay in the center of the chest, surrounded and half covered by the copper. Sally said, "I think you can see something now, Lindsay."

Lindsay reached down with a tongue depressor and gently tried to lift a plate. The copper was fused to the underlying bone. "I'm afraid the answer may have to wait until the burial is finished and photographed," she said. She tried the uppermost plate. It came loose, and she could see the shape of the object in question and how it had been articulated to the now-vanished costal cartilage. "The sternum," she said.

"Are you sure?" said Thomas with great disappointment but no chagrin in his voice.

Lindsay thought that Ned looked even more disappointed than Thomas.

"Yes. Take a look."

"Looks like a sternum to me," said Derrick.

"Well, your reputation is still intact." Frank was smiling at her.

"Was it ever in question?" Lindsay feigned surprise. "I had no idea. Amazing how you can build it up over the years and almost lose it in a moment." She rose, wiped off her hands on Frank's shirt front, and left with the sheriff and Derrick for another grim task in town.

"As a kid I had an interest in medieval weapons, bows and such," said the sheriff as he drove them to his office. "I thought I knew almost all the different kinds of weapons, but I never heard of an atlatl."

"It was quite an ingenious device," said Derrick, leaning forward from his seat in the back. "The throwing stick, in effect, lengthens the thrower's arm. The leverage increases the power of the spear by several times. If you tie a banner stone onto it, the stone increases the mass and you can get even more power in the throw."

"Interesting," said the sheriff. "I guess these Indians were more inventive than I thought." He turned his head to Lindsay. "Pretty touch-and-go for a moment back there for you."

"Not really," Derrick answered for her. "Lindsay knows her bones. At a party in graduate school, some of us took Sebastian—he was one of our skeletons in the osteology lab—took him apart and added a few animal bones to the mix. We blindfolded Lindsay, and she identified every bone, even which side it belonged, by only the feel. But the most fantastic thing was the skull. We substituted Fred, a kind of twin to Sebastian. The department had ordered a male and a female, but got two males. We had to scrounge around for a female. I won't tell you where. But anyway, Fred looked just like Sebastian to all of us, but Lindsay knew the difference as soon as she got her fingers on the skull. We called her the Great

Lindsay after that."

The sheriff, grinning, turned to Lindsay. "Is that true?"

"Yes. But it wasn't that big of a deal. All the diagnostic characteristics of bones can be felt. Still, I wouldn't have been able to live it down if Thomas, of all people, had been right."

"Why him?" asked the sheriff.

"This is Thomas's first course in archaeology," she said. "Since I have a Ph.D. I'm expected to know more." She grinned. "The other day he thought he had a long house. That's kind of like an Indian government building—but it was only a couple of rows of trees."

"A few weeks ago he thought he had found a canoe," said Derrick.

"A canoe?" said Lindsay. "I didn't hear about that."

"That was before you arrived. You should have heard him. He was almost delirious."

"What was it?" asked the sheriff.

"A cache of fallen trees not quite decomposed. It was fairly shallow in the overburden. I expect it was where the paper company who used to own the land piled them up and covered them over a few years ago."

"Thomas is an excitable fellow, I take it."

"Yes," affirmed Lindsay. "But the truth is, we all enjoy the fantastic finds."

"What's the most interesting thing you've found?" the sheriff asked.

"I enjoy the point caches in some of the burials," said Derrick. "You can get some remarkably intricate designs, beautiful ceremonial blades, elegantly flaked points."

"Derrick is a great flint knapper," said Lindsay. "He's made some beautiful blades himself. I found a Spanish sword once. That was thrilling. This burial with the copper should have loads of interesting things in it."

"Come out to the site sometime," said Derrick, "and I'll show you how an atlatl works."

"You have one?"

"Yeah, I made one."

"I'll do that. I enjoy odd weapons."

At the sheriff's department, Derrick transferred to his jeep and drove back to the crime scene. Inside, the sheriff and Lindsay found Sarah and Mike Pruitt waiting in his office. Sheriff Duggan was visibly annoyed.

"We heard you found another skeleton," Sarah said.

"Where did you hear that?" the sheriff asked.

"I … I'd rather not say," she said softly.

"I think it would be better if you went home and let us call you," said the sheriff.

"Now, look here—" began Mike Pruitt.

"Please, Mr. Pruitt, you will be more comfortable at home," interrupted the sheriff. "This could take a while."

"It didn't take that long last time," protested Sarah.

Lindsay answered, "That was because the teeth were clearly different from your daughter's teeth in the photograph. If these teeth occlude properly, like many children's do, I will have to rely on other more time-consuming methods. Please listen to the sheriff and wait at home. You will be much more comfortable, and this could take several hours."

They reluctantly agreed, and the sheriff escorted them to their car. When he returned, Deputy Andy

Littleton took the first brunt of his anger.

"Who told them?"

"I don't know, sir. I didn't. You said not to."

"Find out who did." He turned to Lindsay. "Thanks for the help with the Pruitts. The bones are in the back. I guess you know the way by now."

Lindsay found her way to the back room. Derrick had laid the bones out in a long box. The odor was strong and unpleasant. Most of the connecting cartilage had not yet decomposed, and most of the bones were still articulated. Portions of the scalp—with wisps of blonde hair attached—still adhered to the skull. She looked at the face of the skull, mentally fleshing it out. There was a slight indentation in the chin; the teeth did occlude evenly; the orbits were a little far apart. In her heart, Lindsay knew this was little Peggy Pruitt, but she took out her measuring instruments and the photograph of Peggy and began her work.

The camera measurements she had requested from Mickey Lawson were clipped to the photograph. Lindsay unclipped them and lay aside the figures. She began measuring the photo: nasion to gnathion, orbital height and breadth, nasal height and breadth, bizygomatic breadth, bigonial breadth, symphysis height, and many, many more. On a separate paper she made the calculations that would tell her the actual size of Peggy's head. After the calculations, she made the same measurements on the skull. The measurements on the photograph, adjusted for the actual size of the face, were all consistent with the measurements of the skull. Later, for the report, she would photograph a superimposition of the portrait of Peggy with an x-ray of the skull. Lindsay took a hand lens and carefully examined the teeth in the photograph. After a while, she rose and walked to the sheriff's office.

The door was closed, but the sheriff's voice from inside was clear and angry. "If it turns out not to be Peggy, the Pruitts have had several hours of agony for nothing. If it is Peggy, nothing was to be gained by them knowing ahead of time."

"I just thought—" began a voice that Lindsay recognized as that of the receptionist.

"You just thought your judgment was better than mine. And I won't have that in this office."

"No, I—"

"In this office confidentiality is absolutely essential. Do I make myself clear."

"Yes, sir."

"Good, then this won't ever happen again."

"No, sir."

The door burst open and Winifred hurried out, brushing past Lindsay, red-faced and embarrassed. Lindsay knocked on the open door. The sheriff jerked his head up, then smiled slightly. "Come in, Lindsay. Close the door."

"I need another measurement from the photographer, if he has it. I was wondering if I could use your phone."

"Sure. How is it looking?"

"I believe it's Peggy."

"I kind of figured so," he said. "Truthfully, I was dreading a third missing child."

"I'm not ready to make a definite identification just yet." Lindsay dialed the number written on the back of the photograph. She reached Mickey Lawson and asked him if he kept a record of the lighting distance and angle for Peggy Pruitt's portrait. He left the phone for several minutes. When he returned, he gave her some numbers. Lindsay thanked him and hung up the phone.

"I am going to need an official copy of these numbers from his files, or rather you are," said Lindsay. "Perhaps you could send a deputy over to his studio sometime to take his records and make photocopies of them."

"Sure thing."

"How accurate do you think Mickey Lawson is in his record keeping?" Lindsay asked.

"I think you can probably take them to the bank. Mickey is well known for his obsessive record keeping. He drives his assistants nuts, I've heard."

"I'll be finished shortly."

"I'm sorry about my temper when we arrived. I didn't like seeing the Pruitts put through this."

Lindsay smiled at the sheriff. "I didn't notice."

She went to the back room and performed calculations regarding shadows in the photograph. Lindsay was replacing the remains in the box when the sheriff came in and pulled up a chair.

"I've done all I can do for now with the identification," she told him. "If I can get Peggy's medical and immunization records, I may be able to do something with some calcium deposits in the growth zones."

"So you couldn't make a positive identification?"

"They are Peggy's bones, all right." She smiled at the sheriff. "I like a lot of detail in my records, too. The more corroborating details you have, the easier time you have in court."

The sheriff nodded his head. "Yeah, those defense lawyers will tear into any little sign of uncertainty."

Lindsay took the recordings and showed the sheriff. "All the facial measurements are consistent. See this tooth? The upper left canine? It is slightly forward and casts a shadow on the incisor next to it. The lighting angle allowed me to measure its distance from the incisor next to it in the photograph. It appears to be the same distance forward as the upper left canine in the skull. Also, the teeth in the photograph are the same size and shape as those in the skull. You can see why the accuracy of the photographer's measurements is so important. I thought I would drop by his studio sometime and take a look at his setup."

"What can I tell the Pruitts?"

"You can tell them these are their daughter's remains."

"I'll call them. Then let me take you to the diner for a cup of coffee."

"That would be good." Lindsay leaned toward the sheriff and said in a low voice. "I can tell you this: you have a serial killer. The pelvic damage on these remains is the same as on Amy Lynn Hasting's."

"I was afraid of that." Duggan stood up. "Come on, let's forget about this for a while."

"By the way, before I forget," said Lindsay, "I found this in the cranial cavity of Burial 23." She gave him the bullet. "I'll give you a report on the bones in a couple of days."

The sheriff held up the vial and looked at the bullet. "Small caliber," he commented, then locked it in his desk drawer.

After he called the Pruitts, he took Lindsay to the cafe down the street. They sat in a booth in the back corner.

"This is not easy for you, is it?" he said after the waitress brought them coffee and lemon pie.

Lindsay's eyes misted over. "He hurt them really bad. He had to have gagged them in some way. I don't think he would have trusted that their screams would not be heard, even in a remote location. That may help in your investigation. I don't know."

"Do you get upset over the Indian bones?"

"Sometimes. Child burials are sad, when you think how grieved the parents were. Infant mortality was high, and children were very precious. But mostly at Indian sites you're looking at a normal life cycle. The population lived, were happy perhaps, and died of natural causes."

"They are very real to you, these Indians."

"They were real. Every burial represents a person who once walked around just as you and I. They were happy and sad, loved and hated, worried about making a living, and enjoyed celebrations, just as we do. Mostly, working with the skeletal population is a pleasure. It's like going back in time and talking to them. Their bones tell me a lot about how they lived and died."

"Happier than police work?"

"Sometimes. There was this one site that still haunts me, though. It's dated to the time of European contact." Lindsay took a sip of coffee and a bite of pie before she continued. "You find that sites of the same time period range from wealthy villages with an abundance of fancy artifacts and large populations, to tiny villages that were very poor. This one was small and poor. It wasn't occupied long; we think it was a seasonal camp. Anyway, the burials were almost entirely women, children, and the elderly. There were only a few young adult males. I don't know how deeply you studied medieval weapons, but European medieval battle wounds have specific patterns. We often find those patterns on Indian burials that date to Spanish contact. Every one of the burials at this particular site had those wounds, even the children. In my mind I could see the mothers, children, and grandmothers running from the Spanish conquistadors, who were on horseback cutting them down while the few males who were left in the village tried to defend them. The males' wounds were in front, whereas the women and children's were from behind. I suppose the other males were off hunting. When they returned, they found their families slaughtered and their village burned to the ground. They buried them in mass graves. After that, they left, and the village was never inhabited again."

"It must have been like uncovering an ancient crime scene," he said. "And there was no one to bring to justice."

Unexpectedly, Derrick appeared and slid into the booth beside Lindsay. "You look kind of pale, kid," he said.

"Just telling stories of ancient crimes," she said.

"I hear that the Indians aren't too pleased with having their ancestors dug up," said the sheriff.

"That's why we have a policy in the archaeology department of examining the bones and repatriating them very quickly."

"I suppose that means that you rebury them. You have any regrets or misgivings about that?" the sheriff asked.

Lindsay nodded. "I regret that the skeletal remains

will be lost to us when they are returned to the ground. The techniques for analyzing bones are improving every day. Once the bones are back in the ground, further analysis is lost. It would be nice if one day we could analyze the DNA and match a site with present-day tribes. Then we could know for certain whose ancestors are whose."

"How do you feel about it?" the sheriff asked Derrick.

Derrick took a drink of the water that the waitress had brought him before he answered. "To Native Americans, archaeologists rank below lawyers and politicians. You can't blame them for feeling that way. In the past some archaeologists have not treated the bones with much respect. In fact, they have been rather haphazard with them, keeping them in boxes on shelves for years. I had one professor intentionally crush a skull to make a point about how bones break. These are the remains of people."

"That's true," said Lindsay. "Not every archaeologist has had the purest of motives or the greatest skill either. Archaeologists, like everyone else, have had to learn some lessons about sensitivity and the strong feelings some people have regarding the excavation of burials." She looked at Derrick a moment, remembering the moment in class when the professor dropped the skull in a parking lot and how they were all shocked speechless. "But we are finding and recovering something that has been lost. Sometimes we are able to set right a historical record that has gone wrong, or document an ancient injustice like the slaughter of the village I told you about. Mostly, we are just recording the details of a lost knowledge. In my mind, it would be tragic to lose the knowledge forever."

"Sounds like you two have had this conversation before," said the sheriff.

"You could say that," agreed Derrick, smiling at Lindsay. He took another drink of water. "I found some things I thought the sheriff ought to see," he said. "They're in the jeep."

The sheriff sighed. "Let's go take a look."

They walked out to the jeep, and Derrick opened the back. "Here is some clothing." He opened a box containing a large plastic storage bag. "This box contains another set. I made this map of the crime scene. It shows the relationship of the clothing to the graves. In with each set of clothing was about a four-inch piece of duct tape." Lindsay and the sheriff looked at each other a moment. "And some rope," he finished. "The rope, tape, and clothes that were found together are bagged together.

"Also, we found this." He pulled out a small box and opened it. An open Swiss army knife caked with dirt lay inside. "It was near the grave of the bones I brought in a while ago."

"The clothes will help identify the remains," said the sheriff.

"There's more." Derrick pulled out several more plastic sandwich bags. "This is a quarter, a dime, several weathered candy wrappers, and a ball point pen." Derrick pointed to a place on the map. "They were found here and here, just a few feet apart. I think it's where he parked his car, and these things were lost when he got out on the driver's side and the little girls got out on the passenger side."

The sheriff looked impressed. "You have a knack

for detective work, son," he said.

"Yes, Derrick," said Lindsay. "I think you were Sam Spade in another life."

Derrick grinned. "If archaeology hits a slump, Lindsay and I can open a detective agency. Anyway, we've found a cart load of other stuff you will have to look at," Derrick told the sheriff. "I think it is miscellaneous trash. It fans out from the immediate scene, but some of it may be important. I also found the rest of the dog's bones."

"This is good," said the sheriff as he studied the meticulously drawn map. "Real good."

"Some scout troops are coming out to work on the dig, so I'm going to ask Frank for a few more crew members. I think I can have this finished in another day or two."

"Great. I appreciate your help." The sheriff hesitated a moment, looking at Lindsay and Derrick. "Are you two related, brother and sister?" he asked.

Derrick looked puzzled, but Lindsay knew what he meant. "The hair," she said. Lindsay and Derrick had almost identical long, chestnut-brown hair.

"Oh," said Derrick. "No, it's just some kind of cosmic coincidence."

The sheriff just grinned.

After Derrick dropped the evidence off at the sheriff's department, he and Lindsay headed for the site in his jeep.

"Wait," Lindsay exclaimed. "I have to stop off at Mickey Lawson's portrait studio. It won't take long."

"Sure thing. I needed to stop at the hardware store anyway to see if my shovels are ready. This guy they recommended does a good job of cutting them off straight and putting a good edge on them."

"I'll walk over to the hardware store when I'm finished," she said as Derrick let her out in front of the studio.

The display windows of Mickey Lawson's studio contained rows of family, school, wedding, and various club photographs. She opened the glass door and walked in. A middle-aged woman sitting behind a mahogany desk looked up with a smile as Lindsay entered.

"Can I help you?"

"My name is Lindsay Chamberlain. I called for an appointment with Mr. Lawson."

The receptionist put on a solemn face. "Yes, about little Peggy. That is so sad. Sarah and Mike are just broken-hearted, just like when she disappeared. Now they have to grieve all over again. But it was so hard for them, not knowing what happened to her."

Lindsay nodded. "Is Mr. Lawson in?"

"He stepped out for just a moment."

"Thank you. I'll just walk around and look at these pictures."

"Mr. Lawson is a good photographer."

"I see that."

"People come from all over. Clubs particularly like him. He has done some nice pictures for the garden club."

The photographs were mostly typical family and wedding portraits: full face and profiles in the same portrait, portraits with silhouettes, and portraits taken with fancy filters.

Beside the wedding photographs hung a series of

portraits of the garden club members, each with a flower in an oval inset. Marsha's picture was there, with a large red rose.

"Those of the garden club are good, don't you think?" asked the receptionist.

"Yes, they are. Did each member grow the flower in her portrait?"

"They certainly did. Many are prize winners, too."

"They are quite lovely."

On the opposite wall hung several pictures taken at various local functions: one of the sheriff giving a campaign speech, which made Lindsay smile, and one of a magician with a large mustache in top hat and tails, thrusting a white rabbit in one hand and his hat in the other toward the camera. The photograph was foreshortened so that the rabbit, the hat, and the magician's arms projected out from the photograph and appeared large. There was a series of circus pictures: clowns, elephants, bareback riders, trapeze artists, all taken with varied camera angles and styles. Some pictures of the clowns, the lights, and the crowd were surreal. These, thought Lindsay, were pretty good, better than the more traditional ones. She wondered how often Mickey indulged his creativity.

When Mickey Lawson returned, he greeted Lindsay with a broad smile. He had a boyish face underneath thick, sandy brown hair. She had seen him with the Pruitts but hadn't paid close attention to him then. She guessed him to be about 30. He was tall, large-boned, and slim.

"Sorry," he said. "I had to go up to Tylerwynd to see Grandmother Tyler. When she talks, we all listen."

He gave a little laugh.

"I was just enjoying your photographs," remarked Lindsay.

He blushed slightly and bobbed his head, pleased. "Thanks. People around here seem to like them. Come back to the studio. Tell me again what you want."

"Just some information for the report. I used many of your measurements in the identification, and I just need to see them myself. If I have to go to court, I can say I saw your studio and how you take your measurements."

"Sure. Can I ask how you use them?"

"I do calculations from the photograph and find out the actual size of the head. Then I can compare the calculations with the skeletal remains."

"I see. I'm glad I keep such good records."

His studio looked like most studios Lindsay had ever been in. He had a large box camera, a stage, and an array of lights. Toys and various props sat neatly on a shelf. A red light above a door in the corner of the room revealed the location of the darkroom. Beside the door several metal filing cabinets lined the wall.

Painted on the floor were measurements from the camera to the stage, from the camera to the lights, and from the lights to the stage.

Lindsay took out a tape measure and measured the floor markings. "They correspond to my tape measure," she said. "That is basically all I needed to know. Why don't you take a picture of the floor here and send it to the sheriff's department?"

"Sure." He grinned broadly, obviously appreciating Lindsay's attention to detail. "I find the way to be consistent with my photography is to take careful notes of each picture. Those filing cabinets are full of information on every photograph I have ever taken. I can use my notes and re-create a photograph exactly as it was made the first time."

"That's good to know. I won't take up any more of your time. Thank you for showing me your studio."

"You're welcome. Just call or come by if you need anything else."

Derrick was looking in the window of Mickey's studio when she emerged. "The shovels weren't ready. That's the bad thing about this guy. He's kind of slow."

They climbed in the jeep, and Derrick headed for the site. After five minutes of silence, Derrick patted Lindsay's hand.

"You okay, Lindsay?"

"Yeah."

She told him about the injuries she had found on the bones of the children.

Derrick took her hand and held it. "I don't understand it," he whispered.

"Neither do I. I told the sheriff about the massacre site. This is the same kind of madness."

"You know what we need to do?"

"What?" asked Lindsay.

"Go dancing. Real dancing."

"Yeah, we do. We haven't done that in at least a year."

"I'll scout around for a place. Maybe good old Marsha knows somewhere."

Lindsay grinned. "Maybe she does."

"You and Frank seem to be getting close again."

"We went to the movie the other night, that's all."

"Did you have a good time?"

"It was nice. Why do you ask?" She gave him a sideways glance.

"I like to keep an eye on you, Lindsay. I have to make sure my best dancing partner is happy."

"I think I would be a lot happier if I hadn't become involved in identifying these bones. I love working with bones, but … it's hard when they are children."

Derrick reached over and took her hand. "I know."

"Well, speak of the devil," said Lindsay, "isn't that Good Ole Marsha's Lincoln parked beside Frank's Jeep? We can ask her about a place to go dancing."

... and the bones came together, bone to his bone ...
the sinews and the flesh came up upon them,
and the skin covered them above:
but there was no breath in them.
Ezekiel 37:7-8

Chapter 4

WHEN LINDSAY AND Derrick arrived at the site, Marsha, Frank, Jane, and Thomas were sitting at the picnic table drinking Cokes and laughing. Marsha's hand was resting on Frank's arm as she ended some funny anecdote about her garden club. Lindsay sat down opposite Marsha and Frank while Derrick got the two of them a Coke from the cooler.

"Marsha. Just the person we wanted to see." Derrick sat beside Lindsay and handed her a bottle. "Is there any really good place to go dancing near here?"

"Oh, yes, is there?" cried Jane. "You should see Lindsay and Derrick dance. They've won tons of competitions."

"I had forgotten that you and Derrick dance," Frank said. "I didn't realize it was that serious. So you've won competitions together?"

"Well, as a matter of fact, there is a place," said

Marsha, before Lindsay had a chance to speak. "Not here in Merry Claymoore, but about 40 miles from here. Why don't we all go? I'd love to see Derrick and Lindsay dance."

Great, thought Lindsay. Marsha just wrangled a date with Frank.

"Let's do it," agreed Jane. "You all are in for a treat."

Lindsay gave Jane a pained smile. "You're building us up quite a bit."

"We can deliver." Derrick grinned and put an arm around her shoulder.

"Speaking of delivery," Frank said. "A package arrived for you, Lindsay. I put it in your tent."

"Oh, I know what it is." She downed the rest of her drink. "See you guys later. Let me know when we're going dancing." She left for her tent just as Marsha invited Frank for coffee in town.

The package was from the forensics department at the University of Tennessee. It was the kit she needed to reconstruct the face of Burial 23. Lindsay laid out the supplies on her desk and began placing the skin depth spacers on the skull. When she finished, she began with the modeling clay, smoothing it to a thickness that just covered the spacers. It was like connecting similar elevation lines on a map.

When Lindsay stood and stretched her stiff muscles, she realized that it was well after dark. She looked down at the rough image of a face emerging from her effort. Coarse though it was, she could see the countenance of Burial 23 taking shape.

It was still early enough to take a walk by the river, and the night was lit by the moon. She put away her work and left her tent. No one else was home in the crew's tent village. The tents were dark and empty. Probably in town, she thought, or taking a moonlight swim. It was cool, and she hugged herself as she walked down the deer trail toward the river. No one was there, and she turned around to return to the tents. Just ahead she could see a dark form coming down the path toward her. For a moment, she had the urge to turn and run. Then she realized it was Derrick.

"You out for a walk, too?" she asked, trying not to sound relieved.

"Yeah. Nice night for it."

Derrick looked good in the moonlight. Of course, thought Lindsay, Derrick looked good all the time.

Unexpectedly, he reached out and gently pulled her to him. For a moment, as if waiting for her to say something, he simply looked into her eyes. When she said nothing, he kissed her. Lindsay slipped her arms around his neck, returning his kiss.

Kissing Derrick was sweet, tender, and exciting, everything Lindsay thought it probably would be. When they finally stopped, she stepped back. She had known Derrick for a long time; he was a good friend. He had kissed her cheek many times and had even kissed her lips to ring in a new year, but he had never kissed her like that.

"Come with me." He held out his hand.

"No."

"Why?"

"Can't afford to."

"But you want to."

"Of course I want to. That's beside the point."

"It will be really good." He kissed her ear.

"I don't doubt that, Derrick." She smiled up at him. "You are one of the most gorgeous...sexiest men I have ever known. And you genuinely like women, really like them. But that's part of the problem."

"How come? I practice safe sex."

Lindsay laughed. "I've never had casual sex, and I don't intend to start, not even with such a terrific partner."

Derrick's eyes were soft and dreamy. He was an expert lover, all gentle and coaxing with the promise of giving the greatest of pleasure, which she had no doubt he could deliver.

"My reputation far surpasses the reality. I'm not casual either."

Lindsay laughed again. "I would fall in love with you, and you would break my heart."

"I would never."

"I'll take one more kiss, if you've a mind, then I'll go to my tent and sleep alone."

Derrick pulled her into his arms and gave her his best.

In the morning the sheriff sent word that the Pruitts had identified some of the clothes Derrick had found at the crime scene. With that and Lindsay's report, he released the bones for burial. Lindsay was glad it was over.

The scouts had arrived at the site and had set up camp in an adjoining field. Lindsay tried to give each a little time working on a burial, because among the site crew burials were considered a treat. But she found to her amazement that some of the scouts were afraid to touch the bones. She watched one boy's hand shake as he tried to use a wooden tongue depressor to scrape dirt away from a long bone. She was astonished that he was afraid of the remains of a people she thought of as friends.

Most of the scouts' time, however, was seized by Ned to remove the overburden in the new section he was so impatient to uncover. Lindsay thought he would be happy now, or at least less combative, but Frank's refusal to give him the number of professional crew he wanted and Frank's insistence that he supervise Ned's work made Ned furious. Lindsay overheard them argue on a number of occasions.

"Dammit, you act like I can't lead an excavation!" Ned yelled.

"Ned, we need to have consistent methodology throughout the site. I don't question your abilities, only your stubbornness."

"Great, that's just great..."

All the arguments usually ended with Ned stomping off to his corner of the site.

Lindsay had looked forward all day to her work that evening on the skull of Burial 23. She smoothed and refined the formerly roughed-out features, willing her fingers to bring an expression of life into the clay. Late into the night, she stopped and looked at the face that stared back at her with blank eyes. Whoever she had been, she was a handsome woman with a very proud face and a well-shaped head. Lindsay wondered what her story was, wondered if anyone she once knew was here in this town or if she were now an anonymous person who could only talk to archaeologists. Even to them her ability to communicate was reduced by lack of context. Burial 23 couldn't tell Lindsay as much about her life as could the 500-year-old Indians with whom she had been buried.

Derrick knocked on her tent pole. "I saw your light on," he said as he entered. He was wearing a pair of shorts, and his mane of hair was in disarray as if he had just risen from sleep. "So that's 23," he said, pulling up a chair and raking his fingers through his hair. "Nice looking chick."

"Yes," agreed Lindsay, "I wonder who she was and who shot her?"

"Has it occurred to you that there's been entirely too much murder on this dig?" Derrick commented as he studied the roughed-out clay face.

"Yes, there has. I'm glad you're about finished with the crime scene."

"Me, too. I'm ready to get back to the Indians. They were quite gentle people, compared to the citizenry of Merry Claymoore. I'm going back to bed. Wanna come?"

"I'm too tired."

"Always an excuse. By the way, this Saturday night suit you?"

"Dancing? Fine. I can't wait. By the way, we're going to have to practice a little before we go. How long has it been since you've done any lifts?"

"Since we last danced. I'll find a place. G'nite, Lindsay."

"Sweet dreams, Derrick."

Derrick found another body at the crime scene the next day. From the far side of the site Lindsay saw the sheriff and him as they drove up. Derrick ducked into the lab tent with a box under his arm. The sheriff spotted her and walked in her direction.

"No," she whispered, "not another one."

She met the sheriff half way, hoping he would tell her something different from what she knew in her heart.

"I want this kept absolutely quiet. That's why the coroner agreed we could bring it here," he told her as they walked to the lab.

Derrick was waiting for them. Fortunately, because so many of the professional crew were working away at the crime scene, Frank had pulled all the lab personnel to work the site. Lindsay, Derrick, and the sheriff were alone in the laboratory tent.

"Sorry, Lindsay." Derrick smiled grimly at her when she entered.

She walked to the table and for a moment stared at the box of bones. Finally, she lifted out a femur and examined it. "These bones are older. Right off, I would say they've been in the ground at least ten years, perhaps longer."

"There are some contextual differences," Derrick told her. "I found buttons and some fabric with the bones. On top, but not underneath. It looked as if the hands were bound when the victim was buried, and there were traces of fabric on the maxillary bones."

"Ten years or longer. Damn!" exclaimed the sheriff. "With that long a span of time between this victim and the others, there could be many more out there."

"There may be other burial sites, but I believe we've found all the holes at that site." Derrick said. "We've covered the area pretty well, measuring the resistivity of the ground."

"Resistivity? Is that what you were doing?" asked the sheriff. "I thought you were using a metal detector."

"Besides," said Lindsay, "if that many children went missing over the years, wouldn't it have been noticed?"

"Maybe, but the Hastings girl was from another county. When you have children missing from different parts of the state, it would be easy for a pattern to go unnoticed."

"I'll have a look at these bones right away. There are a few tests I can perform to see how long they have been in the ground. Perhaps I can give you a more accurate time frame."

The sheriff started to go, then abruptly turned to Lindsay and Derrick. "You know, the other day when you were describing those Indians who were massacred by the Spanish? You brought what happened to life by just knowing the bones and the lay of the land. Can you do that for the crime scene? I think that you two might bring a perspective to my investigation."

"We can try," Lindsay replied. "I'm not sure it would be different from what you yourself would see."

"Maybe, but I would like to hear it, just the same." The sheriff left, and Lindsay began to unpack the bones.

"You want some help?"

"You better go see what you can do for Frank," Lindsay suggested. "I guess he is beginning to regret loaning us to the sheriff."

"Let me know if you need to talk." Derrick gave

her a quick hug and a kiss on her cheek.

"Sure," she said and stared after him as he walked out of the tent.

The laboratory tent was hot, even with all the flaps open. Lindsay tied her T-shirt under her breasts, exposing her bare midriff to any cool breeze that might come through the tent. She put on latex gloves, laid out the bones, and began examining each one carefully. After a while, she blinked away a tear and began her meticulous measurements.

Lindsay thought she heard a scream. She stopped what she was doing and listened. She heard it again, then shouting. She hurried out of the tent and saw Derrick and Alan running through the woods toward the latrines with Frank right behind them. Lindsay ran to the edge of the woods. Some of the remaining site crew were not far behind.

"What happened?" she asked the few crew who had arrived, also alerted by the scream.

Jane shrugged. "It must have been Sally. She went to use the bathroom. Maybe she saw a snake."

Lindsay followed the guys into the woods. Jane called after her to be careful. She found Sally standing by one of the outhouses trembling.

Lindsay put an arm around her. "What's wrong?"

"Some sons-a-bitches came up through the woods and started shaking the latrine," she answered breathlessly. "I screamed and went out to find out who it was, and they grabbed me and tried to drag me off into the woods." Lindsay couldn't tell if she was more frightened or angry. "Brian was in the other one and heard me scream. He came out and ran after them. They let me go and ran off. Brian still chased them, and I think he caught one, but I'm not sure."

A moment later Lindsay saw Brian, Derrick, Alan, and Frank walking back. Brian was rubbing his jaw.

"They got away," Alan told them.

"Who was it?" asked Lindsay.

"Dunno," said Brian. "I heard Sally scream, and at first I just thought some insect or something scared her. Then I heard laughing and ran out, and these two guys had hold of Sally. They ran when they saw me. I yelled and chased them. Caught one and decked him. But the other one came back and decked me. About that time Derrick and the others showed up, and we chased them down to the river. Couldn't tell who they were. They wore stockings over their heads.

"Could these be the same guys that came though the woods wearing masks a few days ago?" Frank asked.

Brian and Derrick shrugged. "Could be. These guys wore different masks," said Brian. "I doubt they were pothunters. Probably just some locals out having what they consider entertainment."

"Thanks for rescuing me, Brian," said Sally.

"No problem. Sorry I didn't catch them."

"I'll call the sheriff," said Frank. "Are you all right, Sally?"

"Sure, just scared." She laughed slightly.

"Look," Frank told them. "From now on I don't want the women to go to the latrines alone. Go in pairs."

"Great," said Sally. "Now we can't go to the bathroom by ourselves."

Ned and some of the scouts met them as they walked back to the site. He was red-faced, apparently from running. They all were breathing hard. "We went down to the river to see if we could see anything," he said. "We caught sight of a red outboard, but it was just a flash."

"I'll tell the sheriff," said Frank. "That may help."

"Is everyone okay?" asked Ned.

"Sally is a little shaken, and Brian has a sore jaw," Frank replied.

"This is a little more serious than pothunters," said Ned.

"Yeah," Frank answered. "It is."

Lindsay finished analyzing the small skeleton from the crime scene late in the evening. She carefully laid the bones in their box, wrote up the report, and went to bed. *I don't want to do this anymore,* she thought as she drifted off to sleep. *There is such pain in those little bones. A person had to be hurt terribly for it to show up in their bones.*

The next day, Lindsay helped with the flotation at the river while Michelle, the flotation supervisor, began the chemical flotation in the lab. Lindsay emptied a bag of dirt from the floor of Structure 3 into a bucket with a fine wire mesh bottom. She took the water hose and washed the dirt through the wire mesh, leaving a collection of objects too large to pass through the mesh. She ran her fingers over the objects: chert, broken pottery, daub, rocks and other miscellaneous debris. She was placing the artifacts on a flat screen to lie in the sun to dry when she saw the sheriff walk out into the field with Derrick. Derrick was putting a target on one of the rolls of hay.

"Do you guys think you can finish these bags?" she

asked the scouts who were working with her.

"Sure."

"Come get me or one of the other supervisors if you have any problems." She climbed from the dock onto the shore and walked across the site to the field. Frank and several of the crew were already there watching. Derrick had his bow and arrows, several handmade spears, and his atlatl. He had just hurled a spear into the target when Lindsay arrived. The spear stopped with only its point embedded in the hay. He picked up the banner stone-weighted atlatl and placed another spear on it. Drawing back his arm, he threw the spear hard. It flew from the atlatl and embedded halfway up its shaft into the roll of hay.

"That's a big difference," muttered the sheriff.

Next Derrick took his bow and placed an arrow on it. He drew back the string, aimed, and let the string gently roll off his fingers. The arrow embedded into the bull's eye.

"I'm more accurate with a bow," said Derrick. "But a spear and atlatl can get the job done."

"Sure can," said the sheriff. "Do you hunt?"

"Nope. Never killed anything more dangerous than a roll of hay."

"Those are nice spear points. Did you make them?"

"Yeah. I like to get the feel of what it's like to use the same tools the Indians did. It's hard. I'd hate to have to make my living by my skill with the atlatl."

Lindsay caught the sheriff's eye, and he came over to her. Derrick joined them, having offered to let anyone who wanted to have a go with the weapons. The three of them walked toward the lab.

"I've finished with the preliminary examination."

"What've you found?"

"The damage to the bones is not quite the same, but similar. The most striking thing I found was a pattern of physical abuse."

The sheriff looked up at her sharply. "It was an abused child?"

"Yes. Chronic. There is significant damage to the bones." Lindsay handed him her report.

"If we can find out who it is, that could be our big break," the sheriff said. "Whoever was the chronic abuser of this child could be the killer of the others. This may have been his start. Maybe he killed this kid accidentally and found out he liked it." The sheriff looked satisfied. "I'd like a go at that atlatl."

"Sure," said Derrick. They left the lab and headed back to the field.

"By the way, I haven't got a line on those guys yet. I think they were probably local punks who thought it would be fun to scare some outsiders."

"It's strange," said Lindsay. "We've had problems with pothunters at sites, but never with this kind of thing. They might have hurt Sally."

"I'll keep looking. In the meantime, take care and don't go too far into the woods alone. You never know what is in somebody's mind."

"I didn't mention this before," said Lindsay, "but the other night I had a persistent tailgater. I didn't think too much of it at the time, but, well, he went just slightly over the line of normal tailgaiting."

Derrick frowned. "You should have said something."

"Did you see what kind of car it was or anything?" asked the sheriff.

Lindsay shook her head. "It was too dark, and his

lights were too bright."

"Don't anybody travel alone until I can figure this out," the sheriff warned them.

The field crew had left for the day, and Lindsay sat in the picnic area, gazing over the site. Derrick walked over and sat down beside her.

"You okay, Lindsay? Maybe you ought to bow out of identifying any more bones."

Lindsay shook her head. "I'm fine. Tell me about the crime scene."

"You sure you want to hear it now?"

"Yeah. Let's get it over with."

"The scene itself is a small clearing in a wooded area about five miles from the paved road. Off the paved road, a three-mile dirt road dead ends in an old overgrown roadbed. The old roadbed is two miles long and leads to the clearing. The oldest burial— the last one I found—was the deepest. Three feet, 10 inches, but I'd say about an inch accumulated since the burial. The remains were extended. It looked like the hands had been tied behind, and it looked like she was gagged. The clothes had been removed and laid on top of the body before it was buried. You sure you want to do this?"

"Yes. Let's get it over with."

"Amy Hastings' grave was shallow, about a foot and a half. The sheriff's men measured it, and I don't know how accurate they were. Her dog was buried with her. I didn't see the burial, but the sheriff showed me the pictures. You don't want to see the photographs, do you?"

"No, I'll rely on your narrative. I'll look at your

map later."

"The bones were found by a hunter. Some animal dragged them out and disturbed the burial. So some bones were sticking out of the ground."

"Could you tell when the burial was disturbed?"

"No. The dog bones had been gnawed. You can have a look to see what kind of animal it was, if it's important. Her clothes were buried four feet from the foot of her grave. They had been neatly folded."

"What?"

"Yeah, isn't that a kicker. He folded their clothes. The pants first, the shirt, the socks, and underpants and duct tape, pieces of rope, and the shoes."

"Obsessive personality, or is it compulsive? I forget the difference."

"Me, too. The last grave, Peggy Pruitt's, was three feet, two inches deep. Her clothes were four feet from the foot of her grave and were also folded neatly. She was also extended, her hands crossing her chest."

"Sounds like some kind of ceremonial behavior."

"That's what I thought, too. The knife was found one foot from the head of Peggy's grave. It was slightly warped. I think he put it down after he cut the rope and stepped on it accidentally, mashing it into the ground. That and the shallowness of Amy's grave make me believe that something made him hurry both times."

"Was the ground hard to dig?"

"Not with a sharp shovel, but how many people other than us sharpen their shovels?"

"He was fairly strong," Lindsay said, almost to herself. "He could have dug a deeper grave for Amy. He must have been in danger of being interrupted."

Derrick nodded in agreement.

"How do people get that way?"

Derrick put an arm around her shoulders. "I don't know. I suppose they are abused themselves. They certainly can't have had a normal childhood."

"How'd we get into this?" asked Lindsay, shaking her head.

Derrick pulled her to him and kissed her hair. "I got into it because you volunteered me."

"Oh, right, I forgot. I'm sorry."

"That's okay. I don't think the sheriff's department was up to a thorough search. He loaned me a couple of deputies. Meticulous digging is definitely not their forte."

They were both quiet for a moment, then Derrick said, "Let's go eat."

"Frank was supposed to come by and take me to a movie and dinner."

"All right. Catch you later then."

"Ask me again later," she said.

"I'll do it." He kissed her cheek and headed off to the river.

About ten minutes passed before Frank came. "Sorry I'm late. The flotation crew thought they had mislabeled some bags. Turned out all right, though."

Lindsay stood up and stretched. "Derrick was filling me in on the crime scene."

"I'm sorry I got you involved in this, Lindsay. I didn't think it would go so deep."

"That's okay. Where do you want to eat?"

"How about Mexican? There is a nice place about ten miles from here. We can eat and still have time to make it to the movie. I thought we'd see *Blazing*

Saddles. Have you seen it?"

Lindsay shook her head. "No. That sounds fine to me."

They walked to his car, and she climbed in the passenger side, then buckled her seat belt.

"Tell me something," said Frank when they were on their way. "What is it about Derrick that makes him appealing to so many women? This is not just for my information, you understand. A lot of us guys would like to know."

Lindsay smiled. "I assume you mean besides the fact that he is drop-dead gorgeous."

"Yeah, besides that."

"Derrick respects women. He understands them. He is not a whiner if he doesn't get what he wants. I'll bet you have never heard Derrick bragging about any conquests."

"No, he just smiles if anyone asks him anything."

"Nor will you find any posters of naked women in his tent."

"There are none in my quarters either. And I never whined."

"When we uncover a burial in which dirt action has forced open the jaws, he never makes that dumb joke about it being a woman because her mouth is open."

"I never make that dumb joke," Frank protested.

"You didn't ask me about you. You asked me about Derrick," Lindsay responded.

"Is that all?"

"That's basically it. He is a gentleman, and he is sexy. That's a pretty powerful combination. Not all women like bad boys. I think that is probably just an excuse some men use for being bad."

"How do you feel about him?"

"Derrick is one of my best friends." Lindsay glanced over at Frank, trying to read his expression.

"Is that all?"

"What do you mean?" she asked.

"Well, you and he are hanging around a lot together these days." Frank turned onto the highway and headed toward Cullins.

"We are working the crime scene." Lindsay felt uncomfortable talking about herself and how she felt, preferring to live in the present, at least with her social life. She changed the subject. "What about you and Marsha?"

"Marsha's really a very nice person."

"I know, but that wasn't what I asked." Lindsay enjoyed turning the tables on his interrogations and smiled when Frank seemed uncomfortable, too.

"She has a great deal of enthusiasm about the site," Frank said and asked no more questions.

Comedy was Lindsay's favorite type of movie. When Frank brought her back to the site and walked her to her tent, she was in a good mood. No thoughts of the crimes in Merry Claymoore entered her head.

"I had a great time, Lindsay." He bent his head to give her a kiss.

"Hey, guys, enjoy the movie?" They turned toward Derrick, who looked as if he had just come from the shower—or a late night swim.

"Yes," said Frank. "We had a great time."

"Good," said Derrick, making no move to leave. "We'll all have to go next time. It'd be a nice break."

Lindsay grinned.

"Don't you have someplace to go?" Frank asked.

"Sure do." Derrick walked into his tent and turned on a lamp. "Don't let me disturb you guys," he said. "Go right on with what you were doing."

"We should have gone to my house," said Frank.

"I have to get up early," said Lindsay. She kissed Frank on the cheek and went into her tent.

"Goodnight everybody," said Frank.

"Goodnight," came several voices from their tents.

Lindsay was beginning to dread seeing the sheriff's car. It was 3:00 in the afternoon, and the workday had just ended for them. She was sitting with Frank and Derrick drinking a cold beer when the too-familiar brown-and-tan vehicle with the big star on the doors pulled into the parking area.

"What now?" Frank groaned.

Lindsay said nothing. She just waited. The sheriff got out of his car and came walking up with a large envelope in hand.

"I think we might have the girl," he said, sitting down at the table with them. "I searched the missing person reports for the time frame you gave me and came up with a couple of possibilities. This one"— he tapped the envelope on the table—"is the same age and general description as the others. Her name is Marylou Ridley. She was seven when she disappeared, and she was blonde. I know you thought she was five, but her medical and school records show her to be small for her age." Lindsay reached for the envelope. "These are her x-rays," the sheriff continued. "I dug them out of old Doctor Pritchard's basement."

Lindsay opened the envelope, pulled out the x-rays, and studied them. "It's her. I'll make the measurements to verify it." She rose and started for the lab, but the sheriff stopped her.

"Her mother lives about 20 miles from here on the other side of the county. I'd like to go see her and take you with me. I may need you to describe the pattern of abuse in case she denies it."

"Is this necessary?" asked Frank. "Lindsay has been working a lot of overtime lately."

"No, it's not necessary, but I'd appreciate it."

"I don't mind. I'll go do a few comparisons, then change clothes."

Lindsay and the sheriff stood in the living room of the small white frame house waiting for Mrs. Greenwood neé Ridley to join them. The man she lived with said she was visiting a neighbor, and he would go get her.

Lindsay wore the one suit she had packed, an off-white linen pant suit with an emerald green silk blouse. The man invited them to sit, but Lindsay decided not to because of her white suit. She looked around the room as she waited. The furniture was dirty and worn. Accumulations of dust under the chairs and in the corner wafted as the man opened the door and went outside. On an old end table amid a clutter of bric-a-brac sat a few photographs, one of little Marylou. Lindsay picked it up. It was a school picture. An unsmiling Marylou with puffy eyes and uncombed hair looked back at Lindsay. She set the picture down on the table as the door opened and a woman entered by herself.

"He said you wanted to see me."

Lindsay turned and stared at a thin, haggard woman in a faded house dress. Her mouse-brown hair was streaked with gray and hung in her face. Her frightened brown eyes darted from Lindsay to the sheriff as she absently wiped her hands on her apron.

"Yes, Mrs. Greenwood. I'm Sheriff Duggan, and this is Dr. Chamberlain. I know this is going to be a shock to you, and I'm real sorry to have to tell you, but maybe after all these years it will ease your mind. We found the bones of your daughter, Marylou. Dr. Chamberlain here identified them."

Mrs. Greenwood's eyes grew wide. She stepped back and put a hand over her heart. "Marylou?" she whispered. "It's been so long. I don't understand."

"We have finally found her remains. Would you like to sit down, Mrs. Greenwood?" asked the sheriff. He stepped over to her and took her elbow, then guided her to a chair.

She sat and twisted her bony fingers in her lap. "You found her?"

"Yes, and we need to ask you a few questions. Someone took Marylou twelve years ago," the sheriff said, "took her out in the woods and killed and buried her. We need to find who did it."

"That was a long time ago. I talked to the law then and told them all I knew."

"Mrs. Greenwood." Lindsay spoke for the first time. The woman looked startled a moment, then stared up at her. "Your daughter was abused."

"What do you mean? I was good to Marylou. She was a little clumsy." Mrs. Greenwood looked down at her hands.

"No, Mrs. Greenwood. Your daughter's injuries were not due to clumsiness. The break in her arm was from being twisted, not from falling out of a tree like it said in her medical records. Her fingers had been broken, and she wasn't taken to the doctor to have them set, so they healed misaligned. She had been shaken so severely it damaged the bones in her neck. She was also undernourished."

"That's not true."

"It is true, Mrs. Greenwood. There is no doubt. Her injuries could only have been from abuse, not from falling down."

"You don't understand." Mrs. Greenwood's mouth twisted as she tried to think of how to make them understand. "Marylou was a headstrong, whiny child. You don't know how it was for me."

"Mrs. Greenwood," said Lindsay, taking a step toward her. "There is no circumstance you could possibly have been in that would justify the treatment Marylou received. There is no behavior Marylou could have exhibited that would justify her being mal-treated so severely that it showed deep in her bones."

"You don't know what my life has been like."

"It doesn't matter what your life has been like. You cannot use it as an excuse to abuse your daughter or allow her to be abused. There is no acceptable reason to abuse a child. Your daughter suffered horrendously during her short life. I doubt there was a time she was not in pain."

Mrs. Greenwood stared at Lindsay with liquid cow eyes. "She's got no right to talk to me that way."

"Mrs. Greenwood," broke in the sheriff. "Who were you living with at the time Marylou disappeared?"

"No right a'tall. You don't come to a body's house with news their child is dead, then talk to them like that. It ain't right."

"Who were you living with when Marylou disappeared? Was it her father?"

"Him? He disappeared before she was born, and good riddance."

"Did you live by yourself, or did you live with someone? That fellow we just met. Did he live with you at the time?" the sheriff persisted.

"No. He come about a year ago. Twelve years is a long time." She looked down at her hands. "I've been grieving for 12 years. How can I remember?"

"You need to try," said the sheriff. "Who helped you look for her, for instance?"

"Oh, yeah, that'd be Bobby, Bobby Whitaker. But he's been gone a long time. He didn't like all the police hanging around back then. Say," she brightened, "you don't think he's the one who hurt my baby? He sure hurt me a lot."

"Do you know where he is now?"

"No. His folks live down at Flint Rock."

"Thank you, Mrs. Greenwood. We'll be in touch."

"What about my baby. If you've found her, she needs a Christian burial."

"I'll be in touch as soon as possible, Mrs. Greenwood."

The sheriff and Lindsay left Mrs. Greenwood sitting alone in her small clapboard house, twisting her fingers in her lap.

They were quiet on the drive back. The sheriff concentrated on driving. Lindsay watched the trees going

past and pressed the bridge of her nose trying to drive
back a headache. Suddenly, she asked the sheriff
to pull over. He found a wide space in the road and
stopped. Lindsay jumped out of the car, ran to the
woods, and threw up. She stood with a hand on a tree,
taking deep breaths. The sheriff handed her his handkerchief. It was wet and cold.

"I always carry a cooler in the trunk," he said.

Lindsay put it on the back of her neck for a few
seconds, then wiped her face.

"Thank you."

The sheriff opened a cold drink and handed it to
her. She took several sips. "I can't believe I talked to
that poor woman like that. I was appalling. It's a good
thing I didn't have a rubber hose."

"We did a pretty good job with the good cop/bad
cop routine," said the sheriff, smiling.

"We should have asked a neighbor to stay with
her," Lindsay said.

"She'll be all right. She's the kind of woman who's
good at suffering."

"I should have been kinder."

"She probably abused her daughter. It's hard to be
nice to someone who hurts her kid. The woman I go
out with is a teacher. Teaches kids the same age as
Marylou. Dee may have taught Marylou. She sees
them come to school with black eyes, bruises, sore
arms. Some are thin and hungry, wearing only a
sweater in the middle of winter. They always say they
ran into a door, or fell down the steps, or forgot their
coat. Dee finds them winter coats, enrolls them in the
free lunch program, and reports them to the welfare
folks. But nothing much ever happens. She gets real

frustrated. One of the fathers went so far as to threaten Dee one time, and I had to have a talk with him. He didn't bother Dee anymore, but he still beats his kids. It's hard to work up a lot of sympathy for folks like Mrs. Greenwood."

"She was probably one of those thin little kids with bruises, black eyes, and no winter coat herself," said Lindsay. "I should have behaved more professionally. I owe her an apology." She walked back to the car. They rode in silence.

"I heard you and Derrick are professional dancers," said the sheriff after a while.

"No, we're strictly amateurs. We enter contests now and then. We haven't lately, though. Marsha said there is a place about 40 miles from Merry Claymoore. We're all going dancing there."

"Yeah, that's what she told me. That ought to be a nice break from all this."

"You ought to come and bring your friend."

"I might do that."

I knew a woman, lovely in her bones…
—Theodore Roethke
I Knew a Woman

Chapter 5

THE FIRST THING Lindsay had packed when Frank told her he had hired Derrick was a dancing dress and shoes. It had been almost a year since Derrick and she had danced together, and she hoped for an opportunity to start again.

The dress was not flashy like some of the dresses she used for dancing. It was basic black with a full skirt, tight bodice, and spaghetti straps. The shoes were plain black heels. The shawl she draped over her shoulders had come from Paris. She had purchased it when Derrick and she had competed in a contest there. It was trimmed in black fringe and covered with great red, blue, green, and yellow flowers woven from a shimmering metallic material onto a black background. Lindsay tied her hair into a smooth bun at the nape of her neck. She was putting on dangling silver earrings when she heard Derrick's voice.

"You look stunning."

Lindsay looked up to see him standing in the doorway of her tent.

"You're no slouch yourself." He was dressed in black slacks and a white poet's shirt. His hair was pulled back in a low ponytail, making him look like a seventeenth-century highwayman.

"Frank and Marsha went in her car. I hope you don't mind."

"No." She was not sure if she did or not, but when she looked at Derrick again, she felt very glad to be going out with him.

It was still daylight outside, but the sun was low on the horizon. Derrick took her in his arms and spun her around into a dip. When he brought her back up, he kissed her, lingering for a little longer than a friendly kiss. He released her after a moment, and they walked to his car.

"I'm glad we're doing this," he said as he drove out to the highway.

"Me, too. Tell me something, Derrick. We've known each other for a long time. We were in school together, we've been dancing partners off and on for, what, six or seven years? Until now, you have never seriously tried to seduce me. Why?"

"That's a good question. Why don't you think about it?"

"You're infuriating sometimes ... and tempting. I'll admit that ..."

"Why don't you give in then?"

"I suppose because you're my friend."

Derrick took her hand and kissed it. "We'd still be friends."

Lindsay laughed. "Is this the way it's going to be all evening? You keeping up the sexual tension?"

"You started this conversation."

"I guess I did, didn't I?"

Derrick reached into his pocket and pulled out two rings. He handed one to Lindsay and put one on his own finger.

"Ah, you brought them," she said, slipping the wedding ring on her finger.

"Well, I thought if we went dancing, we might need them."

The Locomotion was a popular place. The parking lot was full, and a stream of people flowed through the double doors. Jane and her boyfriend, Keith, and Sally and Thomas pulled in behind Lindsay and Derrick.

"Wow," said Jane when she saw them. "You two are gorgeous."

"I'll say," chorused Sally and Thomas.

Derrick paid the cover charge for Lindsay and himself, and they fell in with the crowd flowing into the club. They stopped in the entryway to let their eyes get accustomed to the darkness.

The dance floor was large and extended out onto a deck for those who wanted to dance outside. There was no band tonight, but the sound room behind the bandstand had a disk jockey.

Marsha and Frank had already arrived and reserved a large table. Frank wore jeans and a dress shirt. He looked dashing. Marsha's pale blonde hair was fashioned in a silk-smooth French twist. She wore a snug strapless dress that looked like it was painted with pastel brush strokes. It glittered when she moved.

"Don't you two look great," she said when she saw Lindsay and Derrick. "I love that shawl."

"Thank you. It's nice to dust off and get dressed up for a change."

"You can say that again," agreed Sally. "I'm so tired of being covered in dirt and mud."

Frank and Lindsay's eyes met for a moment, and she smiled. "I'm anxious to see you dance," he said. "Jane has talked about it all week."

"Then we will have to dazzle you," said Derrick, putting an arm around Lindsay's shoulder.

"I'm glad Derrick is so confident. He's leading."

Unaccountably, Lindsay felt uncomfortable. I've got to get away from the site more, she thought.

"Hello." They looked up to see the sheriff. On his arm was a petite woman with short, dark hair streaked with gray. She had large, friendly brown eyes and a bright smile. "This is Dee Marlar." He introduced her to everyone around the table. Lindsay was surprised that he knew everyone's name.

"I'm glad you came," she told the sheriff.

"It's to you I owe this night on the town," said Dee, smiling broadly. "Thank you so much. When Greg suggested we go dancing, I was about to search for pods in the basement."

It sounded strange to hear the sheriff addressed by his first name, but it was comforting. This was a night to forget all things frightening.

"I understand you're a teacher?" Lindsay said.

"I teach first grade, and please don't let that end the conversation. Telling people you teach first grade is like telling them you're a nun. I never get to hear any good jokes or have any adult conversation."

"You won't be getting any adult conversation here," Frank said, grinning.

"Greg tells me you and your friend are dancers, as well as archaeologists." Dee and the sheriff sat across from Lindsay.

"We dance a little," Lindsay answered, smiling.

"A little? Don't you believe it," said Jane. "They're great."

"Derrick, it's going to be embarrassing if we fall down after all these raised expectations," Lindsay said.

"I guess I'll have to be really careful not to drop you."

"Mind if I join you?" Ned pulled out a chair and sat next to Lindsay. He was alone.

"Not at all," said Lindsay. "I didn't know you danced."

"I don't really, but I watch real good." He smiled. It seemed to Lindsay that he was making an effort to be congenial with everyone.

The dance floor was half full, and Lindsay and Derrick turned their attention to the dancers. After a few numbers, Derrick rose, whispered to Lindsay, and walked over to make a request. When he returned, he took her to the dance floor.

"When a Man Loves a Woman" began to play, and everyone immediately started dancing.

Lindsay and Derrick waited several beats while they looked at each other, smiling and waiting for space to open around them. They began with Lindsay's back to Derrick. He slid his hands down the length of her arms, then grasped her hands and slid them up her sides and placed them around his neck while they moved slowly to the music. Next, Derrick put his arms around her waist and spun her around as Lindsay bent backward in his arms. As he brought her up, Lindsay put one leg up next to his waist and he swung her around. Many of the dancers stopped and watched. Derrick picked her up and held her above him; she slid down the front of him, and he swung her around again. It was slow, beautiful, and sensuous. At the end of the song, they walked back to their seats amid a round of applause.

"You two are good!" Marsha gushed.

"Didn't I tell you?" Jane said.

"I've never seen anyone dance better," Dee said, still clapping. "It was beautiful."

"I'll have to say," said Frank, "you two certainly delivered."

"You haven't seen anything yet," Derrick replied. "That was just a warm-up."

"Where did you learn to dance?"

"I took classical ballet when I was a kid," he answered. "And a little ballroom dancing when I was a teenager."

"Same for me," agreed Lindsay. "Ballet, tap, and modern dance growing up. I didn't do much ballroom. Derrick taught me most of those steps."

"How did you get to dancing together?"

"Derrick's danced competitively for a long time. We were in graduate school when his dancing partner quit. I asked him if I could try. It turned out we dance well together."

"You sure do that," the sheriff agreed.

The disc jockey played "Stand by Me," and Lindsay and Derrick got up and danced. After that they danced to a string of Elvis songs, then "Hit the Road, Jack." Lindsay and Derrick danced independently, acting out the parts of the lyrics of the song. It was popular, though they didn't do many of their more sensational moves.

"Getting tired?" Derrick asked as they walked back to their seats.

"No. This is invigorating. I really needed to do this, but I think the women would like to dance with you," she said.

"I thought I would ask a little later."

They sat down. Frank had ordered them drinks.

"Thanks." Derrick took a long drink. "It's getting hot out there."

"Hey, did you two get married on the way over here?" asked Sally, pointing to their rings. Frank noticed Lindsay's ring for the first time and looked quizzically at her.

"We wear them when we dance in clubs," offered Derrick. "There's always a few guys who make inappropriate assumptions when they see us dance. The rings stop a lot of hassles."

"How sweet," said Dee.

"It's easier than having to beat someone up," responded Derrick, grinning at her.

"Do you ever dance the Lambada?" Jane asked.

"No," Derrick answered. "The Lambada is a very inelegant dance." Lindsay noticed the sheriff nod his head as if he agreed.

Marsha and Frank got up to dance. So did Jane and Keith. Derrick asked Dee to dance. She wanted to but was hesitant. "I don't dance that well."

"Derrick will lead," Lindsay coaxed. "Just follow

him. It will be easier than you think."

Derrick gave her a few dips and spins, and she looked thrilled.

"I take it you don't like to dance," Lindsay said to the sheriff.

"Not much. I've got two left feet. Dee likes it. She's having a great time."

A few guys came up to Lindsay and asked her to dance. She declined, and they left.

"Do you only dance with Derrick?" the sheriff asked.

"I only dance with people I know."

A young man came up and held out a large hand to Lindsay and asked her to dance. When she refused, he complained, "Come on. I saw you dance. You can dance with me."

"No," said Lindsay.

"That's not friendly. I don't dance as good as that fellow, but I got some of the moves."

"She said no, Patrick," the sheriff said, leaning forward from the shadows. "How is your grandmother?"

"Oh, Sheriff. Hi. I didn't see you. Grandmother is fine." He bent his knees in a slight bow and backed away.

"Who is he?" asked Lindsay.

"Patrick Tyler. Isabel Tyler's grandson. They live up at Tylerwynd. I imagine you've heard of it. He's harmless, just socially clumsy."

Derrick brought Dee back, out of breath. "I don't see how you dance so many dances," she said. "What a workout!"

When Derrick asked Marsha to dance, Frank asked Lindsay. He was a good dancer, though he did nothing fancy. It was a slow dance, and he pulled her close.

"You're full of surprises, Lindsay," he whispered in her ear.

"I thought everyone knew about our dancing."

"I knew you danced, but, well, I guess I didn't know you were so good."

"Thanks."

Frank pulled her a little closer. "I never realized dancing was so intimate."

"It can be."

"It's almost like sex."

"Derrick wrote a paper about that once. I think it was published in *The Journal of Ritual Anthropology*."

"I guess I'd better read it."

"It's a good article." She smiled up at him.

Frank looked as if he wanted to ask her something. Lindsay saw indecision in his hazel eyes and wondered what it meant. She wondered why she couldn't talk as freely with Frank as with Derrick. He was starting to speak when Ned tapped him on the shoulder.

"May I cut in?"

Frank hesitated a moment. "Sure." He left the dance floor, and Ned put an arm hesitantly around Lindsay's waist and took her hand.

"I don't do this very well," he said.

"Sometimes it is nice just to move with the music. The kind of dancing Derrick and I do is very tiring."

"I can see. You two are very good." They danced for a few moments, mainly swaying to the music. "I wanted to apologize for what I said about your helping the sheriff. I shouldn't have gotten so bent out of shape."

"That's all right. We are there to dig the site."

"I know, but you were right. They need our help.

It's just that…"

"What?" asked Lindsay when he stopped.

"Nothing. We shouldn't talk about business tonight." They danced in silence for the remainder of the music. When it ended, they walked back to the table.

It was three in the morning when they left. Lindsay and Derrick's last dance was to "Jailhouse Rock." It was spectacular. The manager invited them back and, after acknowledging the applause, they left with the others.

"You okay to drive?" she asked Derrick as they walked to the car. "Not too tired?"

"Sure, I'm fine."

Lindsay saw Frank put Marsha in the passenger side of the car and go around to the driver's side. It was clear to Lindsay that Marsha was falling in love with him. Lindsay wondered if Frank realized it. After a moment of watching them drive off, she got in the car and buckled her belt. Derrick slid behind the steering wheel but didn't start the car.

"There's Ned," Derrick said.

Lindsay looked out the window at Ned walking alone to his car and felt a stab of pity. "I wonder why he didn't bring anyone?" she asked.

Derrick shrugged. "He's always in such bad temper. Who would go with him?"

"I feel sorry for him."

"Me, too. But all he needs to do is control his temper."

Derrick started the car and pulled out of the parking lot and onto the road. "This was fun. Let's do it again," he said.

Lindsay nodded and smiled. "Yes. I had forgotten

how well we dance together."

"I hadn't," he said.

They were quiet for several minutes as Derrick drove down the highway toward Merry Claymoore. There were a few cars on the road. Lindsay wondered where people were going so late at night. A gentle rain began to fall, making the road a shiny black in front of them. Derrick turned on the wipers.

"You okay?" he asked

"Sure, why?"

"You seem a little low about Frank and Marsha."

"No, I'm not really. I was just realizing that I wasn't looking forward to going back to the site. And I used to love this dig. I still do, mostly." She shook her head. "I don't know. I'm just tired, I suppose."

"Move to the middle and put your head on my shoulder."

Lindsay unbuckled her belt and scooted over. Buckling the center one around her, she put her head on Derrick's shoulder. She stayed there as he drove back to the site.

Lindsay awakened abruptly, terrified. Then she remembered the nightmare. Someone was strangling little girls with a tape measure. An idea struck her with absolute clarity. She shoved off the sheet and jumped out of bed. It was only a few feet to Derrick's tent. She didn't even stop to put on any shoes, and the grass between their tents was wet and cold on her bare feet. She stepped into his tent. Although the moonlight filtered through his screened window, she could only make out his dark form on the bed. Like hers, his bed was a twin-sized mattress lying on a thick plywood board held off the ground by bricks. She kneeled down and gently shook him.

"Derrick." He moaned in his sleep. She shook him harder. "Derrick."

He opened his eyes halfway. "What?" he mumbled. "Is that you, Lindsay?"

"Yes. Wake up, I need to talk to you."

Derrick pushed himself to a sitting position and rubbed his eyes. "Is this business or pleasure?"

"Business." She sat down on his bed.

"Give me a second to wake up."

"I had a nightmare."

"You okay? If you want to stay here, I won't bother you … unless you ask."

"I'm fine. It just made me realize who the murderer might be."

Lindsay watched Derrick's face become alert, and she smiled. The sight of him pushed away some of the frightening feelings left over from the nightmare. He was in his shorts, and she could feel the warmth from his mostly bare body. It would be comforting to slide over to him and snuggle up to that warmth, but Lindsay knew she would lose herself there. Instead, she told him about her dream.

"Mrs. Greenwood's boyfriend, Bobby Whitaker, was a slob, from what the sheriff said. I couldn't imagine someone like him neatly folding the clothes and burying them exactly four feet from the grave. I think my brain was putting the evidence together in my sleep, and I woke up remembering the neatly marked measurements on the floor of Mickey Lawson's studio and his reputation for compulsive detail and neatness."

"Let me see." Derrick rubbed his eyes with the heel of his hand. "You think the killer is Mickey Lawson because he has the same personality characteristics we've given to the murderer. Is that what you're saying?"

"Not just that...those photographs of the children. He is in an occupation that brings him in contact with children on a regular basis. I'd like to find out who made Amy Hastings' portraits and who took the school pictures of Marylou Ridley. We know he took the picture of Peggy Pruitt."

"Okay, I can accept your reasoning, but it is very circumstantial, even if he was the photographer of all the girls."

"It's a place to start. Right now the sheriff has only Bobby Whitaker, and I don't think he's the one."

"Are you going to the sheriff with this?"

"Not now. The Tylers are a pretty prominent family. I think I'll do a little investigating on my own first. Anyway, I just needed to talk to someone."

"Come talk to me anytime." He reached out and grabbed her arm. "And Lindsay, let me know before you do any investigating on your own. It is a murderer you're looking for, remember?"

"I will."

She half expected Derrick to pull her to him or say something seductive, but he merely released her. It seemed colder on the way back to her tent. She crawled back into her bed and went to sleep wondering not about the murders, but what it would feel like to be warmed by Derrick.

On Monday Lindsay called Guy Hastings and told

him that to complete her report she needed to know where his daughter's portraits were made. He asked his wife, who said the last one was a special at a department store in Cullins. Before that, it was at school, but she hadn't had a school picture taken in a year. Hastings gave her the approximate date and the name of the store. She called the store and talked to three people before she found someone who would look up the photographer for her. When the curt voice said Mickey Lawson, a chill went up Lindsay's spine.

Next she called the school Marylou Ridley had attended. Lindsay doubted that Marylou's mother had a professional portrait made of her child. She told the school secretary essentially the same story she told the Hastings. "I just need to know the photographer," she said. "Since I used her picture in the identification, I've to get official information on it from the photographer."

The woman had worked at the school for years and was quite friendly. "That'd be 12 years ago, you say? We used Adam Bancroft until about four years ago, then we changed to Mickey Lawson. I guess the photographer was Adam Bancroft. If it wasn't, he might know who it was. We just don't keep that detail of information."

Lindsay thanked her for being so helpful. She called Mickey Lawson's studio and made an appointment to have her portrait taken.

"It occurred to me while I was in your studio," she said as he was setting up the shot, "that a portrait would make a good Christmas gift for my parents. They are always after me to give them one. I was going to get Derrick to do it. He's the site photographer. But I thought I'd go ahead and have a professional one made."

"I'm glad you decided to have it done here. Photographs make good presents. I do some of my best business before Christmas."

"I wouldn't think there are enough people in Merry Claymoore to keep you in business making portraits."

"If it were only portraits and only in Merry Claymoore, it wouldn't. But I do clubs, civic functions, schools, department stores. I cover a pretty wide area."

"Did you go to school to learn photography?"

"No. I got interested in photography in high school, then got a job working with a photographer when I graduated. In about three or four years, I struck out on my own and have been doing pretty good ever since."

He snapped several poses of Lindsay, carefully recording the measurements after each shot.

"I imagine you were pretty lucky to get a job with a photographer right out of high school."

"Yeah, I was. Adam taught me a lot, but we sure had different styles of photography."

"Adam?"

"Adam Bancroft. He has a studio between Flint Rock and Cullins. He likes to experiment a lot, and I'll tell you, it's cost him business. Around here, people don't want anything unusual. They just want a good picture of themselves."

"It sounds like your business is better than his."

"It is. I suppose he thinks I stole his customers, but you've got to give people what they want. We should get some good pictures from these. I'll have the proofs in a couple of days."

"Thank you."

Lindsay left the studio and found Derrick waiting outside for her. "I had Thomas drop me off. Thought you might need some muscle if you were going to do much detective work."

Lindsay laughed at his feigned Bronx accent. "I'm not doing anything dangerous, Derrick, but you're welcome to come with me."

Derrick climbed into the passenger side of the jeep Lindsay was driving. "I'll ride shotgun," he said.

"Look in the glove compartment for a map. We need to head in the direction of Flint Rock and Cullins."

"No problem. The quarry I believe is the source for the black flint the Indians used in making points is in Flint Rock, so I've been out there."

"We need to find a phone book anyway, because I need to look up an address."

"Stop at the store up the road, and I'll get us a couple of cold drinks while you look up the address."

Adam Bancroft's studio was a refurbished barn a mile off the main road. No one was at the reception desk when Lindsay and Derrick entered. They waited, looking at the pictures lining the walls. These photographs were quite different from Mickey Lawson's. Some were landscapes, some were candid wedding portraits, others were of people at the bus station. All possessed a startling presence, as if each had a story to tell. Lindsay and Derrick were struck by a photograph of a girl in a wedding dress. The apprehension on her face was a powerful testament to her misgivings.

"I didn't even show her that proof," a man behind them said. "I always wondered if she ever got divorced."

Lindsay and Derrick turned to see a tall, slender man with shoulder-length black hair streaked with gray. He wore jeans and a T-shirt with Georgia O'Keefe's painting of a horse skull and a white flower on the front.

"I'm Adam Bancroft." He stretched out his hand to Lindsay and Derrick.

"I'm Lindsay Chamberlain, and this is Derrick Bellamy. We're archaeologists at the Jasper Creek site."

His jaw dropped open. "You're kidding! That's amazing."

Lindsay was a little taken aback by his reaction. He seemed truly surprised that they were archaeologists.

"Yes. I was asked by the sheriff to identify some bones found in the woods. Perhaps you have read about it in the papers."

"Yeah, those three little girls. I read about it. My daughter wanted to come down for a visit and bring her five-year-old. I told her to stay away until this is solved. So you identified the bones. I'm amazed."

"Besides x-rays, I used photographs. Marylou Ridley's photograph was an old school picture. Her school said your studio was the one they used. For the final report, I'd like to get some detailed information about the pictures—negative size and focal length—and I was wondering if you have them."

"Probably not. I don't keep detailed records now. I'm sure I wouldn't keep any around for...what...ten years?"

"Twelve. It's not critical. I just like to put as much information as I can in the report."

"I probably did have that information once. Mickey Lawson worked for me then. I usually sent him on all the school commissions. He drove me crazy with the detailed data he kept on each photograph. I tried to teach him that you have to feel a good shot. Anyway, I burned all his records when he left."

"That's too bad. But, as I said, it isn't critical." Lindsay turned to the photographs again. "Your style is a lot different from his."

"Yeah. People seem to like his better, but it would be hard for me to go back to doing more traditional photography. Not that it would do me much good. When he opened his studio, his grandmother, Isabel Tyler, talked a lot of my customers into going with him. But it forced me to carve out a new niche for myself."

"I think you're an artist."

"Thanks. So do I, actually— "Can I show you something?" He led them into his studio. It was cluttered, unlike the neat studio of Mickey Lawson. Adam went back to the dark room and came out with several eight-by-tens. He laid them on a table, and this time Lindsay's jaw dropped. They were of her and Derrick dancing. "That's why I was so surprised you are archaeologists. You dance so well. Not that archaeologists can't dance, but I thought you were both professional dancers. Obviously, I was at the Locomotion the other night."

Lindsay picked one up. They had just done a lift and she was doing a body slide down the front of Derrick. It was a side view, and they were looking into each other's eyes. It was a very sensual picture. She picked up the others. The motion in each of them could almost be seen: the whirl of Lindsay's dress, the spins, the lifts, the touches. There was also a passion in them that shocked Lindsay.

"I'm glad you came by. I was about to call the sheriff and ask who you were. I would like to send some of these off and needed to get a release."

"These are beautiful," said Derrick. "May we have copies?"

"Sure. I'm trying some things with the developing. I'll make you a set when I'm satisfied and bring them to you."

"Who's this?" asked Derrick.

Lindsay and Adam looked at the photograph. It was one showing the audience in the background. A face stood out from the rest. It had a sinister leer that made Lindsay shiver.

"Patrick Tyler," said Adam. "Isabel Tyler's grandson by her daughter Ruth. Creepy little beggar, isn't he? I couldn't decide whether to crop this picture or not. It gives the whole scene a different mood."

"He kept after me to dance with him while you were dancing with Dee. The sheriff had to run him off."

"You didn't tell me that," said Derrick.

"There wasn't much to tell. He wouldn't take no for an answer, and the sheriff shooed him away. He seemed to threaten him with his grandmother."

"That would do it," laughed Adam. "By the way, could I come to the site and take a few pictures of the crew working?"

"I don't see why not," said Lindsay. "We'll have to

ask the principal investigator first, but I don't foresee a problem."

Lindsay and Derrick signed the model release forms and left Adam's studio.

"Some pictures," Derrick said on the way back to the site.

"He's a good photographer. Too bad the people around here can't see that. His photographs make Mickey Lawson's seem so ordinary."

"I agree," said Derrick, "but Lawson is right. Most people just want a flattering picture of themselves."

"Mickey Lawson photographed all three girls," Lindsay said abruptly.

"Probably. What are you going to do now?"

"Take the information to the sheriff and drop the whole thing. I've reached the limit of my detecting ability."

"Good."

Lindsay sat in the sheriff's office while he finished a phone conversation. She looked around his office for the first time. His desk and chairs were ordinary and worn, the kind one might find in any sheriff's office. Decorating his walls were illustrations of various weapons, many medieval. On the wall behind him was a pair of dueling pistols under a glass covering.

"Dee and I had a good time the other night," he said when he hung up the phone.

Lindsay directed her gaze at him and smiled. "We did, too."

"What can I do for you?" he asked.

"I don't quite know where to begin. I know I should have come to you first, but ... well, I didn't."

"Lindsay, so far you have been a direct person. Just tell me what you did."

"I woke up the other night with an idea I had to follow through on. It was the way the clothes were folded and the way they were buried exactly four feet from two of the graves. It reminded me of my visit to Mickey Lawson's studio. It was so neat, and he had all the measurements and angles marked on the floor so carefully. Several people had mentioned his fanaticism about detail. And then there were the pictures of the girls. I realized that a photographer would have access to children of that age."

Lindsay stopped and took a breath. The sheriff said nothing, his face unreadable.

"I called to find out who took the pictures of Amy Hastings and Marylou Ridley. I said it was to get the official camera readings for my report. I was discreet, and I didn't say anything that wasn't in the newspapers." Lindsay told him in detail of her detective work and her visit to Adam Bancroft's studio. "I just wanted to give you the information. I don't intend to do any more detective work."

The sheriff sat quietly for several moments. "You should have come to me first."

"I know. But I felt I needed a little more than speculation. Even now it is circumstantial. Not much more than a feeling."

"What you were doing was potentially dangerous. Someone who has murdered several times would have no qualms about doing it again."

"That's essentially what Derrick said. That's why he went with me."

"Derrick was more levelheaded than you were.

Nevertheless, he should have stopped you, and you should have come to me. I am not a man to shirk my responsibilities."

"I didn't think you would. I just thought I needed more to back up my suspicions."

Finally, after a moment, he smiled at her. "Well, you did a competent job of it anyway. I agree it is a good lead, and I have very few. I don't have a thing to link Bobby Whitaker. And frankly, I can't see him taking the time to fold the clothes."

Lindsay smiled with relief and rose to leave.

"Take care and come to me if you again feel the need to be a detective." The sheriff rose and walked her to her car.

Derrick and his crew were back at the site. Lindsay was back in charge of the burials, and all was normal again. The scout troops were still there, so removal of the overburden was going quickly. Ned hadn't had an outburst in several days. In fact, he and Frank went together to the university to pick up some supplies. The crew had exposed another large section of the site and were shovel-shaving the ground. Derrick's sharpened flat shovels worked like razor blades, shaving a smooth surface and exposing the underlying patterns. Another house structure, two smaller structures that looked like outbuildings, and five more burials were discovered.

Everything was perfect again, except for Ronald Moody, a scout who thought it was uproariously funny to play "Picking Up Bones" over and over again on his boom box. He took no threats seriously, having decided that archaeologists are mainly pacifists.

No rain was predicted for the next five days, and Lindsay was sitting in the middle of the site with her clipboard, deciding how many burials to open up. Thomas came over and asked her to look at something he had discovered. He was calm. Frank was finally having an influence on his unbridled enthusiasm.

She walked over to the section that Frank and Derrick had given him to dig, and he showed her two stains on the ground. One was about ten feet long and eight feet wide. The stain beside it was smaller. Both were oriented in the same direction, east/west.

"The smaller one looks like a burial," said Lindsay. "I'm not sure about the larger one—maybe a trash pit, but they wouldn't have buried someone next to where they dumped the trash."

"It is outside the village boundary. Maybe the person was an outcast."

"Start digging, and we'll see. This will be Burial 31, and we'll call the larger stain…" Lindsay looked at her clipboard, "…Feature 29."

Both looked up to see Derrick marching over to Ronald, the boom box scout.

"What do you think Derrick is going to do?" asked Thomas wistfully.

"Kill him. It's what I'd do," Lindsay replied.

Whatever Derrick said fell on deaf ears, for he went away with Ronald laughing behind him.

"Derrick is going to do something, isn't he?" Thomas declared.

"I hope so."

• • •

The next morning the site crew started at the usual

time. They were removing the black plastic from the features when a wail came from the scout camp.

"My radio! Someone stole my radio!"

The lament drifted from the field to the site. It seemed that in the dead of night someone had spirited away Ronald's boom box.

After a thorough search of the scouts' campsite, helped by only one or two people, the whereabouts of Ronald's boom box remained a mystery. He made his way over to the site, grumbling and threatening to call the sheriff.

"Who was it?" he demanded, standing in the middle of the site with his hands on his hips. "I know it was one of you."

No one confessed.

The sun was coming over the horizon, and daylight was breaking over the site. Everyone was busy at their assigned tasks when suddenly Brian shouted, "There it is! Isn't that it?"

He pointed to the top of a tree. The crew gravitated over to him and looked up. There—way out on a thin limb—the boom box was hanging by a rope.

"Oh, no! Who did that? Whoever did it, go and get it down, now!"

"That's a long way up," Derrick said in a matter-of-fact tone. "I expect you will have to climb up yourself."

Lindsay looked at him. He was dressed in his usual cutoffs, work boots, and no shirt, but today he also wore mirrored aviator sunglasses and a camouflage bandanna tied around his head like a headband.

Lindsay sidled up to him and whispered, "Are we Rambo today?"

He grinned.

Ronald stood at the base of the tall tree, looking up at the dangling radio. "Look, somebody put it up there, and they are going to have to climb up and get it!"

Frank and Ned arrived about that time and asked what was going on.

"Well, sir," replied Derrick in a clipped military tone, "we have the kid's radio-tape player hanging in that tree. I don't recommend anyone climb up and retrieve it. Too dangerous. I suggest we shoot it down."

"Shoot it down?" exclaimed Ronald. "Shoot it down! That will break it!"

"Why is it up in the tree?" Ned asked.

"We assume," Thomas said, "that someone did it because he was playing the same song all day long yesterday."

"The way I see it," Derrick continued, "we can either have some of the crew hold a blanket to catch it or get a few of the extra mattresses from the laboratory. I suggest the mattresses. The radio could hit someone when it falls. However, we do have the hard-hats we wear to the quarry."

"The mattresses," Frank said.

"Right," Derrick agreed.

"What! You're going to break it!" cried Ronald again.

"Maybe not," Derrick said. "Let's see. The radio is hanging about 75 feet from the ground. It is starting at velocity zero and falling at a rate of 32 feet per second squared, which means it will hit the ground roughly in 2.2 seconds at the speed of 70 feet per second. I can live with that. We'll use three mattresses. It will probably bounce off, but the mattresses will absorb the primary shock. The secondary shock won't be nearly as great."

"You did this!" Ronald shouted. "You have this all figured out!"

"No, son," Derrick said. "I'm just good at math."

Frank turned his back a moment to suppress a smile. Even Ned looked amused. Frank ordered Thomas, Jim, and Alan to get the mattresses from the lab.

Derrick turned to Ronald, pulled his sunglasses down so he could look over the rim, and said, "I'll be back." He turned and walked toward his tent.

Derrick returned with his bow and several arrows tipped with large, steel hunting arrowheads. Thomas, Alan, and Jim placed the mattresses where Derrick ordered, and they all stood back.

"You can't do this. If it breaks, you're going to have to pay for it."

"Not I," Derrick said as he put an arrow in the bow and aimed. The first arrow whizzed by, barely missing the radio.

"You're going to hit it!" Ronald cried.

The second arrow flew about six inches above the radio.

"Need to practice," Derrick commented.

The third hit the rope, and the radio fell, bouncing on the mattresses and off to the side. Brian and Alan rushed for it, almost falling on it. Brian stood up with the prize, walked over to Ronald, and handed it to him.

"This better not be broken." Ronald turned it on, and music flowed from the speakers. He tried a couple of other stations and several controls. It worked perfectly. "You're sure lucky," he told Derrick.

"No, son. You are lucky."

• • •

After a light-hearted workday, the supervisors and some of the professional crew went to dinner together that evening.

"I can't believe the thing still worked after a fall from that height," said Michelle.

Derrick and his cohorts in crime grinned wickedly. "That was an illusion," Derrick said. "His radio was never up in the tree. That was a broken radio I picked up at the Potter's House last evening. His radio was hidden under the mattresses. Brian and Alan made the switch."

"I don't believe it," Jane laughed. "You certainly had us going, not to mention Ronald. What did you do with his tape, by the way?"

"It's safely hidden away."

"How did you get the dummy radio up in the tree?" Lindsay asked.

"A magician can't give away all his secrets." Derrick grinned. "I have to keep my audience fascinated with me."

"Well, Derrick," said Michelle, "I like your headband and sunglasses." She slid closer to Derrick and put a hand on his arm. "I think you could fulfill a lot of fantasies with your military persona."

"Yeah, Derrick," said Sally. "When will you give us a break and take some of us out? I haven't noticed you dating anybody while you've been here."

"He and Lindsay were pretty hot on the dance floor the other night," Jane said.

"Yeah, but that wasn't a date," Michelle said. "That's just something they do."

Lindsay felt an unexpected stab of anger toward

Michelle and started to say something when Frank sat down by her. He looked upset.

"What's up?" Derrick asked.

"I just came from a meeting with the power company about our contract. There is this prig—an attorney for the company—who has something against us digging at the site."

"I thought that was taken care of," Lindsay said.

"I did, too. We have a contract. We have the historical recovery laws in our favor. I don't know what his problem is. It's puzzling. He sits there with his mouth all puckered up like a butt hole and expresses a completely irrational opinion." Frank stopped and took a drink of Lindsay's beer. "Now he's accusing us of being into drugs."

"Drugs?" they all said, simultaneously. "Where did he get that notion?"

"He said he had been getting anonymous calls."

"That's ridiculous," Lindsay said. "Who would do that? None of us are into drugs."

"That's what I told him and the contract committee. Has any of the field school been into anything?"

"The students?" asked Michelle. "No. I'm sure. That Jeremy kid I told you about is a pain in the butt, but I don't think he is into drugs."

"And none of the professional crew."

"Us? Of course not," said Lindsay.

"You don't think the scouts?"

"I think we can clear them," Derrick answered. "The only thing they get into is repetitious music. Besides they are mostly 14- and 15-year-olds, for heaven's sake. This whole thing is absolutely unfounded."

"I know," said Frank wearily.

"The sheriff and his men have been practically living at the site, for heaven's sake," Jane said. "Surely they would have sniffed us out if that had been true."

"Is that all the reason he gives, drugs?" Lindsay asked.

"At first he didn't give that. It's as if he just doesn't want us here, period. Fortunately, Marsha has a lot of credibility with the committee, and our work for the sheriff's department hasn't gone unnoticed. Look, folks, I just wanted to suggest that we all keep a low profile for a while until this blows over."

"What's the attorney's name?" asked Lindsay.

"Seymour Plackert."

The evil that men do lives after them,
The good is oft interred with their bones.
— William Shakespeare
Julius Caesar

Chapter 6

LINDSAY HADN'T NOTICED it when she met Seymour Plackert in the sheriff's office, but Frank was right. Plackert's mouth did look like a butt hole. He had chubby cheeks on either side of a small mouth that was perpetually puckered. He stood in the parking lot with the sheriff and two deputies. They had come to search the crew's tents for drugs.

Frank was there, looking grim. So was Marsha, who was equally grim. Lindsay could say one good thing about her: she was loyal. Ned stood nearby, looking nervous. The professional crew who lived at the site were there. No one was smiling.

Responding to a supposed anonymous call to Seymour Plackert, the sheriff and his deputies had been requested by the contract committee to search the site crew's tents and the laboratory. Only the archaeology crew quarters were to be searched, not the scout campsite. The anonymous caller was very specific about where the drugs would be found.

Derrick walked out of the woods. He was wearing his camouflage headband and aviator glasses.

"Have you gone into permanent combat mode?" Lindsay whispered. He whispered something back that Lindsay did not hear.

They searched the lab first. Lindsay and Frank went with them to make sure that no artifacts were disturbed. It took about thirty minutes. After the lab, they searched each tent. It didn't take long. The tents were small and had few possessions in them.

All the while, Derrick leaned against a tree with his arms folded. Lindsay couldn't tell what he was watching behind his mirrored sunglasses.

"Nothing," pronounced the sheriff.

Seymour Plackert's mouth pinched together in an even tighter pucker. "That's impossible!" he insisted in a high squeaky voice. "I know it's here."

"How do you know?" the sheriff asked. "Did this anonymous caller tell you exactly where it was? How did he know?"

"I don't know. I guess he saw the stuff." Plackert looked down at his feet, studying the ground. Abruptly, he looked up as if an idea occurred to him and pointed to Derrick. "I saw him in town yesterday. He was smoking marijuana in the park."

Derrick took off his glasses and stepped forward. He was angry. Lindsay had seen him angry only once previously, when a professor made fun of another student's work in class. Lindsay braced herself.

"If it was only yesterday, it will still be in my system. Let's go pee in a jar." He stepped close to Plackert, staring down at his face. The man retreated a couple of steps, visibly shaking.

"That won't be necessary," said the sheriff. "Mr. Plackert, come with me to my office."

"Me? Why? It's them. Filthy degenerates, look at them."

"I need to ask you a few questions," said the sheriff. "Come with me. A deputy will drive your car back for you." Seymour Plackert's eyes darted around the group of people. It appeared to Lindsay that he was searching for a way out.

The sheriff and the accuser departed, leaving everyone in a bad mood, especially Derrick. Lindsay didn't like to see his usual calm disposition overcome by anger, nor did she like seeing him unjustly accused, even with so feeble an accusation.

"I think that will be the end of this nonsense," said Frank. "Let's get back to work." He turned to Derrick. "You all right?"

"Sure."

"No one believed him," Frank said.

"Certainly not the sheriff," Marsha added.

"I know. I'll get back to work in a little bit. I'm going to chill out a while." He headed for his tent.

"I'll go talk to him," said Lindsay, following him to his tent.

"Derrick? Can I come in?"

"Sure." He was lying on his bed with his hands behind his head.

"Derrick. What's wrong?"

"What makes you think something's wrong?"

"The way you're acting. You're always so ... so tranquil." She sat on his bed and put a hand on his bare chest. She felt his heart beating slowly and steadily. He put a hand over hers.

"Tell me what's wrong," she repeated.

"I'm thinking."

"What about?"

He raised himself up to a sitting position. "If I tell you, you must keep it a secret, or I'm likely to be in trouble."

"Trouble? You?"

"Yes, me."

"I can't imagine what you could have done that could get you into trouble."

"Late afternoon yesterday when everyone was gone, I was in a tree, of all places, down by the creek, at the pool."

"In a tree?"

"Yeah. I was putting up a rope to swing into the water. Anyway, someone drove up on a motorcycle, carrying something. At first I thought he might be a pothunter, pardon the pun. He went into my tent, then Brian's, and left. I climbed down from the tree and searched the tents and found two small plastic bags of pot."

"What? What did you do with them?"

"Destroyed them."

"Why? Why didn't you tell the sheriff? Or Frank?"

"I don't know. The packets looked so incriminating, and there was only my word that they had been stashed. I suppose I had an attack of paranoia."

"Derrick, no one would believe those were yours, or Brian's."

"I know. I feel really foolish, but it's too late now."

Lindsay put her arms around Derrick's neck. After a moment, he slipped his arm around her waist

"Derrick," she whispered, "that was foolish, but I

won't tell anyone." She kissed his cheek and disengaged herself.

"The point is," he said, "why does someone want us off the site?"

"I don't know."

Three o'clock came quickly. The crew quietly went about the tasks of covering the area and putting up the equipment. Angry shouts suddenly brought everyone to attention. The raised angry voices carried across the site.

Lindsay and Derrick ran over to the dock. Frank and Ned were squared off, yelling at each other. Brian and Michelle were standing, watching, uncertain what to do.

"What's up?" whispered Lindsay.

Brian shook his head. "Frank came with this letter and started yelling."

"Damn you, Ned!" The two were oblivious to anyone else present. "All this time when you've been going to your appointments, you've really been going behind my back." Frank was red-faced. "This is the most underhanded thing you have ever done. We have been working hard out here with everything that has been going on, and you've been working against us."

"Should we do something?" whispered Michelle. "They look very angry."

Lindsay shrugged. They all stood frozen, watching.

"Someone had to do something. And I haven't been working against the site. I've been trying to save it."

"Save it? Save it! It has never been in any danger except in your mind. Don't you think I keep track of what's going with the water project? It's a long way off, Ned."

"They are going to start testing different water levels…"

"That's what you keep saying, but you are wrong. I don't know where you have been getting your information. It doesn't even make sense. But you may have single-handedly stopped the digging." Frank slapped the letter he held in his hand. "This says the archaeology department is going to review the proposal."

"They are going to put me in charge," Ned said.

"You? Are you some kind of idiot? You may have convinced them the dig is unsalvageable."

"That's not true!" Ned yelled back.

Lindsay noticed that Ned almost sounded childlike in his denial.

"It's true," Frank yelled. "I've got to go defend it. As for putting you in charge, you won't be in charge of the backdirt pile. I'll see to that."

Ned lunged at Frank, pushing him backward. Frank started forward, fists ready to pummel Ned. Derrick, Brian, and Lindsay ran to them. Brian grabbed Ned, while Derrick and Lindsay stepped in front of Frank.

"Stop this." Derrick ordered. "It's scaring the field crew."

Frank looked at Derrick as if he were the enemy. "Do you know what he has done?"

"I think we're getting the picture."

"I suppose you are behind the so-called pothunters and everything else that has been going on," Frank yelled at Ned. "And the anonymous calls about the pot. Was that your doing as well?"

"That's right, blame everything on me." Ned pulled back from Brian's grasp.

"Hold on, guys," said Brian.

"Why don't you two go to opposite sides of the site for a while?" Lindsay suggested. "Frank, can I read the letter?"

Frank handed Lindsay the letter, and she began reading. "It says here that due to the number of irregularities and sampling errors ... Sampling errors?" reiterated Lindsay, then continued reading, "... we find it necessary to review the research design and its execution." Lindsay looked up. "I don't understand."

"It's simple," said Frank. "I got this letter when I picked up the mail at lunch. Ned's been reporting to the contracting agent and the archaeology department that we're doing a piss-poor job of excavating the site, and they may just shut it down. And the stupid little beggar thinks they are going to put him in charge."

Ned started to lunge toward Frank, and Brian held him back again.

"Well, Frank," said Lindsay, "I think you and I can convince them otherwise. We are all doing a good job." Frank had a stubborn set to his jaw. He said nothing. "Besides, look at the date they set for the review. It's not for several months. You know what that means. This letter is just to satisfy some bureaucrat that they are addressing the issue." She looked to see who got copies: the board members of the power company. "Frank," she said in a low voice, "I'll talk to Ned and find out who else is involved in this. I don't think this is just his doing." Frank relaxed a little and nodded. "Derrick is right," she continued. "The crew are a little taken aback by all this yelling."

Brian talked Ned into going to the house. Lindsay and Derrick stayed with Frank down by the dock.

"I just don't understand him," said Frank. "I know he has his little theories, and he thinks he won't be able to prove them unless the whole site is finished. But it will be finished. This is one of the better planned sites I've worked on."

"OK," said Lindsay. "You know most of the archaeology department will back us up, and I know several people on the contract committee. Everything's going to be fine. We'll just convince them they have the wrong impression. I'll talk Ned into helping."

"Over my dead body—"

"We get him to convince the committee at the department that they misunderstood what he was talking about. They won't want to make a big deal out of this anyway."

"Lindsay's right, Frank," Derrick said. "Besides, they aren't going to ditch the whole site after this much is done. You know that."

"Yes, I know all of that. It's just that he was betraying me … us … behind our backs."

"I know," said Lindsay. "Ned's paranoid. I don't know why, but he is. He's just gone a little overboard. It may be that someone else is pushing his buttons. Someone at the power company."

It took until lunchtime the next day for the camp to get back to normal. Derrick was back in stride. Ned and Frank didn't speak, and Frank put Derrick in charge of overseeing Ned's work. The site was quiet again. Most of the crew were eating when Ronald the Radio came up shyly to Derrick, who was sitting with

Lindsay.

"Some of the scouts are saying I called the sheriff and told him lies about you, and now we won't be able to dig anymore. I didn't. I wouldn't do anything like that, honest. Sure, I was mad at you, but I wouldn't have done anything like lie about you to the sheriff."

"That's all right. I believe you, kid. And nothing's going to happen to the dig."

Ronald relaxed, then became solemn again. "I did cut your bow string."

Derrick's sandwich was halfway to his mouth. "You what!" he cried. Ronald stepped back with renewed anxiety. "My bow string. You cut my bow string? Do you know how hard it is to make a bow string? Now I have to go kill a deer, and it isn't even hunting season. Then I have to dress it and strip and cure the sinew. I hate that."

"I'm sorry. I'm really sorry."

"Well then, I guess I can go to Wal-Mart, instead." Derrick grinned at him, and Ronald grinned back. Lindsay rolled her eyes at the two of them, picked up the remains of her lunch, and tossed them in the trash can.

After lunch, Lindsay helped Jane with a burial. It had been a while since she could relax and excavate a burial herself. She was brushing dirt away from a long bone when a shadow suddenly blocked out the light. She looked up to see Thomas.

"I have something," he said, calmly. "Really, this time. I know I have hollered wolf many times before, but this looks really neat."

"Have you finally been taking your medicine, Thomas?" Lindsay asked.

"No, ma'am. I'm just working on a new image."
She followed him across the site. When they arrived,
Sally was standing beside the excavation looking
down into it and beaming with a smile. "There," he
said.

Lindsay was astonished. The smaller feature had
indeed been a burial. The skeleton was in a flexed
position facing the larger feature. It was the larger
feature that was astonishing. It was a horse.

It was not completely excavated yet, but Sally and
Thomas had done a good job so far. The finished portions stood out in clear relief. She noticed the horse's
teeth were worn down, indicating advanced age at
death, but the most surprising attributes were a clay
pot by its head and a healed break in one foreleg. An
identical looking clay pot was in the burial with the
human bones.

"I've never seen anything like this," Lindsay said.

"We thought it was rare," said Sally.

"It's unique," Lindsay observed. "Have you shown
it to Frank?"

"Not yet."

"I'll go get him," Sally said.

"This is really nice," Lindsay told Thomas.
"You've found something significant here."

"Yeah, Sally and I thought so, too."

Lindsay lay down on her stomach and peered into
the excavated pit to get a closer look at the bones.

Frank came with Marsha, who was now working
at the site.

"Look what Thomas and Sally found," Lindsay said.

"I'll be damned," said Frank.

Derrick came to see what was going on. He leaned

over the edge and examined the horse. "It has a healed break," he said.

"I know," said Lindsay.

Others drifted over to have a look at what the excitement was about.

"Are you sure this belongs with the site?" Ned asked.

"Look at the pots buried with them," answered Sally, who was not going to allow her find to be reduced in any way.

"Were the man and the horse buried together?" Marsha asked.

Sally shook her head. "These were two discrete holes."

"It's a woman," Lindsay said. "She was old when she died. She may have had arthritis." Lindsay pointed to features of the skeleton as she talked. She examined the burial goods: a single pot and an obsidian knife.

"Aren't stone tools rare in a woman's burial?" Thomas asked.

"This kind is," Lindsay replied, turning the knife over in her hand.

"Is there any other evidence of horses at this site?" Thomas asked.

"No," Frank said. "None."

"The space between the graves makes it unclear whether they were buried together, or even at the same time," Derrick said. "But Sally's right. The presence of grave goods with the horse definitely places it contiguous in time with Indian habitation."

Lindsay lifted out the pot in the woman's burial and examined it.

"Let me see the other one," she said.

Thomas gently lifted the ancient pot out of the horse burial and gave it to Lindsay.

"I think they were made by the same person. Or at least the same tool was used to stamp in the design. Look, it had a nick in the bottom that is repeated in the design of both pots."

"The pots look identical," said Thomas. "Maybe they were both made by her."

"This certainly raises as many questions as it answers," Frank said. "Quite a set of mysteries."

Lindsay sat rubbing her fingers across the design on the pot, lost in thought.

"Tell us what happened, Lindsay," asked Derrick.

"Yes, tell us what happened." Frank smiled at her.

Lindsay sat beside the burial. Derrick sat beside her. All the others sat, too, and Lindsay began her story.

"The conquistadors were riding in the distant woods looking for a village that could tell them where to find gold. One man was riding too fast on the uneven ground, and his horse stepped in a hole and fractured its leg. The man abandoned the horse and rode one of the pack animals. The conquistadors continued their search for the gold and gave no thought to the injured animal. The horse hobbled on three legs looking for water and comfort.

"Meanwhile, there was a woman in the village. She was approaching old age, but she was not yet old. Her husband was dead. He had no brothers, and she had no family, so taking care of herself was very hard. She was a medicine woman, and she traded her cures for food and hides. One day she was in the woods looking for herbs when she happened on a wondrous being. He must be a spirit, she thought, for she had never seen such a beautiful being. He was large, bigger than a deer or a bear, with a broad chest and long back. His fur was black and shiny. He had long hair flowing from a gracefully arched neck, and he had a beautiful long tail that touched the ground. The spirit had hooves—not split like a deer's, but a single piece—and they were very large. He had large, dark eyes and a white patch of fur in the middle of his forehead. Large, sleek muscles moved easily under the shiny coat. The spirit was powerful, but he was injured.

"The woman drew her doeskin skirt up to make a container and poured water into it. The spirit smelled the water and let the woman come to him. He bent his head and drank from her skirt. She searched her pouch for the right herbs and made a poultice. She took her most valuable possession, an obsidian knife that her husband had traded several of her pots for, and cut a strip of leather from her skirt. She put the poultice on the broken leg and wound the strip of leather around it.

"The woman walked back to her village, and the spirit followed, walking slowly on his three good legs. The other people in the village were frightened of the spirit when they saw him and would not let her bring him into the palisade, so she made her home outside where she could care for him. She discovered he liked grass, corn, grain, nuts, and berries. She fed the spirit well, and he healed, though he always walked with a limp.

"The woman found that the animal could pull a travois, so when she went to the woods to gather food and herbs, she could bring back much more than she did when she had to carry it herself. The spirit could drag trees and do the work of many braves, and the people became less afraid of him. He allowed children to sit on his back and ride when he pulled logs or the travois laden with food. He would take nuts, berries, and corn from their hands, gently caressing their palms with his soft lips.

"In the winter, the spirit's coat became shaggy and he could work, no matter how cold or harsh the weather. In the summer, his coat was slick and shiny, and he was very beautiful.

"The spirit lived with the old woman for many years, and both grew very old. One day the spirit died and, because he had done so much work over the years, the men in the village helped the old woman bury him. They dug a large grave for the spirit, and the old woman made a special pot and put corn in it. She set it beside his head.

"The woman was very old and lonely without the spirit, and though the people in the village took care of her, she was so sad she died soon after her friend. The people buried her beside the spirit and put her best possessions in her grave with her, and she was happy."

"I'll bet they were impressed with horses when they first saw them," said Sally. "I remember when I saw a real live horse for the first time. I was five, and it was running in a field. I thought it was the most beautiful creature in the world."

• • •

Lindsay was delighted with Thomas's find. So much of the time, archaeology is about looking for the patterns of a people that define and separate them as a culture distinct from other cultures. Rarely did they uncover an example of idiosyncratic behavior. She was looking forward to analyzing the bones.

Lindsay dreamed about the horse. It was running, chased by conquistadors. They didn't want the Indians to have it. They trampled the corn fields, waving their swords, but the horse was fast. One conquistador took aim and shot just as the horse jumped safely inside the palisade. Lindsay woke up. The sounds of crickets were loud, and outside her window she could see lightning bugs blinking on and off. In the distance she heard the river sounds. This was a good site, one of the best she had worked on. If only all the mysteries were archaeological and not criminal.

The next morning, after the old woman's and the horse's graves were photographed, Frank and Derrick came to help Lindsay, Sally, and Thomas take up the bones.

"Where is Marsha?"Lindsay asked, surprised not to see her with Frank as usual.

"She said she wasn't feeling well this morning. I think it's aches and pains from digging. You remember how it is at first."

"Yes," said Lindsay aloud, but she thought to herself that, unlike Marsha, they were required to continue working, aches and pains or not.

"The lab crew floated the contents of the pot from the horse burial. It contained corn cupules," Frank said. "How did you know?"

"I just guessed. It's not all that uncommon to find corn in a pot, you know. Don't read anything into it."

"I won't, but I think some of the others are. You're

in danger of becoming famous, Lindsay."

Lindsay just laughed and shook her head.

"Take one last look," she said. "We're going to take up the bones."

As she reached into the pit and touched the horse's skull, a piercing scream split the relative silence of the site. They all froze.

"That was from the flotation dock," said Derrick. They ran toward the dock.

Carrie, one of the flotation crew, stood on the dock pointing toward an object floating in the water.

"Good, God," exclaimed Frank. "It's a body."

Lindsay went to Carrie and led her off the dock and away from the river. She was shaking and started crying. By then the remainder of the site crew had gathered and were staring into the water.

"Go back to the site," Frank ordered. "Michelle, you and Jane take everyone to the picnic area and call the sheriff."

Lindsay gave Carrie to Jane. "Take her with you and give her some water or a Coke or whatever she wants." Lindsay went back to the river.

"What should we do?" Brian asked.

"I suppose we should pull it out of the water," Frank answered.

"We who?" asked Derrick.

"Aren't you supposed to leave a dead body where you find it?" asked Brian, hopefully.

"Not when it might float away. I know this is not pleasant, but you, Derrick, and I have on gloves. We are just going to have to do it."

They pulled the corpse from the water and dragged it onto the dock, where they turned it over.

It was Seymour Plackert.

They all stared at each other for a moment.

"What do you think happened?" Brian asked. "Do you think he fell in and drowned?"

"I'm sure the sheriff will sort it out." Frank stayed with the body and sent the others to wait for the sheriff, who arrived half an hour later. The crew were sitting with their arms folded, grim-faced and quiet.

"Where is the body?" he asked.

"It's down at the river, on the dock," Lindsay said.

"Who found it?"

"I did," Carrie said quietly.

"Can you tell me about it?"

Carrie shrugged. "I dipped the flotation bucket into the water—the pump is broken—and was bringing it up when, it … it just came from under the dock. I screamed and dropped the bucket. I guess the artifacts are lost."

"That's all right, Carrie," Derrick comforted her. "Don't worry about the artifacts."

"What happened then?" asked the sheriff.

"When we heard her scream," said Lindsay, "we rushed down to the dock and saw the body. Brian, Derrick, and Frank pulled it out of the water onto the dock. Frank's with the body now. All of us came here to wait for you."

"I want all of you to stay here until I examine the body. I may have some questions."

The sheriff, one of his deputies, and the two men who drove the ambulance walked to the dock carrying a stretcher and a body bag.

"What's going to happen now?" asked Jane.

"I don't know," Lindsay answered.

"Will they think we did it?" Jane asked.

"No," answered Lindsay. "Why would we?"

"Well, he accused us ..." She let the sentence trail off.

"We were proven innocent," said Lindsay. "We had no reason to kill him."

"Will the sheriff see it that way, though?" Jane persisted.

"I've found him to be a reasonable man."

Derrick rose and walked away from the others, stretching his legs. Lindsay walked over to him.

"I'll have to tell the sheriff about the stashed pot," he whispered to her.

"It will be all right."

"Sure."

"It will."

He smiled at her. "You sure are pretty."

"Where did that come from?"

Derrick shrugged. "I just notice it sometimes." He caressed her cheek with the back of his finger tips, walked back to the tables, and sat with the others.

Before long, the sheriff and his crew came up out of the woods carrying the body across the site. Frank directed them around the artifacts and features.

The sheriff let the others go to their quarters and asked to talk with Derrick, Lindsay, and Frank alone. He looked at each of them before saying anything. Frank and Lindsay waited for him to begin. Derrick stared absently at the wooden deck of the picnic area.

"Was it an accident, you think?" asked Frank.

The sheriff shook his head. "He was shot." The sheriff took a breath. He seemed to be weighing his words. "Plackert was surprised that we found no drugs," the sheriff said. "Perhaps bewildered would be a better word. I can think of several reasons he could be so sure there were drugs. One is that he put them there himself. Does anyone know anything about that?"

"I do," said Derrick, not taking his eyes off the ground. Frank looked over at him in surprise. Lindsay wanted to take his hand, but he was too far away.

"Why don't you tell me about it?"

Derrick looked at the sheriff and told him what he had seen from his perch in the tree and what he had done about it.

"I know it was stupid, but at the time it seemed like the right thing to do."

"If I had known this when I interrogated Plackert, it would have been a great help," said the sheriff.

"Yeah, I know."

"Would you recognize the fellow if you saw him again?"

"I doubt it. He had on a helmet, and I wasn't that close."

"How about the bike? Would you recognize it?"

"Maybe."

"A little later you can drive around with me to some hang-outs, and we'll look for the bike."

Derrick nodded.

"Why?" Frank replied. "What could anyone gain from running us off the site?"

"Perhaps they didn't want you to find a body?" said the sheriff, and they all looked at him in astonishment. Burial 23. It had not occurred to any of them. No one off the site knew they had found Burial 23.

"Then you think it has to do with Burial 23?" asked Frank.

"I think it highly likely," said the sheriff. "Lindsay, you said the burial could have been in the ground anywhere from 25 to 100 years. For example, say it was 25 years and the perpetrator committed the crime when he was 20. He would be 45 now."

"Or it could have been Plackert," said Lindsay. "He was what? Sixty-five?"

"That was my first idea. After questioning him at length, I finally told him we had found the body and he should come clean. He appeared genuinely shocked, but he stuck to the story that he had received several anonymous calls about the people at the dig. I had my deputies follow him. He went straight home. The next day they lost track of him."

"You think he was working for someone else but didn't know why they wanted the crew off the site?" asked Frank.

"I believe that is a reasonable explanation," the sheriff replied.

"Why do you think the murderer dumped Plackert's body here?" asked Frank. "To scare us?"

"I'm not sure they knew you would find it. There are many remote places up river to dump a body."

"I think he was killed near here," Lindsay said abruptly.

They stared at her. "How do you know?" the sheriff asked.

"I heard the shot. At least I think I did. I was dreaming, but you know how dreams are. They incorporate outside sounds into the plot. I heard a shot in my dream."

"Do you have any idea what time it was?"

"I don't know. I think I woke up shortly after the shot, but I didn't look at the clock. I didn't hear anything suspicious when I was awake. Maybe it was nothing."

"Maybe and maybe not. Derrick, did you hear anything?"

"No, but I sleep like the dead."

"I'll ask the others before I leave. They may have heard something and not realized it. I also think Lindsay should move into town or someplace more protected. Everyone knows she is the one who identifies bones."

"Are you saying someone may come after her?" Frank asked.

"It's a possibility I can't discount," answered the sheriff.

"You can move into my house," said Frank. "The doors all have good locks. You can sleep on the second floor, and I'll be there in case—"

"I think you're overreacting a bit," Lindsay declared.

"Frank and the sheriff are right," Derrick said. "You should move to a safer place. Perhaps with the field students. We could be talking about a person who has killed twice already and would not hesitate to kill again."

"There is no room with the field students," Frank said. "There is plenty of room where I'm staying." Frank and Derrick eyed each other for a moment.

"Look," said Lindsay, "I have Derrick, Brian, Jane, Allen, Jim, and Sally living here. I should be safe."

"Tents are too easy to get into, and someone could easily shoot through the tent at you," said Frank.

"Listen to yourselves," said Lindsay. "Aren't you going overboard just a little? If someone wants to kill me, I don't think they would march into camp where they would likely be seen. Besides, there are many bone experts in the United States. Killing me would only delay things."

"They may not rationalize things that way. And as far as not wanting to be recognized, they could send the fellow who planted the pot," said Derrick. "Or they could send someone else. It is best if you stay at Frank's."

"What about you and the others?" Lindsay argued. "He could make a mistake and get Jane or Sally. He could see only your hair, Derrick, and think it was me."

"Jane and Sally should stay at the house, too," Derrick said. "Brian, Jim, Alan, and I can take care of ourselves."

"Look, this is just supposition, and I'm not going to move my quarters based on it." They started to protest again when Lindsay turned to the sheriff. "I made a cast of the Burial 23 skull and am reconstructing her face. Would you like to see it?"

The sheriff looked surprised. "Yes, by all means."

They followed Lindsay to her tent, and she pulled the box from under the table. She took the reconstruction, set it on her table, and uncovered it.

"Nice job," said Frank.

"That's her?" asked the sheriff.

"Pretty much," said Lindsay. "There are things like the exact shape of the nose and lips that I may not have captured. I have no way of knowing her eye and hair color. The face is still rough. I'm still working on it.

The sheriff stared at the face. "That's pretty good. If it's been in the ground around 60 or 70 years like you said in your report, there may be some old missing persons report. When I can spare someone, I'll have them look in the morgue at the newspaper office and see if there are any articles. I have to go now. I don't have to tell all of you to keep an eye out." He left, and Frank turned to Lindsay.

"Come stay at the house. The sheriff is right. Everyone knows you identified the skeletons of the children."

"Do it," said Derrick. "I want you to be safe."

"I'll think about it." She smiled at him.

A fool there was and he made his prayer
To a rag and a bone and a hank of hair
(We called her the woman who did not care)
But the fool he called her his lady fair.
　　　　　　　—Rudyard Kipling
　　　　　　　The Vampire

Chapter 7

THE THOUGHT OF the digging season coming to
an abrupt and ignominious end distressed Lindsay, for
she expected the students from the field school and
the scouts to flee in terror from the site. However,
they did not take the discovery of Plackert's body
with the same gravity as everyone else. They were,
in fact, fascinated by it. They were in the middle of
a mystery, and they reveled in the gory details, even
made up worse particulars on their own.

Things started taking an upturn when the sheriff
and Derrick found the motorcycle that had been used
to deliver the pot at a local hang-out. The sheriff took
the owner in for questioning, and they all believed the
solution was near. Lindsay felt safe and pushed the
events to the back of her mind.

Marsha Latimore had undergone a transforma-
tion. The metamorphosis had happened gradually, but now it was complete. Her hair, no longer

the bright blonde, lacquered bouffant style that all Merry Claymoore Garden Club members wore, was now a chin-length, subtle golden blonde with bangs that stopped just above her eyebrows. Nowadays, she often wore it pulled behind her ears and covered with an Atlanta Braves baseball cap. The nails, too, had changed. The once long, bright pink talons were short and polished with clear polish. Marsha was more relaxed, and she no longer followed Frank around the site, nor did she make a lot of small talk while she worked.

She stood in front of Lindsay in shorts, a T-shirt, and sneakers, a trowel in her hand. Marsha was good at assimilating.

"Frank said to ask you if I could work on a burial."

"Okay. I have one here I was about to open up." Lindsay indicated a dark tan stain on the lighter tan surface of the site floor. "The way we excavate a burial is one end at a time so we can map the cross-section of the burial fill. I'll start until I find bone, then let you work."

Lindsay began digging gently into the burial, taking shallow shovelfuls and putting the dirt in a pile near the burial. She stopped frequently and tested the burial with her trowel.

"I'll get a crew member to screen your dirt for artifacts." Lindsay tested the burial again with the trowel. "I've found bone." She shoveled as much dirt from the top of the bones as she could without endangering them. Marsha sat beside the hole and looked into the burial, staring at the yellow brown shaft.

"Is that the bone?" she asked.

"That's it." Lindsay handed Marsha a collection

of tools. "Take the trowel and remove the dirt from around the bones, but try not to touch them. Use the spoon or tongue depressor to loosen the dirt close to the bones. Try not to scrape them. Use this paint brush to brush the loose dirt away. Remember, always work from the known to the unknown, from where the bone is exposed to where it is covered. Take care. It is a slow task, even for someone with a lot of experience. Ask for help if you need it."

As Lindsay talked, she was looking not at Marsha but at Jeremy, the troublemaker she had taken off Michelle's hands. Lindsay had assigned him to screen fill dirt from Sally's burial, and he was picking things out of the screen and throwing them on the ground. "Just a minute," she told Marsha. She rose and walked over to Jeremy. He was a big boy, almost six feet tall, but much of his behavior looked adolescent despite the fact he was a college student.

"What are you doing?" she asked.

"Taking the pebbles out." He did not try to hide the derision in his voice.

"Save everything that doesn't go through the screen."

"Even rocks?"

"What looks like rocks to you may have meaning for archaeologists." Lindsay reached down and picked up a small stone. "This is a section of a chunky stone, a gaming stone. See the rounded edge. Don't throw anything away. Your job is to sift and to save everything that doesn't pass through the screen."

"Well, do you want me to put the rocks back in?"

His arrogant attitude was beginning to irritate Lindsay. "No, they have lost their provenience. You have mixed items from different batches. They are useless."

"They were useless to begin with."

"That's not for you to decide. Just do the job as you were instructed. It's an important job." Lindsay turned to go but looked back in time to see Jeremy turn, grin at a fellow student, and throw a few more pebbles away. "All right, that's it, you are not going to destroy artifacts from my burials. Get out. You are not working here anymore."

"You can't do that. You're not in charge here."

"That's where you're wrong. I'm in charge of the burials, and I'm telling you to leave."

"I paid good money to come and do this, and I'm earning course credits. You can't make me leave just because you don't like my attitude."

"It is not because of your attitude that I'm kicking you out. It's your behavior. You deliberately disobeyed my instructions and threw away artifacts. Now, get out!"

Jeremy stepped up to Lindsay, staring intensely at her as if his eyes were a weapon. "If you want me to leave, you'll have to throw me out." Lindsay's five feet, eleven inches were almost as tall as Jeremy's six feet, and she stared back at him.

They were attracting the attention of the other diggers, who stopped and watched. Derrick came over from his transit. "Having trouble, Lindsay?" he asked.

"So? You can't handle things yourself, can you? You have to get a man to do it for you!" taunted Jeremy, not taking his eyes off Lindsay.

"I don't care who throws you out, just as long as you go."

"Well, we'll just see about that."

Jeremy stomped off, apparently in search of Frank.

"Do you think he is really going to tell the head archaeologist that he was throwing away artifacts?" Derrick asked.

Lindsay shrugged. "Michelle said he was a troublemaker." She smiled at Derrick. "Thanks."

"Don't mention it."

Marsha had been watching the scene with surprise. "Do you frequently have people like that?"

"That's the first time, and I've worked on many digs," Lindsay said.

She and Marsha looked up to see Frank and Jeremy coming across the site. "What happened?" Frank asked when he reached them.

"Jeremy was throwing away things from the burial he identified as useless rocks. I told him to stop, and when he thought my back was turned, he continued."

"She's lying," Jeremy sneered.

"Lindsay doesn't lie," said Frank. "I think you had better pack up your things."

"It's her word against mine, and she's lying."

"She isn't lying," Marsha said. "I saw it, too."

"I paid my tuition. You can't tell me to leave."

"You'll have to take the matter of your tuition up with the university. But you're off this site."

"What about my grade?"

"Since you were on Dr. Chamberlain's crew, it will be up to her what grade you get on your performance. If I were you, I would withdraw gracefully and cut my losses."

"Aw, this is stupid. Just wait till my father hears about this. He'll shut this site down so fast—"

"Derrick, tell Brian to drive Mr. Reynolds into town." Frank turned and went back to the structure he had been excavating.

"He's an unpleasant young man," Marsha said, when she and Lindsay returned to the burial.

"He certainly is. You may have to sift your own burial fill," Lindsay said. "It looks like I'm short one crew member."

"Oh, I don't mind. I think that will be fun."

"I hope you keep your enthusiasm in the heat of the day. When you finish the first half of the burial, I'll come and show you how to smooth the cross-section."

Lindsay picked up the surveying rod Brian had left and helped Derrick with mapping for the rest of the workday.

"Lindsay," Frank said as they were closing the site for the day. "I know I haven't been giving you the attention you deserve." He ran his fingers through his hair. "Damn, that didn't come out right. What I mean is, I have wanted to spend more time with you."

"A lot of things have been happening," she agreed, shoveling dirt into a burial from which bones had just been removed.

"Come stay at my house. If not for yourself, for me. Hell, for the sheriff and Derrick. We all are worried about you."

"But Frank, Burial 23 has been found. The damage is done. If they're smart, whoever they are, they'll just sit tight. It's been in the papers that I use x-rays, dental records, and photographs for identifying bones. They would know that I don't have any of those things in this case. The bones are too old."

"Come anyway."

She sighed, "All right, I'll give it a try."

"Good." He seemed to relax. "I'm sorry about Jeremy. Michelle's been complaining about him, and I talked to him, but it obviously didn't do any good."

"No big deal."

"I hope he didn't do too much damage."

"I don't think so. We would have noticed major artifacts strewn around."

After work Lindsay and Derrick lounged on the makeshift beach the crew had built on the bank of the river.

"I'm going to try moving into Frank's house," Lindsay told him.

Derrick didn't say anything for several moments. "You'll be safe there."

"I'll miss being here."

"I'll miss having you here." Derrick smiled at her and took her hand.

"Don't let anyone get my tent," she said.

"I'll guard it with my life."

They were silent for a long while, watching the sun go down.

"Lindsay, I think you and I need to go to Atlanta or Savannah this weekend and go dancing."

"I've got Burial 23 to analyze."

"It can wait. Come away with me. I'll keep you safe."

Lindsay looked over at him, surprised. "You really believe I'm in danger, don't you? If Burial 23 might get me killed, I should get the examination completed so I'll be safe."

"It's not just that I believe you're in danger. I would just like to spend time with you. Work on 23 during the week."

Frank had said the same thing about wanting to spend time with her, Lindsay thought. She looked at Derrick in his jeans, white T-shirt, and ponytail, and was tempted.

"We do need to get away and forget everything," she said.

"Then you'll go?"

"Yeah, I'll go."

Derrick settled back comfortably in his lounge chair and closed his eyes.

Lindsay moved into the upstairs bedroom Frank had prepared for her. "This is fine," she said, looking at the double bed, desk, and throw rugs on the hardwood floor.

"I'm glad you're here." Frank kissed her gently on the lips.

"I still am not convinced of the need."

"I am. Listen, I have to go out tonight. The mayor and his wife invited me to dinner. Under the circumstances, I think it is a good idea to go, or I wouldn't leave you."

"You're going to leave me alone after all this talk about my safety?"

"I'll lock the doors. No one knows you're here."

"I was joking. I'll be fine. I brought Burial 23 with me. She'll keep me company."

"I'm going to get dressed," he said. "Marsha is picking me up in an hour."

"Say hello to the mayor for me."

Lindsay cleared off the table in the corner of the bedroom and set out the clay bust she had been working on. By ten o'clock, she was ready to go to bed. Frank hadn't returned, she noted. Still out with Marsha. She put on a night shirt and slipped between the covers. The sheets were cool, and the bed was soft. She drifted off to sleep quickly.

Lindsay's dreams were fearful, and she awakened with a start. She wanted to get up and run across to Derrick's tent, then realized she was not in her tent. For an alarming moment, she did not know where she was. Suddenly she remembered. Frank's house. The room was dark, full of unfamiliar shadows moving with whatever source of light there was outside. As her eyes grew accustomed to the darkness, a shape in the corner emerged, a tall body with broad shoulders, wearing a hat. Lindsay's heart pounded. Slowly and silently she reached for the light and turned it on. It was a hat and coat hanging on a hat rack.

She put a hand over her heart and took a breath. *This is just great, Lindsay,* she thought. *You might as well go back to the site.* Suddenly, she heard the front door open and close. *Frank.* She sat up in bed listening and heard only muffled sounds. Leaving the questionable comfort of the bed, she tiptoed across the hardwood floor. It was cool on her bare feet and creaked as she walked across it. She opened the door only slightly so it would not make noise, slipped out, and peered over the landing.

It was Frank and Marsha, and they were kissing.

Lindsay quietly backed into her room. She crawled into bed and turned out the light. Only a few minutes later she heard a car door shut and a car drive off, then footfalls ascending the stairs. The footsteps stopped for a moment in front of her door, then passed. Lindsay fell asleep and didn't awaken until 4:00 in the morning.

She showered and dressed quickly. Frank was already downstairs. She packed her things, including Burial 23, and carried them down to the living room. Frank was in the kitchen. The aroma of fresh coffee and pancakes flowed through the house.

"Hi," he greeted her when she came through the door.

"Do you do this every morning?"

"Hardly. This is for you. Sit down."

She sat in front of a plate and a glass of orange juice. Frank put several pancakes on her plate. He heaped his own plate and sat opposite her.

"This tastes good," she said, tasting the warm pancakes. "I appreciate it."

"It's nothing." Frank seemed to want to say something to Lindsay, but instead he picked up his fork and began to eat.

"I'm going back to the site to stay."

"Why?"

"I'm more comfortable there."

Frank was silent a moment, studying her face. "Is there a particular reason?"

Lindsay shook her head. "I'd rather stay at the site. I never believed I was in danger there. Anyway, did you enjoy your evening with the mayor?"

"Wasn't too bad. But I had to spend the evening explaining to him and his wife that the Southeastern Indians were perfectly capable of building large mounds and earthworks without the help of aliens or lost people from Atlantis."

Lindsay smiled broadly. "I'm sorry I missed that."

Frank looked at her and raised his eyebrows. Again he looked as if he wanted to say something, yet didn't.

When they finished breakfast, Frank helped Lindsay carry her things to the Jeep. It was dark at 4:30 A.M. and cool, but it made Lindsay feel good. She walked back into the house with Frank.

"It was scary here anyway," she told him. "I kept seeing ghosts and villains in the shadows."

Frank hugged her. "Take care."

"I'm all right. I'll see you at the site."

She walked out to the Jeep and was getting into it when someone grabbed her shoulder painfully hard. Lindsay instinctively elbowed the attacker, knocking him back slightly. He came forward and pushed her hard. She fell against the Jeep and slid to the ground. The large, dark form advanced on her, his hands curled into fists. Lindsay hooked the instep of her left foot behind his right calf and kicked his knee with her right foot with all her strength. He fell back, screaming. Frank came flying out of the house.

"Lindsay!" He rushed to help her up. "Are you hurt? What happened?"

"He attacked me. I'm all right." But she was about to lose her pancakes. She leaned against the Jeep and took slow deep breaths.

Frank turned to the attacker, writhing on the ground, moaning and crying. He wore a ski mask. The students flowed out of the house next door and gathered around the scene. Frank pulled the mask off.

"Jeremy!"

"Oh, man, it hurts, it hurts. I'm gonna die. Help

me."

"What the hell were you doing?" Frank demanded.

"Just scare her. Just meant to scare her, that's all." His breaths were coming in ragged gasps.

"Someone call an ambulance," Frank ordered. "And get a blanket." He turned to Lindsay, who sat on the ground with her head down between her knees. "Are you all right?"

"Yes," she replied. "I'm just a little sick."

In a few moments a student appeared with a blanket, and Frank covered Jeremy up. "Get another blanket for Lindsay," he said.

"The ambulance will be here soon. They'll give you something for the pain," Frank told Jeremy.

"What happened?" someone asked.

"He attacked Lindsay," answered another.

"He said he was going to do something to scare her. I thought he meant to put a snake in her bed or something," someone else said.

Jeremy was still groaning on the ground when the ambulance came. Frank had also called the sheriff's office, and a deputy arrived as Jeremy was being carted off to the hospital. After Lindsay gave her story to the deputy, several students jumped in with what they knew. It was 6:15 before Lindsay, Frank, and the students arrived at the site.

Derrick was emerging from the laboratory when he saw Lindsay carrying a suitcase to her tent. "I thought I was going to have to go looking for the whole crew. What happened? What are you doing?"

"Moving back into my tent."

"Why?"

"Among other things, I was attacked at Frank's

early this morning."

"What? Are you all right?" He started to look her over.

"Yes, I'm fine, but that's more than I can say for Jeremy Reynolds." Lindsay went into her tent and sat on her bed, shaking.

"Tell me what happened." Derrick sat down beside her and put his arm around her as she explained. "Well, that's what can happen when you attack someone," said Derrick. "You don't know if the other person is stronger. Don't give the bastard another thought."

"I probably ruined his leg."

"So what? He shouldn't have attacked you."

"I know. I'm going to lie down for a while. Would you ask Jane to take charge of the burials?"

"Sure. Can I get you anything?"

Lindsay shook her head.

"Call if you need anything." Derrick kissed her head.

It was 11:00 before Lindsay felt like working. She went out to the site, feeling tired and depressed. "Thanks, Jane. I appreciate your taking charge so much these days."

"No problem. I'm sorry all this stuff is happening to you. What a jerk. I hope his leg falls off!"

Lindsay winced and went to check on the burials.

Marsha was working on the other half of her burial. Jane had shown her how to smooth the cross-section with her trowel and how to draw the pattern of layers.

"I am so sorry about what happened," Marsha said. For a moment, Lindsay didn't know which incident she was talking about, Jeremy, or her and Frank. "You certainly have been seeing the bad side of our town lately."

"This was someone we brought."

"Well, with all the killings … It's just too much."

"I'm inclined to agree."

Lindsay saw Marsha search her face for any signs of knowledge or hostility and smile slightly when she saw none.

"Can you tell me something about my burial?" Marsha asked.

"Well, let's see. You don't have the pelvis uncovered yet, so I can't be definitive on the gender, but it is probably a male." Lindsay pointed to the brow ridge. "Females have a more gracile forehead. Notice the prominent brow ridge on the skull. When we're at lunch today, look at the women and men. You'll see that most of the men have prominent brow ridges and squarer jaws. Some look positively Neanderthal."

Marsha laughed.

"The pelvis is a better indicator because some women have large brow ridges and some men have small ones." Lindsay looked at the teeth. "He is older than 21. He has his wisdom teeth. I'd guess he's less than 45 from the wear on them." Lindsay took a brush and brushed off the skull. "Oh, dear, it looks like the poor fellow had syphilis."

Marsha's eyes widened. "Really?"

"Yes. That probably pushes his age up some because the syphilis was fairly advanced."

"Wasn't that something brought by the Europeans?"

"I think this is probably a New World variety."

"It must be wonderful to know all the things you

know."

"Lately it's been damn inconvenient."

"I guess it has, but you like it, don't you? I mean, looking at these bones?"

"Yes, I do. Very much. I'll leave you to it. You're doing a great job."

At lunch Frank told Lindsay that Jeremy's knee would require surgery and would eventually be all right. But he would need a lot of therapy. "Don't feel bad about him," Frank said. "He'll have a long convalescence to think about his behavior."

"I'm relieved to hear he is going to be all right."

"You need to sign a statement at the sheriff's office and bring charges against him. That will protect you from anything his parents might want to do."

"Okay," Lindsay said. "I'll do it when we finish today."

After work Lindsay and Frank went to the sheriff's office and filed charges against Jeremy Reynolds. While they were there, they learned that the person who planted the pot in Derrick and Brian's tents was working for Seymore Plackert, but he did not know who Plackert worked for. He said Plackert just showed up in the bar looking for someone to do a job. It was another depressing bit of information in a thoroughly depressing day for Lindsay.

She waited in Frank's car with the windows down as he went into the hardware store for supplies. A car pulled into the parking lot beside her, cutting off another car trying to get into the parking space. Lindsay glanced over at the driver. It was Patrick Tyler, and he was grinning at her.

"Hi, Miss Lindsay. Do you want to go dancing this Saturday?"

"I have other plans."

"Why don't you change them?"

"I don't want to." Lindsay kept her eyes straight ahead.

"I'll bet we could have a real good time."

"No."

"I've been taking dancing lessons."

Lindsay said nothing. Patrick got out of his car. Lindsay thought he was going into the hardware store. Instead, he came around and got in the driver's side of Frank's car.

"What are you doing?" Lindsay's hand gripped the door handle. "Get out! Right now!"

"I just thought if you had the opportunity to get to know me—"

I don't believe this, thought Lindsay. "Get out, or I'll tell your grandmother!" It sounded foolish. Lindsay had meant to say sheriff, but the threat got the desired effect. Patrick got out of the car and closed the door. He started to say something, but Frank came out of the hardware store and got in the car. "The screen ought to be in next Wednesday," he said.

"Good," said Lindsay. "I'm ready to go back to the site."

It was 4:30 when Lindsay got back. The site was vacant and covered, and no one was in the crew village. She thought she heard laughter and splashing down at the dock. Some of the crew apparently were swimming in the river.

She smiled to herself as she changed into her swimsuit and walked down to the pool in the river. Jane was there, and Brian and Sally, Thomas and Michelle. Suddenly, Derrick broke through the water. Lindsay smiled upon seeing him. Michelle swam toward him, and he picked her up in the air and threw her into the water. Michelle came up laughing and turned to swim away, Derrick chasing her. The feelings—the jealousy, the pain—that Lindsay hadn't seemed to feel at the sight of Marsha and Frank came to her with a gut-wrenching force as she watched Derrick and Michelle. She turned and walked back to her tent. It definitely had been a thoroughly depressing day.

During the night, it rained, a hard driving rain. Lindsay lay awake worrying about the two burials that were half finished and worrying that the black plastic covering was not anchored well enough. She turned over on her bed and thought about how long she had had a crush on Frank, about their few promising dates last year, and now about her feelings for Derrick. Her good friend Derrick. When had her feelings started to change? What exactly were her feelings anyway? She was still awake when her alarm went off.

"Some rain we had last night," Derrick said when Lindsay came out of her tent.

"I hope the burials didn't fill up," she replied.

"Let's go have a look."

They walked across the site to a burial. The ground was muddy, and pools of water stood everywhere. Derrick shined a flashlight on the burial. It was still covered. They looked under the plastic at the dry bones.

"That's a relief," Lindsay said. They walked to the other one. "Damn," she said when she saw that the rain had puddled on top of the plastic covering and collapsed it into the burial, filling it with water.

"I'll get the pump," Derrick said.

They had drained most of the water by the time Frank and the van arrived.

"How much damage?" Frank asked.

"One burial flooded," Lindsay said. "The structures look okay, just small pools of water here and there. It's not too bad, considering how much rain we had."

"It came down in torrents, didn't it!" he said.

"Yeah, I'm surprised we didn't have more damage."

"You all right?"

"Sure, my tent stayed dry."

"That's not what I mean."

"I'm fine. I just have to salvage this waterlogged burial."

Frank studied her face for a moment, then went to check the structures.

A letter came for Lindsay. Frank handed it to her at lunch. She didn't recognize the handwriting on the envelope. It was a spidery scrawl, and the i's were dotted with small hearts. What in the world, thought Lindsay, as she tore the envelope open:

> Dear Beautiful Lindsay,
>
> I think if you got to know me you would find we have a lot in common. I know you probably feel self-conscious dating a member of the community, not to mention a member of the Tyler family, but I assure you no one would think any-

thing about it. I have made reservations at
Le Jour for us. If I don't hear from you,
I'll assume you have accepted my invita-
tion and will pick you up at 6:00 Tuesday
evening.

Sincerely,
Patrick Tyler

"I don't believe this!" Lindsay exclaimed.

"What?" Jane asked.

"This letter from Patrick Tyler. Read this." She
handed the letter to Jane.

"Cheeky." Jane laughed and shook her head. "What
are you going to do?"

"Nothing. I don't feel obligated to call him. If he
wants to get all dressed up for nothing and drive out
here, let him."

"Le Jour is an expensive place. He must be trying
to impress you."

Lindsay threw the letter into the trash with the
remains of her lunch and went back to work.

Tuesday evening, Lindsay and Jane returned from a
shopping trip in Cullins. They had stocked up on groceries, toilet paper, soap, and paperback books and
were putting soft drinks in the refrigerator when Derrick came up to Lindsay, looking puzzled. "Lindsay,
were you supposed to have a date with Patrick Tyler
this evening?"

"No."

"He came by at 6:00, all dressed up. Said you and
he were supposed to go to Le Jour."

"He wrote a letter saying he had made reservations, and he would take it for granted that I had accepted if I didn't contact him. I did not feel obligated to accommodate his fantasies and just ignored the whole thing."

"What was it he said, Lindsay?" laughed Jane. "You shouldn't feel self-conscious dating a Tyler."

"Something like that."

Lindsay took a sack of supplies and walked toward the storage tent.

"Wait up," said Derrick, following her. "Isn't he the guy in the picture?"

"Yeah."

"Is he bothering you?"

"Not really," she said as she quickly marched to the supply tent.

"I'd say he is. You're obviously worried about something."

Lindsay stopped and looked up at Derrick. His brown eyes were narrowed, and his face was creased in a concerned frown. Lindsay smiled.

"I'm fine. He is just an annoyance, that's all."

"You want me to talk to him?"

"No. If he comes around again, I'll talk to him." She took the groceries into the supply tent, and Derrick helped her put them up.

Lindsay took a paperback to bed with her. She was deep into a Dick Francis mystery when she noticed the top drawer of her cardboard chest-of-drawers was slightly open. She rose from the bed, taking her battery-powered lamp with her. Setting it on top of the chest, she pulled open the drawer. Her underwear was in disarray, and deep among the panties was a ring box. She opened the lid. It contained a heart-shaped locket. Inside the locket was a small picture of herself on one side and Patrick Tyler on the other.

"Damn little bastard," she swore out loud.

Lindsay threw the necklace in her trash can and paced around her tent, steaming. She stopped pacing, looked at the necklace among the crumpled paper, and retrieved it. She threw it on the chest and got back into bed. Despite her anger, she fell asleep quickly, but jerked awake when her alarm rang. First thing after she dressed, she took the drawer of underwear outside, emptied the lot into a ditch, and set fire to it.

"What'cha burning, Lindsay?" Brian asked, coming up behind her from the direction of the latrine. He squatted down and looked at the burning apparel. "It looks like your underwear. You don't have lice do you?"

"No, Brian, I don't have lice. Get lost."

Brian shrugged, hoisted his shovel over his shoulder, and walked toward the site.

When the clothes had burned, Lindsay shoveled dirt over the smoldering fire and went looking for Jane. Lindsay found her with Derrick and Sally, who were taking the plastic covering from a structure.

"Want to go into town with me when the stores open?"

"We forget something yesterday?" Jane asked.

"I need to buy new underwear. I just burned mine."

They all stopped and looked at her with open mouths.

"Why?" Derrick asked.

"Because that little creep Patrick Tyler had his

hands in my underwear drawer."

"Oh, gross!" Sally exclaimed.

"What? How do you know?" Derrick asked.

"He left me a locket with my picture and his in it. Obviously, he has been hiding and photographing me as well."

Derrick scowled. "I'll have a word with him."

"No. I'm going to the sheriff and let him have a word with him."

"I've heard about people like that. They can be dangerous," Sally said.

"I'm going to be dangerous if he doesn't leave me alone."

Lindsay helped them pull the plastic off the excavation of the structure, then went to the flotation dock, taking several of their specially adapted buckets with her. The crew had found five structures so far, and the volume of material needing floating was increasing. She was hooking up the pump when Frank and the field students arrived, flowing onto the site like worker ants. Lindsay glanced up through the trees and saw Patrick Tyler with Frank and Marsha. Dammit, she thought. She left the dock, climbed up the bank, and headed toward Frank, who was starting on Structure 5 with Marsha's help. She saw Patrick making a beeline for the outer trench that Derrick was cross-sectioning.

"What is he doing here?" Lindsay demanded.

"Who?" asked Frank absently.

"Patrick Tyler."

"Oh. He asked me if he could work on the site. I thought it would be good community relations."

Lindsay watched Patrick sneaking up on Derrick.

Only the top of Derrick's head could be seen as he knelt in the deep trench. She started running toward the trench as Patrick knelt down and stretched out his hand to Derrick's head. Lindsay stopped when she saw Patrick run his fingers through Derrick's hair, a wry smile playing on her lips. Derrick turned around, saw Patrick, and jumped from the trench in a fury. Patrick backed away, stuttering.

"I—It's a m-mistake, really."

He fell backward, and Derrick pulled him up by the front of his shirt.

"Do something like that again, you little pervert, and I'll break your neck."

"It was a mistake. You don't understand."

"Oh, I understand, all right." Derrick grabbed a piece of satin and lace hanging half out of Patrick's pocket.

"That's mine."

"Yours? Yours? Get off the site, you piece of puke. If I ever see your face again, I'll smash it in."

"But, but I—I don't have a car."

"Then walk! Now!"

"Nonsense," said Brian. "I'm the official creep chauffeur around here. I'll take him back to town." Brian grabbed Patrick by the collar and began dragging him toward the parking lot.

"What the hell is going on?" swore Frank, hurrying to the commotion. "Brian, let him go!" Brian stopped, but still held onto Patrick.

"He was running his fingers through Derrick's hair," said Marsha, who had watched the incident in puzzled fascination.

"What?" asked Frank. "Derrick. What is going on?

Do you know who that is? His grandmother is Isabel Tyler."

"I don't care if his grandmother is Queen Elizabeth. He's a disgusting little creep."

"Derrick, don't you think he was probably just horsing around?" Frank asked.

"No," Lindsay answered. "He thought it was me."

Frank stared at Lindsay. "You? What do you mean?"

"All he could see was the hair," she said.

"Am I missing something?" Frank asked.

"He had this in his pocket." Derrick held out a pair of panties to Lindsay. "Are they yours?"

"Yes," she said without touching them.

"What in God's name is going on?" Frank asked.

"Patrick has been harassing Lindsay," Derrick said. "Apparently, last evening he went through her underwear and stole these."

"He's lying!" Patrick cried. "He's a dirty liar."

"Oh, God," Marsha exclaimed.

"Brian," Frank said. "You can escort Mr. Tyler off the site."

"Yes, sir."

"Lindsay," said Frank, "why didn't you tell me?"

"I haven't had a chance. Besides, I was going to the sheriff's office today to tell him."

"Well, I'll go with you."

"So will I," Derrick said.

"Me, too," said Marsha. "I think I recall him harassing a girl when he was in high school. The sheriff might remember it."

"What brings you all here? You haven't found another

body?" the sheriff asked as he looked up from his desk and grinned.

"I need you to have a word with Patrick Tyler," Lindsay said. She set the box with the necklace on the desk. Derrick, who had put Lindsay's panties in a plastic bag, lay them on the desk beside the box. The sheriff looked at them in surprise as Lindsay and Derrick detailed the incidents with Patrick. "I didn't save the letter," finished Lindsay.

The sheriff looked dumbfounded for a moment. He picked up the plastic bag that held Lindsay's panties, then put it down again. "I'll have a talk with him," he said. "It is probably just an infatuation."

"Do you remember how he was fixated on Wilma Harrison's daughter in high school?" put in Marsha. "They finally had to send her to live with her aunt in Michigan, he was so persistent."

"Yeah, I remember, but that was a long time ago." Marsha started to protest, but the sheriff raised his hand to cut her off. "Leave it to me. I'll talk to him. He has no business sneaking around in Lindsay's personal things and taking her underwear."

Later Derrick and Lindsay sat in the diner drinking coffee while they waited for Frank and Marsha to join them after Frank paid the bill at the hardware store for the last order of screens and shovels.

"Calm down," Derrick said. "The sheriff said he would sort everything out."

"What are you talking about?" Lindsay asked, with sudden unexplainable exasperation.

"Look at yourself. Your shoulders are hunched up. Your expression looks like you're ready to kill the next person who walks in the door."

Lindsay smiled. "If it's Patrick, maybe I will. Let's not talk about murderers and perverts anymore."

"Suits me. Let's talk about you. What's going on in your head?"

"All those things I don't want to talk about. Give me a diversion, Derrick."

He smiled and reached for her hand. "I would love to divert you if you would let me. When we go to Savannah..."

A clever reply played on Lindsay's lips, but it was lost as she looked up and saw Frank and Marsha pull into a parking space in front of the diner. She took back her hand.

It was hot and humid at the site the next day as Lindsay worked on excavating a structure. She knelt between the strings that marked off a grid on the structure floor, putting the dirt from each square into a bag labeled with the number of its square. As she finished each bag, a scout took it to the dock to have the dirt and debris separated from the small artifacts by use of the floatation screens. She looked up through strands of sweat-dampened hair to see the sheriff coming toward her. Not today, she thought. Please, not ever again. No more death. Lindsay had a strong urge to run in the opposite direction.

The sheriff waved to her. "Good news," he said. "Patrick Tyler has been sent out of town for an extended stay."

"How did you manage that?" Lindsay asked, stepping out of the grid strings to stand with him.

"I went to see his grandmother, Isabel Tyler, and took the locket, your underwear, the bill for the flowers he ordered for your 'date,' and the bill for the locket. I laid them out on her coffee table and told her that he was harassing you and would not stop. I reminded her of Linda Harrison and how her parents had to send her out of the state to get away from Patrick. I told her that because of Patrick's past and present behavior, he had attracted the attention of the Georgia Bureau of Investigation's psychologist as a suspect in the child murders. I admit I stretched it a bit there, but it had the desired effect."

"What did she do?"

"She sat in her high-backed chair as rigid as could be, without saying a word. Occasionally, her mouth would twitch. The old lady thought I should leave the locket, since her money had bought it. I told her that since it was found in your underwear drawer, it was evidence. Believe me, she did not like that one bit. Yesterday evening I got word that Patrick and his mother, Ruth, left on a trip to an undisclosed location for an undetermined amount of time." He laughed.

"That means he'll stay gone? He'll do what she says?" Lindsay asked.

"Isabel Tyler controls all the money, and she rules with an iron hand. I imagine she tore into his butt real good."

Lindsay suddenly put her arms around the sheriff's neck and kissed him. "Thank you so much!"

"No problem," he said, blushing. "Is there anything else I can do for you?"

Lindsay smiled. "No. This really takes a big load off my mind."

"I doubt you'll hear from him again. I don't believe

Patrick is dangerous, just a damn nuisance. But you never know."

"I really appreciate all you've done to help."

"Actually, I rather enjoyed mortifying the old lady. But don't let that get out."

The day was beautiful. The weatherman said there would be no rain. Indeed, the bright sun and cloudless sky confirmed the accuracy of his prediction. It was a perfect day. Lindsay went from burial to burial, checking her diggers. Satisfied with the progress, she helped Sally with the mapping.

Derrick and Brian had gone into town to pick up supplies at the hardware store. As Lindsay was drawing a corner posthole of a small outbuilding on Derrick's map, she saw Brian and Derrick drive into the parking area.

The survey rod Sally was holding leaned severely as she watched them emerge from the Jeep. Lindsay yelled at her to pay attention, and Sally grinned sheepishly. "Come on, Lindsay, it is almost lunch time."

Lindsay grinned back. "Okay. We'll let Derrick and Brian finish the mapping after lunch."

"What do you think of Brian?" Sally asked as she brought the rod to Lindsay.

"What do you mean?"

"Well, I was thinking about asking him out. Do you know if he is seeing anyone?"

"Not that I know of. I thought you and Thomas were getting along."

"Yeah, but we are not serious. I kind of like the way Brian saved me from the masked outhouse shakers and dragged Jeremy and Patrick off the site."

Lindsay laughed. "I see. Well, if you're interested, why not ask him out?"

"You don't think he minds forward women? Some men are funny about being the one to do the asking."

"Ask him and see. I think he'll be flattered."

Late in the day as the sun was beginning to fall behind the trees and the heat of the day had begun to dissipate, Lindsay was working with bone identification in the laboratory tent after most of the crew had scattered. Suddenly, the triangular dinner bell that hung from a tree near the picnic tables sounded. Lindsay and Sally both looked at their watches and at each other. "What the ..." Sally exclaimed.

Derrick and Brian were sitting on a table, looking grim. Lindsay had a sinking feeling that something else had gone wrong. When the crew had gathered, Frank spoke.

"We've been told a five-year-old girl is missing. The sheriff wants us to help look for her."

Lindsay thought she was going to be sick.

His bones are as strong pieces of brass ...
—Job 40:18

Chapter 8

THE FOCUS OF the search for Jenna Venable was a large wooded area behind her house. "She likes to play in the woods," her mother tearfully told the sheriff. "I told her to always stay in sight of the house ... not to go in the woods ..."

No one mentioned the possibility that Jenna might be another victim of the killer, but the fear of that prospect was in everyone's eyes.

Lindsay looked at the map the sheriff laid out on the hood of his car and noted that the place where the skeletons of the little girls were found was just five miles through the woods.

The sheriff marked off the map into quadrants and assigned teams to the quadrants.

"This is a big area," he said. "This neighborhood borders on about three thousand acres of wilderness. The terrain gets rough around a thousand feet into the woods. We won't be able to cover the entire area before dark, so everybody come back before sundown.

It is near impossible to find your way out of the woods at night, and I don't want to have to search for anyone else."

Lindsay checked her compass before she started into her assigned section of woods. Derrick was twenty yards to her right, Brian about the same distance to her left, but he was hidden by thick brush. She examined the ground, trees, and bushes for signs of previous passage, making sure she maintained a relatively straight line of travel through the heavy growth. As she progressed deeper into the woods, the undergrowth grew more dense and she lost sight of Derrick. Occasionally, in the distance she heard Jenna's name called out by another searcher.

Lindsay entered a heavily eroded area where water had cut deep gullies through the earth. The terrain was forested over, and Lindsay looked down into a gully thick with trees, vines, ferns, and an abundance of other plant life. It looked dark and forbidding now that she was searching for a lost child, but Lindsay remembered that as a little girl she loved places like this. To her right she could see a monadnock rising as a rocky hillock dotted with small trees and shrubs. She saw Derrick climbing among the rocks, searching. She wanted to signal her position, but he was too far to call to, so she gathered up stones and made a cairn on the edge of the gully. After scratching her initials in the dirt next to the cairn, she descended, holding onto the ropy vines with her gloved hands to keep from falling.

The overhanging trees screened out most of the light, but Lindsay could see the winding passage the gully cut through layers of sedimentary strata. A small stream about a foot wide and just a few inches deep flowed through the bottom of the gully. Lindsay made another mound of marker stones by the creek and walked downstream away from the rise.

The roots of trees that grew on the edge of the gully were eroded from the earth so that they made gnarly, snaky appendages in front of small caves in the side of the gully. Lindsay shined her light into the holes, and sometimes the glow of animal eyes shone back at her. Along the way she built small cairns to show her passage.

It was growing darker, and Lindsay guessed the searchers had already started back. She tried to remember the map the sheriff showed them and how far the gully continued before it emptied into the river—at least two miles, too far to continue to the end. The creek was becoming wider and deeper.

"Jenna," she called softly. Nothing. Lindsay was loath to give up. She decided to go a little further before starting back.

Around a bend, Lindsay thought she heard a muffled sob. She stopped and listened and heard it again. "Jenna, is that you? Your mother is looking for you." Again she heard the soft sobs. She searched the brush with the light from her flashlight, and the patch of canes growing on the other side of the creek seemed to move. Lindsay stepped through the small stream and shined her light in among the foliage. A small, dirty, tear-stained face peered back at her and began whimpering.

"It's all right, Jenna sweetheart. You're safe now. My name is Lindsay, and I'm going to take you back to your mother." As Lindsay stepped forward, Jenna shrank back.

"Would you like to take my flashlight and have a look at me?" Lindsay lay the light near Jenna and stepped back. After several moments, Jenna hesitantly grasped the light and shined it at Lindsay.

"Let me take you home," Lindsay said.

Jenna sobbed, and Lindsay stepped forward again. This time the little girl didn't shrink back, and Lindsay took her in her arms and held her.

"It will be all right." Lindsay took the flashlight and stood up with Jenna, who now held to her tightly.

Carrying the child, Lindsay retraced her steps back along the creek through the winding gully. It was dark, and she needed the flashlight to find her way through the vines and heavy growth. She stopped to rearrange Jenna so she could walk more easily.

"Don't let the bad man get me," Jenna whimpered.

Lindsay went cold. "What bad man, sweetheart?"

"The bad man that chased me."

Lindsay held Jenna tighter. "No bad man is going to get you." Her words were firm and sure, but a wave of fear swept over her. The bad man would be one of the searchers, she was sure. Wasn't that a pattern: the perpetrator joining the search for his victim? Lindsay turned off the flashlight and stood for a moment to accustom her eyes to the darkness before she continued.

As she walked, Lindsay thought she saw a point of light in the distance. She stopped and watched. The light was coming closer. Lindsay looked around for cover, but she was standing in an exposed area with only tall ferns and leafy vines hanging from the bank. She hid Jenna among the ferns and told her to be very quiet. Lindsay took her knife from its scabbard and waited in the shadow of the foliage. Soon she heard the sound of someone walking along the creek, but she couldn't make out a shape because of the bright flashlight. Her hands were sweating and her heart raced.

"Lindsay," a voice called out.

"Derrick," Lindsay sighed heavily. She replaced her knife and picked up Jenna, who started to cry.

"You found her!" exclaimed Derrick.

"Yes, and I'm so glad you found us. I've never been so glad to see anyone in my life."

"I just followed your markers."

"Someone chased Jenna into the woods."

"I see," Derrick quietly said.

"Jenna, this is a friend of mine. His name is Derrick. He is a good man."

Jenna held onto Lindsay's neck with one arm. She had her other fist in her mouth, sobbing and hiccuping. Lindsay shined her light on Derrick so Jenna could see him. She rocked her in her arms.

"He's like you." Jenna pointed to his hair.

"Yes, he's like me, and we are going to take you to your mother."

Derrick led the way to the place where they had entered the gully. He tried to take Jenna so that Lindsay could climb out, but the little girl clung fast to Lindsay's neck.

"I can make it," Lindsay said. "You go first and give me a little help."

Derrick climbed part way up the embankment. Holding onto a vine, he reached out for Lindsay. She held tightly to Jenna with one arm and gave Derrick her other hand.

There was more light at the top of the gully and

glimpses of red sky left by the setting sun showed through the trees. "We need to convince her to let me carry her," said Derrick. "You must be tired."

"It's all right. I would prefer that you have your hands free."

Derrick eyed her a moment, then scanned the darkening forest. He gave her a reassuring smile and led the way back toward Jenna's house. It seemed to Lindsay that the walk out of the woods was much longer than the walk into the woods. Her arms were tired, and she stopped frequently to shift Jenna.

"I'll take her," Derrick said the last time she stopped.

"I'm fine. We're almost there. I can see lights through the trees."

They emerged from the woods amid a storm of camera flashes, shouts from reporters, and screams from Jenna's mother, relatives, and friends. Mrs. Venable ran up and grabbed her daughter from Lindsay's arms. "Oh, God, my baby, you're all right. You're all right. Thank God, you're all right." She hugged Jenna as people gathered around. Jenna began to cry.

"Good work." The sheriff beamed at them with obvious relief.

Derrick and Lindsay answered a few questions from reporters, then ducked away, pulling the sheriff with them. "Someone chased her into the woods," whispered Lindsay.

The sheriff stared at her for several moments as if not understanding what she had said. "No," he whispered finally. "No. Did she know who?"

"We didn't question her."

"What did she say?"

"When I found her, she asked me not to let the bad man get her."

"Damn," said the sheriff, then lowered his voice before he attracted the press still gathered around Jenna and her mother. "You two did good."

"I'm glad we found her before someone else did," Derrick said.

"Yeah," the sheriff agreed. "Jenna is one lucky little girl."

Suddenly, a flash went off in their faces and they all looked up to see Mickey Lawson grinning at them. "Great job, folks," he said. He had snapped their picture. Lindsay was glad the picture would not show the look of horror on her face at seeing him.

"He sometimes takes pictures for the newspaper," the sheriff said after Mickey moved on.

"Still ..." said Lindsay.

"The newspaper would want pictures. They would send one of their best photographers," said the sheriff. "Why don't the two of you go back to the site and get some sleep. Come down to my office tomorrow and make out a statement about finding Jenna."

"Good idea," urged Derrick. "Come on, Lindsay. You could use a good night's sleep."

They left the crowd of searchers, reporters, and onlookers and started back to the site, but Lindsay still felt a profound uneasiness.

"Pretty good night's work, Lindsay," Derrick said as they drove along the highway. He reached over, took her hand, and squeezed it.

"I was relieved that you came along when you did," she said. "I was afraid it might be..."

"I know. I'm glad it was me, too."

•   •   •

Lindsay went to the hospital early in the morning to take Jenna a teddy bear. It was a large brown bear, and Lindsay told her it would watch over her. Jenna's mother apologized to Lindsay and Derrick for not thanking them when they brought Jenna out of the woods.

"It was very chaotic," Lindsay said.

"I can't tell you how thankful I am. We are going to visit my mother for a few weeks, aren't we, Jenna?"

Jenna nodded, holding on to her bear. "They said you're an arc ... arc ... arc'olgist," Jenna said. "What is that?"

"I dig up places where people used to live long ago to find out what they did there."

"That's what I want to be."

Lindsay smiled. "It's a fun thing to be."

The sheriff was also there when Lindsay arrived. He had come to the hospital to get more information about the man who had chased Jenna into the woods. He told Lindsay and Derrick that Jenna had been playing in the far corner of her backyard when a man approached her and offered her candy if she would come with him. The only description they got from Jenna was that he had a big moustache. The sheriff suspected that he may have been disguised. Jenna said she ran from him, and he chased her into the thick woods where she hid in the bushes. Afraid that he would find her, she ran deeper into the woods and down into the gully, a place where she had played previously but unknown to her mother, and hid where Lindsay had found her. Again, like most of the other clues, nothing pointed to anyone. The sheriff had someone checking out all the stores that might have sold the disguise, but he held out little hope of finding anything helpful. Lindsay and Derrick left the hospital and followed the sheriff to his office.

After they wrote up and signed their statements for the sheriff, Derrick reminded the sheriff that he needed to finish examining the artifacts that he and his crew had retrieved from the crime scene.

"Good idea. I'd like to send the whole lot to the crime lab in Atlanta to see what they make of it."

Derrick laid all the plastic bags filled with crime scene artifacts on the table in the back room of the sheriff's department. Lindsay wrote down the description of each object beside its number as Derrick made the identification. He already had looked at much of the debris, but he examined each with a hand lens, hoping to find some minute but useful clue.

The yield consisted mostly of old pull tabs and bottle tops, beer cans, and old soft drink bottles. They had also found ten rusted nails, pieces of a barrel hoop, a two-foot length of rusted chain, three-and-a-half feet of barbed wire, three rusted hinges, two small weathered pieces of cardboard that had once been tightly wrapped into a stick, the bones of one rabbit, and parts of two mice.

"Not much help," Lindsay commented as she wrote down the identifications.

"This might help," Derrick said. "It looks like the pan lock from a tripod."

Lindsay looked at the object Derrick was holding. "Another photography connection."

"What's that?" The sheriff peered over Derrick's shoulder.

"A part for a camera tripod," said Derrick.

"Oh, Lord," the sheriff said.

"That means there may be pictures somewhere, if this belongs to the killer," Lindsay said. "Can't you search Lawson's studio?"

"I don't have probable cause to get a warrant for Mickey's place."

"He took the portraits of the children," said Lindsay, "and he showed up at the search for Jenna."

"So did half the town." The sheriff pulled up a chair and sat down. "And it's true he took the school pictures, but he and Adam Bancroft are the only two professional photographers in this area. Mickey is well known. I know you don't like to hear this, but his family, the Tylers, have a lot of influence in this town. I need a little more evidence before I can zero in on a member of the Tyler clan."

"Can you get a warrant for both Adam's and Mickey's studios, so it won't look like you're focusing on Mickey?" Derrick asked.

"You can't just get warrants like that," said the sheriff. "We have absolutely nothing to link Adam Bancroft to the murders, and you can't just focus on someone and point them out as a possible child killer when you have no grounds to prove it."

"Yeah, you're right," Derrick agreed. "I guess even the most liberal of us can turn fascist in the right circumstance."

The sheriff grinned. "Yep, that's why you have people like me to watch out for people like you. How 'bout we go out for lunch?"

A few minutes later, the sheriff, Derrick, and Lindsay sat in a far corner of the diner and, as had become their tradition, finished eating before mentioning anything about the murders.

The sheriff cautioned them. "I know it looks to you like you have a good suspect in Mickey. But you have no hard evidence, and your circumstantial evidence is very thin."

"Who owns the land the crime scene is on?" Lindsay asked.

"The Timberland Paper Company now. They bought it from the Tylers about 15 years ago."

"The Tylers again," Lindsay remarked.

"Yes," the sheriff said, "but they have owned a lot of land over the years. They are the biggest landowners hereabouts, besides the paper company."

"Still, a family member would be familiar with the land."

"And a lot of other folks who might have hunted on the land. Gun clubs have rented it for years. I need something that connects Mickey to the scene or to the children, something besides him being the one who took their school pictures."

"Can you find out if he has a broken tripod?" Derrick asked.

"Yes. I can do that," said the sheriff.

"I was thinking," Lindsay said. "Derrick is well known at the hardware store and other places for scavenging tools for the site. What if he asks around for old tripods to use for parts to fix his surveying tripod?"

"Good idea," the sheriff said. "I don't think that would raise any suspicion at all."

• • •

After lunch, Derrick took Lindsay to the crime scene. He sat on a log and watched as she walked among the children's filled-in graves.

It came to her mind easier than she thought it would, as easily as for archaeological sites. She saw a truck turn into the overgrown road. It was a common pickup truck, like every other one on the road.

He slid out, coins dropping to the ground from his truck seat.

The girl slid out the other side, dropping the pen and candy wrappers. She was sucking on a Tootsie Roll pop. Lindsay couldn't see which little girl it was, nor could she see the face of the man. Even though she thought the man was Mickey Lawson, his face was a haze. The man took his camera from the seat, walked to the rear of his truck, and began setting up the tripod. The little girl played around the site, crunching on her sucker and throwing away the cardboard stick when she finished. When she became restless, the man soothed her, telling about the pretty pictures he was going to take of her and how pleased her parents would be. He picked her up and a large black fog appeared in front of them through which Lindsay could neither see nor hear what he did. When he came out of the fog, he was carrying the little girl, and she was limp.

Suddenly, Lindsay was being shaken.

"Come out of it." Derrick's voice was almost angry.

"Why did you do that?" Lindsay shouted at him.

"Because you're crying."

Lindsay put a hand to her face. It was wet with tears. "I didn't even realize it."

Derrick took out a handkerchief and began wiping her eyes and pulled her to his chest. "I shouldn't have brought you here."

Lindsay felt the steady thump of Derrick's heart. They said nothing, and after a moment she stopped crying and pulled away from him. Derrick guided her back to the Jeep, and they left the crime scene.

On the way back to the site, Lindsay told him of the vision she had seen. "He had to have some kind of truck or Jeep to get out there, and it had to be inconspicuous. The little girls knew him, or he couldn't have lured them out there."

"Then you think they were killed at the crime scene?"

"Yes, I think so. I'll bet the tripod was knocked over in a struggle. Are you going to look for it tomorrow?"

"Yeah, I'll do as you suggest, pretend I'm looking for an old broken one for spare parts. But, if you're right about him knowing the little girls and luring them away, he broke his pattern with Jenna—provided it is the same person."

"That's right," Lindsay agreed. "I didn't add that in as a factor."

"Your story fits the artifacts, though."

"Many stories could fit the artifacts. After all, we never know if any of my stories are right." Lindsay was quiet for a moment, staring out the window. "Maybe the killer was compelled to commit the crime again," she said, "but couldn't do it his usual way by luring a child he knew, so he took an opportunity to kidnap a child he found alone."

"You know, there may be two killers: one who

takes the photographs and the other who ..." Derrick let the sentence trail off.

"Maybe. Who knows? We don't know enough about criminal psychology to be making the assumptions we have been making."

"I agree. Just let the sheriff find the killer. We've certainly done our part already," Derrick said.

The sheriff made an arrest. It shocked everyone when Brian came from town with the news.

"Ned?" Lindsay exclaimed.

"I don't believe it," both Frank and Derrick said.

"Believe it," Brian said. "From what I hear, the sheriff has a strong case. The folks of Merry Claymoore are none too happy about us either. Talk about guilt by association. All that goodwill that Lindsay built is gone now."

"Surely not," said Frank. "Ned is sort of a hometown boy."

"Some of them see us as a bad influence," Brian said. "At least they are not assembling in mobs with torches yet, but between that Plackert guy being found dead here at the site after his run-in with us, and now Ned under arrest for murdering little kids ..."

Marsha's Lincoln slid to a halt on the gravel. She jumped out of the car and hurried to the small group gathered in the eating area. "I guess Brian told you," she said.

"Yes," answered Frank. "It's hard to believe. Ned is a first-class ass, but I can't believe he is a murderer. I hope Brian is exaggerating the town's reaction."

"There is not a ground swell of antagonism, but some people are frightened."

"I'll talk to the sheriff," said Lindsay, "and find out what's going on."

"You want me to drive you?" Frank asked.

"No, I'd prefer to go alone."

"I know what you're thinking, Lindsay," the sheriff said as he stood face-to-face with her in his office.

"No, you don't," she answered.

"Good, because what I'm thinking you're think-ing is that I passed over arresting a resident of Merry Claymoore to get one of yours."

"I don't make snap judgments. Right now I don't know why you arrested Ned."

"I don't make snap judgments either. I arrested Ned because Jenna identified him."

Lindsay's mouth flew open. "What?"

The sheriff nodded his head. "Sit down, and I'll tell you about it."

Lindsay sat down in the brown leather chair in front of the sheriff's desk and watched as he sat down in a matching chair across from her.

"Jenna's mother took her to get ice cream. Ned was there, and Jenna pointed to him and said, 'That's him.' Later, I showed her several pictures." He leaned forward for emphasis. "Mickey's among them. She picked out Ned Meyers."

"I see."

"I doubt you see yet. There's more. Ned fits the profile."

"Profile?"

"Yes. You didn't think I was relying only on you archaeology people to find the killer, did you?"

"No, I didn't assume that," she said stiffly.

The sheriff frowned. "Both of Ned's parents were alcoholics. Did you know that?"

"No, but that's hardly—"

The sheriff held up a hand, and Lindsay did not finish. "He stayed a lot with his mother's parents, who lived in Merry Claymoore until their deaths several years ago. He was here summers and many times during the school year. What with going back and forth between homes and coming from a troubled family the way he did, he didn't make many friends."

"But still," Lindsay said, "I can't imagine Ned as the killer."

"Does Ned date?"

Lindsay shrugged. "I don't know very much about his social life."

"Has he dated anyone this summer?"

"He came to the Locomotion with us," Lindsay evaded.

"Alone?"

Lindsay looked down at the floor, then back up at the sheriff. "Okay, he had a troubled youth and is shy with women."

The sheriff raised his hands in a gesture. "You were ready for me to lock up Mickey Lawson because he's a photographer."

"Lawson took all the pictures of the children."

"That's true, he did. You do know that Ned is a photographer, too?" The sheriff raised an eyebrow and waited for Lindsay's response.

"It is not uncommon for archaeologists to have that skill," she evaded again, then added, "Mickey is excessively neat and precise."

"When you all were looking for housing for your digging crews, Ned didn't volunteer his home, the one he inherited from his grandparents. Have you seen it? It is a very neat place."

"Well, sheriff," said Lindsay, "if you know students, you would not want them staying in your home either. All this is slim evidence."

The sheriff smiled. "I agree, and I'm still building a case. But with Jenna pointing him out, I had to arrest him, even if only for his own protection."

"Have you thought about Patrick Tyler as a possible suspect?" she asked.

"Sure, but these guys are pretty much one dimensional. They usually have only one variety of obsession. With Patrick, it's females his own age."

Lindsay sighed. "Brian says people are pretty mad at us."

"Some are, but you need not worry. I won't allow vigilantes in my county. I'll keep deputies looking in on the site."

"What about bail for Ned?"

The sheriff shook his head. "You won't find a judge around here who will give him bail, not with the chance he's a child killer. It's best if he stays here anyway."

"Can I see him?"

The sheriff nodded. "Lindsay, I don't like any of this. I have a lot of respect for you, but if this guy's guilty …"

"All right, sheriff, I understand."

The sheriff led Lindsay to the lockup. When she heard the steel door slam behind them, she felt panicked. Ned must be awfully frightened, she thought.

She had expected the bars on the jail cells to be

black. They weren't. They were tan, as were the floor and the walls. As she walked down the cell-lined hallway, Lindsay's loafers made hollow clicking sounds on the polished floor. The odor of chlorine and urine were strong, and she involuntarily put her hand to her nose. Someone shouted at her as she went by. Lindsay kept her eyes straight ahead.

Ned was in a cell by himself, sitting on the lower bunk and holding his head in his hands. He looked even more lonely than when she and Derrick had seen him leaving by himself from the Locomotion.

"I won't be very far," said the sheriff. "Call when you are finished." He opened the cell door and allowed her to enter.

Ned raised his head and looked at Lindsay. For a moment she thought he didn't recognize her.

"Hello, Ned. Are you okay?"

"I'm innocent, Lindsay. I didn't do this."

"Do you have a lawyer?"

Ned shook his head. "I imagine the court will appoint one. At least that's what it said on that damn little card they read to me."

"Why did Jenna point you out?" she asked.

"I don't know."

Lindsay thought he genuinely looked bewildered.

"Have you ever seen Jenna before?"

Ned shrugged. "I may have. I go in the drugstore a lot to get ice cream."

"Think back. Have you ever spoken to her?"

Ned shook his head. "I don't know. I don't usually speak to people. I didn't do this," he said again.

"We don't believe you did it," Lindsay said.

"Really? Even Frank? He's so angry."

"What you did about the site is far from murder. No, Frank doesn't think you are guilty."

"I want you to understand about the site."

"That's not important—"

"Please, let me tell you. My parents weren't great, and they palmed me off on my grandparents whenever they could. When I was here, I spent most of my time exploring the woods around here."

"I'm sorry," she said.

Ned's face was red from the sun. It never tanned. Here in the cell it made him look embarrassed. He sat with his shoulders rounded and hunched over. Defeated, Lindsay thought.

"It wasn't bad," he said. "I enjoyed it. I kept coming back to that place, the bend in the river where the site is. Every time after a rain I'd be over there collecting arrowheads. After a while I learned to recognize other things. And I started keeping a map of where I found things. I read everything I could about Indians, and later about archaeology. Do you see what I'm talking about?"

"I think so."

"Jasper Creek is my site. Ever since I learned that archaeologists dig up ancient places to learn about them, I dreamed of becoming an archaeologist and digging up that place at the bend in the river." He seemed to be looking back to the beginning of that dream.

"You felt it was taken away from you?" Lindsay understood and felt sympathy for Ned.

"It was. I should have been principal investigator." He rubbed the palms of his hands on his jeans.

"It had to be a Ph.D.," said Lindsay gently.

"I would've been one and not just a graduate student

if I could have gone to school full time and not had to work. I tried. I studied hard."

"You are a good archaeology student," Lindsay said.

"Humph," he snorted. "I may be a good student, but to get an assistantship you have to have a high GRE." He was silent for several moments. "Derrick."

"Derrick?" Lindsay asked.

"He can't decide if he wants to finish his Ph.D. or not." Ned shook his head. "He can't decide. I sometimes hate him for that. When he does go back, they'll give him an assistantship, just like before, because of that high GRE he has. It's not fair."

"No," Lindsay agreed, "it's not always fair."

"And now," he continued as if Lindsay hadn't said anything, "now, I'll never get to go back. This will ruin me." He put his head in his hands again. Lindsay put a hand on his arm. He looked at her hand, as if surprised that she would touch him. "You know," he said. "It was the high point of this summer when you danced with me."

"Well, I guess you hadn't been having a very good time at the site." Lindsay tried to sound lighthearted.

She stood up, and Ned rose to face her. "Look, Ned. We'll find out who did this."

"How? Do you think you can?"

Lindsay called for the sheriff, then turned to Ned and gave him a hug. "Sure, I can," she said as the sheriff let her out the door. "My GRE score was higher than Derrick's."

Old bones to carry, old stories to tell ...
— Padraic Colum

Chapter 9

WE'VE BEEN INVITED to Tylerwynd for the annual Fourth of July barbecue this Saturday," Frank said at lunch the next day. "In view of the unpleasant things that have been happening, I think it would be a good gesture to go. In fact, we're lucky to be invited, so I expect all of you, especially the professional crew, to be there. And Lindsay, I was assured that your problem person will not be attending."

"What if we have already made other plans?" Derrick asked.

"Change them. This is important, and I expect all of you to be on your best behavior. No pranks or jokes. Lindsay, would you and Sally select an assemblage of artifacts to take? Marsha thought it would be a good idea to show the townspeople what we are doing."

"That means someone will have to watch them constantly," Sally said.

"Marsha's seeing to it that a lockable display case will be there. Write on an index card what each artifact is and what it was used for."

"Perhaps Marsha would help with the cards," Sally whispered to Lindsay. "I'm sure she must have had penmanship in finishing school."

Lindsay grinned.

"I think it sounds like fun," Michelle said. "Will you give me a ride, Derrick?"

"Sure," he muttered.

After lunch, Derrick found Lindsay looking at a cache of animal bones that had been discovered in a pit. "You have photographed this, haven't you, Derrick?"

"Yes, before lunch. I can't believe Frank is insisting we go to that 4th of July thing—in spite of the fact that some of us have made other plans."

Lindsay told Sally she could take up the bones. Then she and Derrick moved away from the other diggers. "We can go dancing some other time," she said.

"You need a break, and so do I. I've seen you, how down you've been lately."

"Just all these things happening," she said. "We must all have done some bad shit in a previous life."

"We'll figure something out about Ned," Derrick offered. "The sheriff has the Patrick thing under control, and you took care of Jeremy. You're finished with the skeletal identifications for the sheriff, and Burial 23 is probably too old to worry about."

"There are still too many unanswered questions," Lindsay said. "The guy who planted the pot didn't know who Plackert was working for, so we don't know why he wants us off the site. And we don't know who killed Plackert." She shook her head. "It must be someone from the power company, something to do with the dam. But why? It doesn't make sense."

"Plackert had lots of clients," Derrick said. "I'm sure the sheriff is talking to all of them. He was the Tylers' lawyer, too, wasn't he? Maybe Mickey Lawson's putting pressure on us, thinking he can somehow keep you from investigating the deaths of the children."

Lindsay shook her head. "The problems with the contract and the harassment of the site started before I was asked to identify the bones ... before the bones were found, even. It's something else."

Derrick massaged her shoulder. "Let me tell Frank that we can't go to his PR picnic."

"I think that would probably disappoint Michelle. You promised to take her."

"I promised to give her a ride."

"We might have an opportunity to look for the tripod," Lindsay continued. "Besides, I understand Tylerwynd is really a showplace. It might be fun."

"We could have more fun together."

"You, me, and Michelle?"

"Michelle?" Derrick sounded surprised and bewildered.

Lindsay regretted the words as soon as she had said them. She felt embarrassed. "I see Brian gesturing, I think he needs to talk to you." Lindsay walked back to the cache of animal bones. Derrick stared after her, then reluctantly went to see what Brian wanted.

What in the world's wrong with you? Lindsay chided herself. Derrick's a good friend, and you're treating him like ... like what? Like a lover who has jilted you, she told herself. She made up her mind to apologize to him.

Just as it was nearly time to close the site for the day, Lindsay observed the sheriff's car, followed by a large bronze-colored Mercedes, wind down the dirt road into the parking lot. She decided to let him come to her. She wasn't going to greet any more bad news. Frank met the cars, and she watched the sheriff introduce him to the man from the Mercedes, who looked angry as he gestured furiously with both hands. She looked back down at her burial and ignored them. When she looked up again, Frank was coming over to her.

"Lindsay, someone is here who wants to talk to you. But you don't have to, unless you want to."

"Who is it?"

"Jeremy Reynolds' father."

"Oh."

"I'll tell him to get lost."

"No, I'll talk to him. I have a few pointers on child rearing I'd like to share with him."

As Lindsay approached the picnic tables, Frank and the sheriff seemed to close ranks around her. The man glared at her.

"Who is this ... this woman?"

"Mr. Reynolds," said Frank, "I have a site to dig, and we are behind schedule. I don't have time to play whatever game you are playing. You said you wanted to see Lindsay Chamberlain, and here she is."

"This is a woman. I understood Lindsay was a

man. My son said he was attacked, and that is how he got his leg so seriously mangled."

"Mr. Reynolds," Lindsay said, "I assure you I don't go around attacking boys. It would be reckless and dangerous. I fired your son for throwing away artifacts after I specifically told him not to. He got mad and attacked me in the dark. My father taught me how to defend myself if a guy ever attacked me, and I did exactly what he said. We have several witnesses who saw Jeremy in his ski mask whining that he only meant to scare me. We also have witnesses who say he was planning something against me."

Mr. Reynolds was a man who clearly did not like being made a fool, and Lindsay almost felt sorry for his son. After angrily searching for something to say, he turned and walked back to his car. He burned up a significant amount of rubber leaving the site.

Lindsay looked over at the sheriff, who was smiling. "You knew he thought I was a guy?" she asked.

"Yeah, I just thought it would be fun to see his face when he found out the truth."

"I don't suppose he'll take legal action now," Frank said. "I don't imagine he wants the humiliation of having the world know his son was beat up by a girl." Frank walked back to the section under excavation.

"That was a good trick your father taught you," the sheriff said.

"That was the first time I have ever had to use it."

"It was certainly effective. You know, I have a daughter in college. She's off campus, as she calls it, this semester. I've tried to teach her a few things, but she doesn't take me seriously."

"I didn't take my father seriously either, but I remembered what he taught me."

"What does your father do?"

"He teaches Shakespeare at a community college in Kentucky. My mother breeds and trains Arabians."

"Not thoroughbreds?"

"No. They are quite expensive."

"Sounds like you have a nice family."

"I do. How is Ned?"

"He's holding up all right."

Lindsay didn't ask him any more about the investigation, and he didn't offer any information. He took his leave, and Lindsay went back to her burial.

"What on earth!" Frank exclaimed, looking into the back of the Jeep that Derrick had just driven into the parking lot.

Lindsay grinned. "Derrick, you're the best scavenger I know."

"Yeah, the good people of Merry Claymoore were very generous in giving me their old camera tripods."

"Why do you want all these tripods?" asked Frank.

"I found a pan lock and just can't rest until I find the tripod it goes to."

Frank frowned at Derrick, and Lindsay explained to him about the broken pan lock found at the crime scene.

"You know the probability is very low that you will find the right tripod," Frank said.

"Right now," Lindsay said, "this is the only clue. We need to find something to help Ned."

"You're right, of course," Frank agreed, "but the site has sure been quiet since he's been in jail."

"It's not only for Ned," Lindsay said. "It's for us, too. We've lost about a third of our scouts and a lot of goodwill from the townspeople since his arrest."

"True," Frank said. "Carry on." He left them with their cache of tripods.

"He's probably right," Derrick said. "Even if the tripod the pan lock came from is one of these, it could have been repaired and we would never be able to make a positive match."

"I know."

Derrick smiled and kissed her cheek. "But we will look. Who knows? We might get lucky."

"Derrick?"

"Yes?" he asked, stacking the tripods out on the ground.

"I'm sorry about the other day."

"What about?"

"About what I said."

Derrick stopped hoisting the tripods out of the Jeep and looked into Lindsay's eyes. He touched her cheek with his finger tips, then caressed her lips with his thumb. "After the Fourth of July thing, let me take you away for a weekend. I'll make you forget about all this for a little while anyway."

Lindsay reached up and took his hand. "I would like to forget about all this for a little while."

Derrick gave her lips a quick kiss, and she helped him carry the tripods into the laboratory tent. Most of the lab workers cataloging the artifacts took no notice of them as they laid out the tripods on the floor. Derrick set about examining each one. None had its pan lock missing, but several looked as if they had had their pan lock replaced. One was from Adam

Bancroft's studio, and one was given to Derrick by the owner of the hardware store where the site did all its business. "Glad to get rid of the thing," he had said. "Been laying around for years." One was given to Derrick by a school teacher requesting that instead of using it for parts, perhaps he could fix it, and she and her students could use it.

"This got you into some work," Lindsay commented. "Can you fix it for them?"

"No, it looks like the center post is pretty well busted, but I imagine I can fix one of the others for them."

"You're too good, Derrick."

"This tripod thing seemed like a good idea, but now I think it may be a waste of time. The one we are looking for was probably carted to the dump long ago or stuck in an old barn somewhere."

"I know, but we have so few clues, and Ned needs good news from somewhere."

"Yeah, I thought about that, too. You know, Lindsay, Jenna did identify him."

"I know. I've been thinking about that. What if I'm wrong and Ned did do it and ..."

Derrick touched her lips. "We'll do what we can, Lindsay. We could just give the sheriff what information we have about tripods and leave everything to him. We'll just concentrate on the site. The sheriff is a good man. He wants the right murderer caught." Derrick sighed. "Let this be the last detective work we do, okay?"

"Okay."

"I mean it," he said.

"Me, too. I don't really know what else to do."

"And no more time tripping at the crime scene."

"No, definitely not."

Soon after 10:00 o'clock the next morning, Ned came strolling into the site, delivered by the sheriff. The crew stopped their work and watched as he walked to the section of the site he had opened up earlier and began giving orders. Lindsay was the first to greet him.

"Hello, Ned," she said.

He nodded. "Looks like they made some progress while I've been gone."

"We didn't think the judge was granting bail …"

"Didn't need it," he interrupted. "Look, I need to check on this section. I'll talk to you later."

"Sure," Lindsay said.

She looked across the parking lot and saw the sheriff standing with his hands in his pockets. She turned and walked toward him. Frank and Marsha came walking toward him from one of the nearby structure excavations. The sheriff did not look happy.

"Hey," Lindsay greeted him. "What happened?"

"Yeah," said Frank. "I thought he was in the pokey for a while."

"So did I," said the sheriff, "but it seems as though he came up with an iron-clad eyewitness alibi for the time when Jenna was supposed to have seen him."

"Who?" asked Lindsay.

The sheriff smiled grimly. "Isabel Tyler."

"Isabel Tyler?" Marsha exclaimed.

Lindsay raised her eyebrows.

"What's the story?" Frank asked.

"Seems our boy made a phone call, and about 20

minutes later Isabel Tyler drives up in her chauffeured limousine and says Ned was with her that afternoon, telling her what places on her property she might find Indian artifacts." The sheriff shook his head. "Never knew the woman was interested in Indian artifacts." He turned on his heels and walked to his car. Lindsay followed.

The sheriff started to get into his car, and Lindsay put a hand on the door. "What does this mean?" she asked.

The sheriff stood up, the car door like a barrier between the two of them. "I don't know."

"Do you believe she was telling the truth?"

"Frankly … no."

"Then, why?" she asked.

"Who knows?" The sheriff's face showed no expression.

He doesn't like being manipulated, thought Lindsay, and that's what he feels Ned has done. Ned and Isabel Tyler.

"He must know something about …"

"Yep," said the sheriff. "He must know something about something." He started to get back in his car again. Lindsay held on to the door.

"Do you think maybe he knows it is really Mickey Lawson?" Lindsay asked.

"If he knew that, he would've told me and not her."

"I suppose so," Lindsay agreed. "Are you going to the Fourth of July picnic?"

"I do every year."

"Perhaps …"

The sheriff stood up, closed the door, and put a hand on Lindsay's shoulder. "Now, look, I don't want you to go snooping around at the Tylers. I can't, and you mustn't. Do you understand?"

"I want to know what is going on."

"So do I, and it is my job to find out. I don't come here and dig up your bones. Don't you go snooping around Merry Claymoore."

"Sheriff, I ..."

The sheriff's face softened. "I don't mean to sound harsh. Well, I suppose I do, too. I just want you to remember about Seymour Plackert's body floating down the river and landing at your dock. Something dangerous is going on in this town." The sheriff got in his car and drove off.

"What did he say?" Frank asked when Lindsay came back.

"Nothing much, except that he doesn't believe Ned's alibi."

Whited sepulchers, which indeed appear beautiful outward,
but are within full of dead men's bones.
—Matthew 23:27

Chapter 10

TYLERWYND WAS A LARGE antebellum mansion at the end of a long, winding drive lined by pecan trees. The lawn immediately around the house was neatly mowed and bordered by shrubs. Live oaks shaded parts of the lawn, their trunks surrounded by wooden and wrought iron benches.

Many cars were already parked in the black-topped parking lot for the guests, and Derrick pulled in beside Brian's car when he arrived with Lindsay, Michelle, and Jim. Jane, Sally, and Alan had ridden with Brian. Ned volunteered to stay at the site "to guard it from pothunters" as he said. Everyone was in good spirits, glad to be away from the site and ready for a picnic. However, Michelle, Lindsay noticed, was a little cool.

"It looks like Tara," Sally observed, looking at the three-story, white-columned house before them.

"I'd hate to vacuum the place," Jane said.

Frank pulled in beside them with Marsha and her

grandmother. Marsha helped the elderly woman from the car and introduced her to the others. "This is my grandmother, Elaine Darby."

Elaine Darby, who was dressed in a blue jogging suit, possessed the most silvery hair Lindsay had ever seen. It sparkled like strands of spun metal. She smiled at Lindsay, Derrick, and Sally.

"It's nice to meet you," she said. "Marsha has told me all about the work you do. It sounds so interesting."

Mrs. Darby used a walker, and they all slowed their pace to walk with her. "It's been a long time since I've been here," she said. "I used to come quite frequently, about ... my goodness, it must have been over 60 years ago. It looked the same then." She stopped, and they all stopped with her. "Except for this parking area, I don't believe there have been any other changes. Imagine that." Elaine Darby shook her head and continued toward the house.

"I had the display case delivered," Marsha told Lindsay. "It's supposed to be outside near the entrance. I hope it wasn't too much trouble to bring some artifacts."

"Not at all," Lindsay replied.

They were greeted at the door by the housekeeper, who ushered them through a wide central hallway. Mrs. Darby's slow pace allowed her and the others to look into the rooms as they passed. The furniture suited the house: highly polished antebellum pieces that looked as though they were never used. The housekeeper took them to a back patio where several long tables were set up amid flags, streamers, and a long banner welcoming the guests to the Tyler's 70th Annual Fourth-of-July picnic. Lindsay recognized several people from town, including the sheriff, milling around and talking to each other.

Marsha and Frank found a shady place for her grandmother to sit, and Derrick and Lindsay stayed to talk with them. The others wandered around the garden.

"Very odd," Mrs. Darby said. "It looks just like it did 60 years ago inside, too. I think I would get bored after a while with the same furniture in the same arrangement."

"Can I get you something to drink?" asked a young woman in a black dress and frilly white apron.

"Why, yes, dear," Mrs. Darby answered. "Bring us some lemonade. Do you have ginger cookies as well?"

"Yes, ma'am."

"Good. Bring us some of those, too. Tylerwynd is famous for its lemonade and ginger cookies," she confided to Lindsay and Derrick.

The display case was where Marsha said it would be. It was a small table with a hinged glass top that could be locked. Lindsay and Sally began setting the artifacts inside with their neatly printed identification cards. Lindsay had selected several potsherds, deciding that a whole pot would be too tempting to any potential pothunters at the gathering. She also decided against bringing the copper ear spools for the same reason. She did, however, bring a shell disk incised with designs; a mica cutout of a hand; two celts, both of which had a nice smooth axe shape; and a stone tool that might have been a hoe. She brought a mano and metatae and placed some corn in the depression of the metatae to show how it was used. Lindsay also selected several ceremonial points from the burials.

"That's a good selection," commented Frank over her shoulder.

"Marsha said you were bringing some of the things you dug up for us to see. That is so nice," said Mrs. Darby, who had walked over to see the artifacts.

"Well, Elaine, how good of you to come. It has been a long time," said an ancient, haughty, female voice.

They turned to see a tall, thin, elderly woman in a dark high-necked dress. She wore a long string of pearls that dripped down to her waist and a porcelain rose pin at her throat. Her hair was blonde and pulled tight into a bun on the back of her head. The thick pancake makeup accentuated rather than hid her deep wrinkles. Despite the careful use of a lip liner, her lipstick bled out into tiny lines around her lips. Large, penetrating blue eyes outlined in black and fringed with long false eyelashes gazed at all of them with what seemed to Lindsay like malevolent amusement. Diamond, emerald, and ruby rings glittered on her fingers gripping the silver head of a black lacquered cane.

"Isabel," said Mrs. Darby. "Yes, it has been a long time."

"You have been offered refreshment?"

"Oh, yes. A nice young woman went off to get us lemonade and ginger cookies. I was telling them how traditional they are at Tylerwynd."

Isabel Tyler smiled, and her eyes glittered. "Yes. Tradition is important. Who are these people you have brought with you?"

"You know Marsha, my granddaughter. This is Frank Carter. He is the chief archaeologist at the Jasper Creek archaeological site. You have read about it, haven't you, dear? This lovely young woman is Lindsay ... is it Chamberlain?"

"Yes," replied Lindsay. "Lindsay Chamberlain." If Isabel recognized the name, she didn't allow it to show.

"And Derrick Bellamy, I believe, but my memory is not what it used to be."

"That's correct," Derrick said. "How do you do, Mrs. Tyler? Your home is quite grand."

"Yes, it is," added Frank. "Thank you for inviting us."

Isabel abruptly turned her attention to Lindsay. "I believe I have read about you in the paper. You have helped the sheriff's office identify those poor children. One was my great grandniece, you know. I appreciate your assistance in helping with a family tragedy. Mike and Sarah won't be here, of course, but have you met the rest of my family?"

What a cold woman, Lindsay thought.

"We just arrived," Marsha replied. "I haven't introduced them to everyone yet."

"I've met your grandson, Mickey Lawson."

"Yes, Mitchell told me about his assistance in your identification."

"The details of camera measurements were a great help."

"It is interesting work you do, but a bit horrifying. Mitchell tells me you do something with the skeletons."

"Yes, I analyze the bones at the Indian site to find

out their age, gender, diseases. You can discover a lot of information about the lives of a people by studying their bones."

"I suppose, if you want to know that kind of thing."

"We do," said Lindsay. "These are some artifacts we have found at the site. We thought everyone would like to see what we were doing."

"Yes, very nice."

But Lindsay noticed that she did not even glance at the display case.

"Oh, this is my son Jacob Tyler. Jacob, these are the people from the ... what did the papers call it? A dig?"

Lindsay smiled at the man who had come to his mother's side. He was a heavyset, round-faced man in his 50s who tried to disguise his thinning hair with a comb-over. He wore dress pants and a short sleeve white shirt buttoned up to the top, but no tie. Jacob reminded Lindsay of a large child. He held out his hand for them to shake. His hands were unusually large, like slabs of pink meat with large protruding sausages. He smiled, shook their hands, and turned to Isabel.

"Mother, Winifred said everything is ready."

"Then we will sit down and eat. Tell her to serve when everyone is seated." She turned to her guests. "You will find your names on cards by the place settings."

Lindsay sat at the head of the table near Isabel. Frank sat beside Lindsay. Marsha and her grandmother, and Derrick had been placed at another table. Across from Lindsay was a woman who was introduced as Isabel's daughter, Esther Lawson, Mickey

Lawson's mother. Esther Lawson had dyed black hair pulled back in a stiff French twist. She wore a short sleeve black dress trimmed with black scalloped stitching. A white choker of pearls wound around her neck like a brace. She might have been a pretty woman, but her carefully applied makeup masked her features. She asked Lindsay and Frank about the site, all the while trying to find just the right place for her silverware, bread plate, and lemonade glass in relation to her dinner plate. The esthetics of her place setting was such a problem for her that both Lindsay and Frank stopped talking and watched.

"Stop it, Esther!" Isabel ordered. "You are attracting attention." Esther put her hands in her lap and grinned at Lindsay and Frank in obvious distress at having to stop without having solved the problem of the right arrangement for her dinnerware.

Two young women in uniforms began serving the food.

Rachel Somerton, another daughter of Isabel's, sat next to her sister and smirked at Esther's frustration while she asked Frank coy questions. Unlike Esther, Rachel wore a white dress covered with stitched eyelets. It had a frilly scooped neckline, puffed sleeves, and a wide yellow ribbon for a belt. Rachel also wore pearls, but they were long like her mother's, and she played with them, running them through her fingers. The Edwardian manner in which her brown hair was styled suited her attire. She was younger than her sister. Lindsay guessed her age to be about 40, but it had sneaked up on her so silently that she had not yet realized she no longer was 20. She reminded Lindsay of Delta Dawn.

"Oh, Mister Carter." Her breathy voice was so low Lindsay and Frank had to strain to hear her. "I thought about working at the site like Marsha. It sounds so exciting, but my skin simply can't take the sun."

"You can always wear a hat and sun block," Lindsay said. Esther tittered and reached for her glass of lemonade to arrange it. Her eyes darted toward her mother, and she took a drink instead.

"Oh, but I am allergic to sun block. My skin is just so sensitive," Rachel explained.

"How unfortunate for you," Lindsay sincerely replied, but the expression on Rachel's face told her that she expected to be admired for this trait.

Lindsay understood that Rachel's twin sister Ruth was the mother of Patrick. No one at the table mentioned either of them. Marsha had explained to Lindsay, when she asked why Patrick's last name was Tyler, that Isabel had made Ruth change his name when Ruth's husband divorced her.

Jacob Tyler sat to the left of his mother so he could be near if she needed anything, he said, and cast a glance at his sisters, who glared back. The sheriff sat on Isabel's right, looking ill at ease.

Marsha had told Lindsay that all of Isabel's children were divorced or had died, and that all of the ex-spouses lived in other states. She had also told her that Rachel had one daughter who had committed suicide and a son in an institution. "I am only telling you this so you won't ask Rachel if she has any children. As you can imagine, it is very painful."

"Your son, Mickey, took some portraits of me to give to my family for Christmas," Lindsay said to Esther.

She smiled broadly. "He is so good, isn't he? I taught him to be orderly and exacting. My teaching has served him well. He is in much demand. He's such a good son. He has never been on drugs or anything like that. I have never had a minute's trouble from him." She cast a sideways glance at her sister, who sat in stony silence. Lindsay wondered if she could bring up any topic that wouldn't lead to competition between the sisters.

Jacob had a son and daughter. The daughter, Lindsay was told, was married and lived in California. His son, Jarvis, sat at the far end of the table next to Mickey. He was a skinnier version of his father. Already his hair was thinning on top, and he had the same large hands. Lindsay shivered as she thought of Patrick's large hands.

"What does Jarvis do?" she asked.

"He helps Mickey in his studio sometimes," Jacob said. "He is quite a good photographer himself." Jacob glanced at his sister Esther, who ate quietly, pretending not to be listening to her brother. "He's thinking about going to the university to study film," continued Jacob proudly.

"That sounds very interesting," Lindsay said. Jarvis appeared about the same age as Mickey, in his early thirties. She wondered why he was so late in embarking on a career but decided not to ask.

"The university has a good film and drama department," Frank muttered, taking a large bite of barbecued pork.

Lindsay relaxed a little, finally believing Patrick was not there. She turned her attention to the bone structure of Isabel's face, trying to draw her into conversation so she could scrutinize it without being obvious, but Isabel was reticent. She preferred to watch her guests talk or to monitor her adult children's behavior. Or perhaps, Lindsay thought, she was piqued at her for bringing Patrick's behavior to the attention of the sheriff.

"That is a lovely pin," said Lindsay about the red-rose porcelain pin at Isabel's throat, making another effort to draw her into conversation. "Is it Dresden?"

"Yes, it is. My father gave it to me. Sixty years ago today, actually." She fingered it and seemed suddenly lost in thought.

Finally, thought Lindsay, some topic she is interested in. "I noticed one of the leaves is broken off. I can give you the name of someone who can repair it. Her work is flawless."

Isabel looked at Lindsay for a moment and almost smiled. Then she must have remembered who she was talking to. "I've been told it can't be repaired." She turned her head, dismissing any further conversation.

Dessert was home-churned peach ice cream. It was fresh and good, qualities that seemed so incongruous with the Tyler family. After dessert, the guests were invited to admire the house and gardens or they could watch Jacob do a few of his magic tricks for the children, play croquet on the lawn, or play softball in a field farther from the house behind a copse of trees.

Frank whispered to Lindsay that he was about ready to go back to Earth and went looking for Marsha. Lindsay found Derrick. "Not a bad barbecue," he said to her.

"You missed the entertainment. I'll have to tell you

about it later," she said.

"There are several outbuildings," Derrick said. "I think I'll do a little snooping."

"Be careful."

He smiled at her. "I will. You take care. Don't go wandering too far into that old house."

Lindsay went with several people to tour the downstairs portion of the house that was open to the guests. She found a large hallway with walls filled with paintings and large photographs. The paintings looked original, but she knew none of the artists. There were several wedding photographs, one for each of Isabel's children. All were formal, the women in long gowns and trains, the men in top hats and tails. It seemed a bit pretentious. The picture of Jacob Tyler in his formal attire standing by his bride looked familiar. It must have been hanging in Mickey's studio, she thought. Lindsay studied the spouses of Isabel Tyler's children, all smiles at their weddings. She wondered if they had any inkling at the time that marriage would not hold all the promise and gaiety of the wedding. Married life with a Tyler must have been a shock to them.

A large portrait of a man similar in appearance to Jacob attracted her attention. She noticed the thinning hair and the large hands.

"That's my father," spoke a breathy voice behind her. Lindsay stood aside, and Rachel came up beside her. She stared up at the picture in adoration. "I was his favorite, you know. He told me. He always said that I was his special little girl."

Lindsay looked over at Rachel's adoring face. She understood the love a daughter felt for her father, for she, too, was her father's little girl. But here in the dark hallway, standing in front of the portrait, Lindsay felt that Rachel was talking about a relationship that was wholly different from the one Lindsay had with her father.

After a moment, Rachel snapped out of her mood and turned to Lindsay. "I just met this gorgeous man from the site. He is tall, broad-shouldered, and has the most beautiful mane of hair."

"That would be Derrick," said Lindsay, smiling.

"Yes, Derrick. That was his name. Do you know him well?"

"Yes. Derrick and I went to graduate school together. Is this your mother?" asked Lindsay, gesturing to a silver framed sepia-toned photograph of a very beautiful young girl with long blonde hair held away from her face with bejeweled barrettes. The girl had a wisp of a smile on her face. She wore a lacy, high-collared dress fastened at the throat with her father's gift of the Dresden pin and a long string of pearls. The Fourth-of-July celebration in the background looked so much like the one occurring today, down to the placement of the tables and flags and welcoming 10th Annual Fourth-of-July picnic banner, it was amazing. These folks never changed anything.

"Yes, that's Mother," said Rachel. "Looks rather innocent, doesn't she?" Lindsay looked at Rachel and for the first time thought that she might be smarter than she let on.

A maid came by with some fresh lemonade and offered Lindsay a glass. She took it and wandered away from Rachel into the living room where another portrait caught her eye: a woman in English riding dress sitting on a horse. She held her derby and crop on her left thigh and her reins in her right hand.

"That is my mother. Isn't she beautiful?" Jacob asked from behind her.

Lindsay jumped. Did all of Isabel's children wander about the house admiring their parents' portraits?

"I didn't mean to startle you."

"That's all right. It is a beautiful picture." Lindsay stared at it in fascination.

"It was painted by a famous painter," Jacob continued.

"Yes, I am familiar with his work." Lindsay recognized the signature and the style of the artist.

"Are you?" Jacob smiled broadly, as if he hadn't really believed it was by a famous painter and was overjoyed to have it confirmed.

"Yes, though I am more familiar with his portraits of Derby winners."

"Derby winners?"

"Yes. Fletcher Kinneston painted the winners of major horse races in the U.S. and abroad in the '20s and '30s. My parents live in Kentucky, and my mother breeds Arabian horses. She has a portrait he did of a horse called Black Gold. This kind of portrait with a person as the subject is rare for him, which makes it very valuable."

"Why, yes, I guess it would, wouldn't it? Almost like one of a kind. I will have to tell Mother. She'll be so pleased. It's so nice of you to tell me that, and so clever of you to know."

Oh, I am more clever than that, thought Lindsay to

herself as she looked up at the painting.

Jacob wandered away, Lindsay supposed, to receive praise from his mother for the information he had learned from her. Only a few people seemed to be in the house. She heard a little boy ask a maid for directions to the bathroom, and she thought she heard Marsha and her grandmother. Alone, she tried a couple of doors that looked like they might lead either down or up but found them locked. To keep out people like me, she thought, and smiled to herself. As she walked into the large hallway and passed the parlor, Lindsay saw Isabel Tyler grab onto a little boy's arm. He looked about five and was clearly terrified.

"And just what were you stealing?" she asked in a raspy voice.

"Nothing ... nothing. Just looking for the bathroom."

"Don't lie to me. Do you know what I do to little boys who lie to me?"

The child tried to pull away, but the old lady held tightly to his arm. Lindsay walked into the parlor.

"Perhaps I can help," Lindsay said. "I heard him ask the housekeeper for directions to the bathroom. When you're five, getting lost in a big house is really easy." Isabel looked up at Lindsay as if she was a cat trying to steal her mouse. "I'm sure you don't realize it," continued Lindsay, "but you're hurting his arm." Isabel stared at her. Lindsay could feel Isabel willing her to leave them alone.

Lindsay said firmly. "You are wrong. He was not stealing anything. He just had to go to the bathroom. Let him go. If you don't, you are going to scare him, and he will go all over your Oriental carpet."

Isabel released his arm, and the kid ran. "Young woman," said Isabel, "this is my house, and I don't tolerate interference."

"I do apologize." Lindsay smiled her most gracious smile. "I would like to ask you a question. That portrait in the other room of the young woman on the horse. Is it you or your twin sister?"

Lindsay could only describe what came next as blind rage. Isabel Tyler shook from head to toe and gave Lindsay a look of absolute malevolence.

Suddenly, it seemed as if everyone had gravitated toward the parlor, for the large double doorway was filled with people. Jacob rushed in.

"Mother! Mother! What happened? Are you all right? What happened?" He put an arm around her shoulders and helped her to a chair. "What happened?" he looked up at Lindsay.

"I'm afraid it must be my fault," she said. "I mentioned her twin sister, and she became upset. I didn't realize it was a sensitive topic."

"Her twin sister?" Jacob looked confused. The two daughters rushed up to their mother's side.

Lindsay walked over to Derrick, who put an arm around her shoulder. Frank looked a trifle annoyed.

"I'm perfectly fine," said Isabel after a moment. "Get away from me, all of you! You are smothering me." She waved her cane, and her children slunk back. "I'm going up to my room. Say goodbye to my guests for me." She marched out, trailing her children in her wake. Everyone cleared a path for her.

"What is this about, Lindsay?" Frank asked.

"Just what I said. I would like to show you something," she whispered. She walked toward the living room. Frank, Marsha, and the sheriff followed her. Everyone else went back to the patio.

"I hope this is good." His voice was angry.

Lindsay whirled around and looked at him.

"It is," she said.

"I think we can trust Lindsay," Derrick defended her. Frank and his eyes locked for a moment, then Frank blinked.

"All right, show us."

Lindsay led them to the painting of the woman on the horse. "I know this artist. He mostly painted horses, and he paid particular attention to the bone structure, which is important in race horses. He actually takes measurements, and he is very accurate. This is supposed to be Isabel, but the only way it could be her is if she painted it herself by looking in a mirror." Lindsay looked around and saw that no one could see it. "This picture is a mirror image of Isabel. Look at the lack of symmetry in the brow ridge and cheek bones and compare it with Isabel's face. Hers is just the opposite. Can't you see it?" Lindsay realized that they couldn't perceive the fine distinctions in the features, and if they could, they had not scrutinized Isabel's face the way she had. "Isabel is left-handed. The person in this painting is right-handed. See how she is holding the reins? If you have to control your horse one-handed, you do it with the hand you have the most control over." Lindsay looked at them. "I guessed that the picture is really of a twin, a mirror twin, and I asked Isabel about it. That's when she became irate."

They all stared blankly, even Derrick. Then a voice

came from the corner. It was Marsha's grandmother. She had been resting on an antique stuffed chair.

"You have a good eye, Miss Chamberlain. Everybody knew, at one time anyway, that Isabel was deathly afraid of horses. She even made Edward tear the stables down. It was Augustine who loved horses. I remember when she had this painted. Augustine was Isabel's twin sister."

"So you have a good eye," said Frank, still not mollified. "Clever, but so what?"

"Don't you see?"

Suddenly Derrick's mouth dropped open. "I don't believe it. God, Lindsay, you're right!"

"What?" asked Marsha.

The sheriff had been studying the painting hard. Then he, too, realized. "Well, I'll be damned! It's her."

"Who?" asked Frank.

"Burial 23," Derrick replied.

They were all silent for a full minute, staring at the face in the painting. The sheriff spoke first. "Mrs. Darby, do you know what happened to Augustine?"

"Why, she disappeared. Let's see, about 60 years ago. Yes, 60 years ago today, in fact. The Fourth-of-July picnic was the last time anyone saw her."

When Lindsay told them she had finished the facial reconstruction of Burial 23, they decided to go back to the site immediately. Marsha's grandmother was delighted to be involved in a mystery, after she got over the shock that the long-lost Augustine may have been found.

"Augustine! After all these years, I can't believe

it," she said, shaking her head as they walked back to the car. "What a wonderful mystery. I get the volunteers to read me Agatha Christie and Mary Roberts Rinehart. I enjoy Miss Marple the most, but this is so much more exciting. Augustine. I can't believe it …"

They gathered around a picnic table and waited for Lindsay to bring out the reconstruction. The site was closed, and the crew who did not go to the picnic were gone for the day. It was about five minutes before she came from her tent with the bust and set it at the head of the table so that they all could see. It was covered with a cloth.

"I smoothed out the face and worked on the features. I painted the skin, put in the eyelashes, and bought a couple of wigs, a dark one and a blonde one. I put the blonde one on a minute ago. I have put in the eyes since you saw it last, sheriff." Lindsay removed the cloth, and they all gasped.

"Augustine, it is you. After all these years, you've been found," whispered Mrs. Darby.

"Mrs. Darby," asked the sheriff, "do you remember any details of her disappearance?"

Elaine Darby smiled slightly. "Oh, yes. It was all we talked about for a long time. And it was also at the same time I met David, Marsha's grandfather. He was a writer come down from the north to write about small southern towns during the Depression. He was part of the Work Projects Administration for writers. That was one of Roosevelt's programs to get the country out of the Depression. I was almost seventeen. Augustine and Isabel were a year older than me."

"I remember the first time I saw David. He was so handsome. He was getting off the train with a small suitcase in his hand and a shock of black hair falling in his face. I think I fell in love with him at that moment. I remember Augustine that day because she was meeting the train, too, and I was afraid that this handsome stranger would see her first and fall in love with her, as most of the boys did at one time or another. But he walked past her without even a glance.

"Augustine had on riding clothes, and I remember that she had Gideon and Victor—those were two of her horses—tied in back of the station, so I guessed she was meeting Edward Tyler. Both of them loved to ride."

"Let me get you something to drink, Mrs. Darby," said Derrick. He and Lindsay went to the cooler and passed around cold drinks to everyone.

"I was meeting Mother," Mrs. Darby continued after she had taken a sip of the cold drink. "She had gone to visit my aunt, who had just had a baby. She got off the train soon after David, so I didn't see who Augustine met. As it turned out, Mother had met David on the train and offered to put him up at our house. We took in boarders back then. A lot of people did. You did about anything you could do. Anyway, I was so pleased with my mother that day. I had picked her up in our old truck, and I didn't even mind that she sat between David and me. I remember looking out and seeing Augustine and whoever it was with her running their horses across the field. Augustine loved to ride.

"Augustine and Isabel Beaufort's father owned a dry goods store where the hardware store is now. If you look close to the top, you can still see the name *Beaufort* in large, faded letters. Their father, Rudolph Beaufort, was a strict man, but it didn't seem to do them any good. Both of them were wild and will-ful. Augustine and Isabel fought like cats and dogs. Teachers never put them in the same classroom if they could help it. Augustine was the nicer of the two, but that wasn't saying a whole lot. They were rich children, and every other child's father in school owed their dad money. They enjoyed their position in the community.

"Edward Tyler, Sr., was the only man in town richer than Rudolph Beaufort. He owned both the sawmill and the bank. His son, Edward, Jr., would have been the most eligible bachelor in town if he hadn't been such a scoundrel. He was always trying to get us girls alone and touch us. We always had to travel in twos and threes if he were anywhere around. But, I'll say one thing," she said, and nodded for emphasis, "he brought David and me together. Edward caught me out by myself, and he had ahold of me with those roving hands of his. That boy had the ugliest hands I have ever seen. Too big, I always thought. Anyway, he had just taken ahold of my arms and pushed me down when David came up behind him and knocked him down. Edward scrambled up and ran. He was a coward when it came to other men, even ones smaller than himself."

Elaine Darby took another drink, then smiled at the memory. "I remember David held out his hand, gallant as a knight. I took it, and he pulled me up." Then she frowned. "The thing that none of us could understand was that Augustine seemed to really love Edward, and he loved her. She was a pretty girl and could have just about anybody, for a while anyway, until her personality caught up with her." She shook her head. "We all guessed that the rich only liked the rich, no matter what kind of ugly rascals they were."

"You never told me these stories, Grandma," Marsha said.

Mrs. Darby shrugged and patted her granddaughter's hand. "It was a long time ago."

"The problem was," she continued, "Isabel liked Edward, too. But Isabel was such a hateful girl. Even a scoundrel like Edward did not like to be around her for very long. I remember overhearing an argument between Augustine and Edward that afternoon. The Tylers had us town folk over to Tylerwynd for the annual Fourth-of-July picnic, same as the one we had today. David and I were out by the stables when we heard Augustine's voice, and she was so angry. I can't remember after all this time exactly what she said, but at first I thought it was Isabel because it was so hateful. I do remember her saying something like, 'It may turn out to be a grand joke on Isabel herself.' She came charging out, Edward following meekly behind. David and I stood back in the bushes. That was the last time I ever saw Augustine."

"No one had any idea what happened to her?" Derrick asked.

"Oh, there were lots of ideas and rumors. There were just no real clues. No one saw any suspicious strangers or anything else. One theory was that Augustine fought with her father and ran away. They were always fighting, and Augustine was always threatening to go up north where there were more things to do. Another was that she got pregnant by some fellow passing through and ran off with him. I always wished it were that one, mainly because I didn't like to think she was dead, and I liked the idea of her jilting Edward. But it would not be like her to just leave her inheritance. One story went that Augustine got pregnant by Edward and he killed her. But he was crazy about her. Some said she was kidnapped and sold as a white slave. That one was popular with a lot of folk."

"What did you think?" asked the sheriff.

Elaine Darby shook her head. "I don't know. At the time, I thought she had just run off to worry everybody, but now ... I guess somebody killed her, didn't they? Isabel got everything she wanted after Augustine disappeared."

Marsha's grandmother shook her head again. "Isabel and Edward became engaged that next winter. After they married, Isabel started going to church. The family always went to church, but now Isabel took an active role. She became much more like her father—stern."

"I can remember always being scared of her when I had her for Sunday School," Marsha said.

"I sure remember her chasing me off her property once with that cane of hers," the sheriff said, grinning. "Me and a couple of buddies were in her strawberry patch. She caught old Billy and walloped him good with that cane. We pulled him away and got out of there fast."

"That's just the way her father was about the strawberry patch. Rudolph Beaufort refused to talk about Augustine. It was as if she never existed. He thought with all the stories going around, she had shamed the family. David and I got married that next year and moved away for about six years. A lot of people moved away from Merry Claymoore looking for work. When we moved back, no one ever mentioned Augustine. A lot of people didn't even know Isabel had a sister. I thought that was real sad." Mrs. Darby hesitated a moment. "Would you think it terrible of me if I asked to see her bones?"

"Of course not," said Lindsay. She rose and they went to the laboratory tent. Marsha, Mrs. Darby, and the sheriff walked in as if they were about to view a body. Lindsay retrieved the box containing Burial 23 and set out the bones on the table.

"Augustine, I'm sorry none of us knew what happened to you," whispered Mrs. Darby when Augustine's bones were laid out. "I know you loved living."

"Are you all right, Grandma?" Marsha asked.

"Yes, I'm fine, dear. It's just poor Augustine … All this time she was right here, and her father was too concerned about the family name to even look for her. That's all I know, sheriff."

"We'd better go back home, anyway," Marsha said.

"Frankly," said the sheriff when Marsha and Frank had gone to take Mrs. Darby back to her retirement home, "I'm going to have to figure out how to proceed on this thing. I don't know how Isabel is going to take it that her sister has been found after all these years."

"Who do you think killed her?" Derrick asked.

The sheriff shook his head.

"Isabel was certainly disturbed when I discovered that she even had a twin sister," said Lindsay. "It seems to me she would be the prime suspect."

"I'll have to see if I can find any old records on the case," the sheriff said. "I don't think I can accuse Isabel of murder based on her reaction to your statement. The woman is well-known for her strange reactions to people."

"It is not remarkable for one twin to have schizophrenia and the other one not," Lindsay said. "I suspect that is where the scenario of the so-called evil twin comes from."

"Are you saying Isabel is schizophrenic?" The sheriff was skeptical.

"No. I'm not an expert by any means, but people can lead relatively normal lives and have mild cases of it." Lindsay threw up her hands. "I don't know. I'm obviously reaching because of Isabel's dramatic reaction to my mention of her twin. I do believe this, however: The Tylers are a dysfunctional family, and Isabel is a sadistic old woman. After talking to Rachel, I suspect the daughters were molested by their father. One grandchild has committed suicide, another is in an institution, and others can't seem to choose a direction for their lives. Oddly enough, despite my suspicions of Mickey Lawson, he seems the most normal."

Sheriff Duggan said nothing. Derrick, too, was silent throughout her dissertation. Lindsay began to feel unsure. "I just find it more than a coincidence that so much seems to lead back to that family—Isabel's sister, Augustine, and her grandniece, Peggy Pruitt, both murdered. Two murders in the same family? What are the odds?"

"You're right. All roads seem to lead to the Tylers these days," the sheriff agreed while nodding his head. "But there is absolutely no real evidence that links them to anything. I'll question Isabel about her sister, but I'm sure not looking forward to that. Maybe some folks are still around who remember Augustine Beaufort's disappearance. Elaine Darby can't be the only one." The sheriff set down his drink bottle and stood up. "Don't get your hopes up that I'll find who killed Augustine Beaufort. After all this time, unless someone confesses to doing it or witnessing it, it's probably a dead end."

Lindsay and Derrick stood, too. "What about Mickey Lawson?" she asked. "I suppose that is a dead end, too?"

"I've been looking into his background. So far, I've not found any complaints of child molestation or anything like it lodged against him. There is usually a history of this kind of thing starting from a very early age, and it escalates. It's hard to believe that if he is guilty the molestation and murder just started as an adult. So far, I haven't come up with anything against him."

Derrick had a smug smile on his face. "This may help. I've been waiting to tell you and Lindsay some news that should make your job easier." He held out a plastic bag containing the rusted pan lock. "I did a bit of snooping around the Tylers' outbuildings. If you get a warrant for the one farthest from the house next to the pond, I believe you will find the tripod that this fits."

The sheriff stared at him for several moments before taking the bag from Derrick's hand. "It is one of them, then," he said quietly. "Probably Mickey." Then he looked up at Derrick. "This is the first direct evidence we have found. I'll get a search warrant."

"Do the Tylers have a lot of power in the community?" Derrick asked. "Maybe they paid people off."

"They used to. They still do with some of the old-timers. To tell you the truth, many of the younger people in Merry Claymoore find the Tylers a little too odd to take seriously. It helps that their financial holdings are not what they once were. They don't own the banks anymore, and the sawmill has a lot of competitors in the area. Most of their holdings now are in land, and I think stocks."

"I wonder," said Derrick, "if Isabel could be behind Seymour Plackert's accusations and murder. We thought it had something to do with the power company but couldn't think of any motive for them. Plackert was Isabel's lawyer, too, and it was her sister buried on the site."

"There's a lot to look into. And I'm still not satisfied that Ned doesn't have something to do with this thing. I'll tell you what I've been thinking," the sheriff said, "and I'm telling you this because since I've been working with you, I believe you really want to find the child killer and won't let friendship interfere."

"Of course," Lindsay agreed.

"I've been toying with the idea that there are two killers." Derrick and Lindsay looked at each other. "One taking photographs and another molesting and killing the children."

"We've had a similar idea," Derrick said.

"I think Mickey may be the photographer, and Ned may be the killer," the sheriff said, "and that is why Isabel sprung Ned—to avoid a scandal in her family."

Lindsay had to agree that it made sense. She hated it, but it made sense.

Lindsay and Derrick watched the sheriff drive off toward town. Some of the crew members were gradually coming back to the site. They could see the Fourth-of-July celebration was still going strong over at the scout encampment. Soon the fireworks would start.

Maybe this will be the end of it, Lindsay thought, but she doubted it would be the case.

Bones make good witnesses,
they never lie and they never forget.
—Clyde Snow

Chapter 11

FRANK BROUGHT THE newspaper when he came
to the site the next morning. Though Lindsay had
expected that Mickey Lawson would be arrested for
the murder of his niece, Peggy Pruitt, it still came as a
surprise. Isabel Tyler took to her bed, and the town was
divided on the issue. For the most part, the evidence
was circumstantial, except that it had been established
that Mickey had been the last person to see his niece
before she disappeared. Her mother had picked her up
from school and had taken her home, leaving her in
the backyard to play. It was thought that Peggy had
disappeared from there.

Upon closer inquiries from the sheriff, however, it
was discovered that the druggist had seen Mickey buy
her an ice cream cone thirty minutes after her mother
had last seen her. The druggist remembered the time
because his watch had chimed for his 3:30 pill. In
addition to the eyewitness evidence, it turned out that

Mickey owned the tripod found at the Tyler estate, the tripod that exactly fit the broken pan lock.

Mickey vehemently denied killing his niece or any of the other children. He did admit to taking Peggy for ice cream, but witnesses and family members reported that it had been a common practice. He was close to his cousin Sarah, and he often looked after Peggy for short periods of time.

"Why didn't you tell her mother that you took her?" the sheriff had asked.

"We often did that," Mickey had said. "She wasn't supposed to have ice cream so close to supper. It was just a thing we did."

When the dominoes started falling against Mickey, they fell quickly, thought Lindsay.

"Will you show me how to identify animal bones?" Sally asked later in the day as she helped Lindsay and Thomas take bones out of a large trash pit near the palisade. "I think I'd like to become a zooarchaeologist."

"Sure. First you divide them into mammal, reptile, fish, bird, amphibian, and unidentified bones."

"That's easy," Thomas said. "It's all unidentified bones to me."

Lindsay smiled. "It's really pretty easy once you develop an eye for it. Bird bone is lighter and has thinner walls." Lindsay looked around in the pile of bones. "This is the humerus of a wild turkey. All humeri tend to look alike. So once you've learned what the upper arm looks like, you can identify it immediately, no matter what animal it comes from."

She handed the bone to Sally. "Feel how light it

is and look down the middle of the shaft where it's broken. See how much smoother on the inside it is than, say, this deer bone?" Lindsay gave Sally a section of deer bone for comparison.

"Okay," said Sally. "Bird bone is light, smoother, and mostly hollow, and mammal bone has thicker walls and is heavier."

"Right. Some species of animals have specific bones that are easily recognizable. Take this for instance." She handed Sally a bone with a very prominent thin ridge running its length. "This is a breast bone, a sternum. Whereas human sternums look like an atlatl ..." Sally laughed, and Thomas rolled his eyes "... bird breast bones have this keel."

"What about reptile bones?" Sally asked.

"They are thick and heavy. I don't see any here, but once you see them, they are easy to recognize." Lindsay looked up to see the sheriff's car pulling into the parking lot. "Oh, dear," she whispered.

Thomas and Sally looked up from the bones. "What now?" Thomas exclaimed.

Sheriff Duggan and two deputies got out of the car and came walking toward the site, as if on a mission. Lindsay automatically looked to see if Ned was in Section 3. He was, and for a moment Lindsay thought he was going to drop his trowel and run. She could see his body tense, but he stood there watching the lawmen come to get him. The sheriff cuffed him, read him his rights, and led him off the site. They could hear the protest in Ned's voice but could not hear his words.

Frank came over to Lindsay. "I guess I had better follow in my car. Do you want to go with me?"

"Yes." She left Thomas and Sally to gather up the bones.

Frank and Lindsay sat in the sheriff's office in front of his desk. Sheriff Duggan sat looking grim, his hands clasped in front of him on top of his desk.

"Why did you re-arrest Ned?" Frank asked.

"I think Isabel Tyler gave him an alibi to protect Mickey. We can't find anyone to corroborate Mrs. Tyler's story that Ned was on her property that day or any other day. We are building a good case for Mickey murdering Peggy Pruitt. We believe we have a good case for Ned trying to kidnap Jenna Venable. If I can get them to tell on each other, I'll have them both for all the murders."

"I hate to hear that about Ned," said Frank.

"I know," the sheriff agreed. "I've known Mickey for a long time, too."

"Can I talk to Ned?" Lindsay asked.

"I don't know what you can accomplish," the sheriff answered.

"Perhaps nothing," Lindsay said, "but I won't do any harm."

The sheriff nodded and stood up. "I'll take you down there."

For the second time, Lindsay walked into the cell block. Nothing had changed. It still smelled and looked the same. She passed by Mickey's cell. He called out to them, and they stopped.

"You've got the wrong guy, sheriff. I didn't do this. Sarah's my cousin, for God's sake. I hardly know Ned. We went to school together when he was in Merry Claymoore, but we weren't friends. Hell, I wouldn't go on a life of crime with him. This is crazy. Dammit, Greg, let me out of here!"

"I know," the sheriff replied. "Everybody I lock up is innocent."

They came to Ned's cell. He was stretched out on his bed but sat up when the sheriff let Lindsay in. This time she didn't sit down but stood in front of him. Ned didn't rise. He looked as if he hadn't the energy.

"You came to see me again?" he asked. "I guess you think I did it."

"Actually, I don't," Lindsay replied, "though the sheriff is convinced you did. Jenna did identify you. That's pretty strong evidence."

"I know. I can't explain that. Why did you come by?"

"I want to ask you two things, and I want you to answer me with the truth."

"What?"

"Why did Isabel Tyler give you an alibi?"

"I guess I can tell you now. Last time I was here and you came, it got me to thinking about the past and staying with my grandparents. I remembered Grandma telling me about Isabel Tyler and her sister Augustine, how Isabel hated Augustine and how Augustine disappeared, how there were lots of rumors about what happened to her. It just dawned on me. That Burial 23. It could be her." He shrugged. "It was worth a chance, and I was right. Old lady Tyler came down here and gave me an alibi."

It has the ring of truth, Lindsay thought. "Okay. Why did you undermine Frank? Why did you think they were going to flood the site ahead of schedule?"

Ned took a deep breath. "Seymour Plackert told me that was their plan, and I thought he knew. He told me he would help me be in charge of the dig."

Lindsay was not surprised. She had thought it was something like that. "He was lying to you," she said.

"I know that now."

"Did you know he was going to plant pot at the site?"

Ned sighed. "He asked me to do it." He looked up at Lindsay, his eyes puffy and bloodshot. "I refused. I did. That's why he hired that other guy."

"What if they had found the pot in Derrick and Brian's tent?" she asked.

"I would've said something," Ned mumbled.

Lindsay wondered if he would have.

"Plackert using you that way gives you motive to murder him."

Ned stood up and faced her. "I didn't, Lindsay. I'm not a killer, for heaven's sake. I'm not a killer."

"Do you know who killed him?"

"I have no idea, and I've racked my brain. I knew how it would look for me if this came out."

"Thanks for telling me."

"You believe me?"

"Yes, I do." Lindsay put a hand on his shoulder. "Take care. I'll see what I can do."

Lindsay called for the sheriff to let her out. The keys clanked loudly against the cell door as he opened the lock. Every noise seems loud down here, she thought. As they walked back to his office, Lindsay told the sheriff why Isabel Tyler gave Ned the alibi.

"Don't you think he heard what happened at the picnic and just made up the story?"

"His story sounds true to me."

"Well-crafted lies usually do."

Lindsay didn't tell him about Ned's association with Plackert.

"Thank you for letting me see him."

"It doesn't make me happy doing this," he said.

Lindsay stopped and looked at him. "I didn't think it did," she said. "We all want this solved with the true solution. It just doesn't feel right to me about Ned."

"I don't imagine he put child killing on his resume," the sheriff said darkly.

"You believe it's him, don't you?"

The sheriff let out a long breath. "The little girl identified him, and he lied about his alibi."

"He was scared, and ... and I don't know about the identification."

The sheriff put an arm around her shoulder. "I understand how you feel." He squeezed her shoulder, then dropped his arm to his side. "How do you think I feel locking up Mickey? I've known him a long time. I've got half the town wanting to lynch him, and the other half telling me I'm a damn fool."

"I know. It's bad any way you look at it."

"Yes, it is. Go back to the site and dig up artifacts and try to forget this. It's not that I don't appreciate the help that you ... and Derrick ... have given me, but now I think you are too close."

Lindsay said nothing as she walked with the sheriff to his office. She wasn't sure she was objective anymore either. When she was talking to Ned, he seemed truthful and she believed him. Away, talking with others, she had doubts.

• • •

Frank took Lindsay to the diner to eat before they went back to the site. She told him everything Ned had told her.

"I wasn't aware until all this came up how much it meant to him to be in charge of this particular site," said Frank.

"Everything he said sounded so true," Lindsay said.

Frank shrugged. "I can't imagine him killing the children. But Plackert, that's a different story. As much as the site meant to Ned, to discover that Plackert was using him and may have cost him all association with the site ... well ..."

"I know," Lindsay agreed. "I think I might hang up this detective business and become an archaeologist. What do you think? Do you think archaeologists run into this much murder and mayhem?"

Frank laughed and bit into his sandwich.

On the way back to the site, Lindsay and Frank passed the entrance to Tylerwynd. "The answers are there," she said. "Everything has led to the Tylers, one way or another."

"Why don't you forget about it?" Frank asked.

"I've tried that."

"Funny, when we began this site, I thought we were becoming close. Now it seems we have grown apart," he said.

"Not so much grown apart," said Lindsay. "You've become involved with Marsha."

"And you have become close to Derrick."

"Derrick and I have always been close."

"This is different."

Yes, thought Lindsay, it feels different. She was going dancing with him over the weekend. They had gone on dancing trips before—to Paris and London—when they were competing. But she had never felt about him the way she did now. She found it strangely unsettling. Lindsay closed her eyes and rubbed them. Perhaps, she thought, because so much has gone on at the site, so much mystery and no closure.

"Why are you bringing this up?" she asked.

"I don't know. Wistful, perhaps, for what might have been, what might be." Lindsay looked over at him. It's caring about two men at the same time that is so disconcerting, she thought.

Everyone had questions when she and Frank arrived back at the site. Lindsay left Frank to answer them and went to her tent. She sat down on her bed, then stood up. The unsettling feeling that the case was not solved, when everyone else thought it was, wouldn't let her rest. If the sheriff were wrong about Ned ... if she were wrong about Mickey ... then there was someone else out there ready to prey upon another little blonde girl. Perhaps he had already. Lindsay couldn't get the image of the damaged little bones out of her head. She hurried out of her tent, walked across the grass, and started into Derrick's tent.

"So, you'll take me then, and teach me to dance—" It was Michelle. She had her arms around Derrick's neck. They both looked at Lindsay standing in the doorway of the tent.

There was a sudden lurch in Lindsay's stomach. "I'm sorry, Derrick, I didn't realize you had company," she said. Lindsay was stunned, confused, and on the verge of tears. She didn't know if she wanted to cry, to shout at Derrick, or to knock Michelle into the middle of next week. She wanted to do all those things. She turned and started to walk back to her tent but instead walked into the woods toward the beach. She hadn't gotten far when she felt a hand grip her arm. She realized then that her heart was pounding. She turned around, and Derrick gripped her shoulders.

"Lindsay," he said, "Michelle wanted me to teach her how to dance. I agreed, and she was grateful." Derrick's voice was steady and firm, with no trace of contrition.

"It's none of my business—" she said.

"Whether it is or not, it has nothing to do with the two of us. Why did you leave so abruptly?"

"Well, you were obviously busy." Lindsay felt like a jealous school girl. She stepped back to free herself, but Derrick didn't let go.

"Look—" she began.

"No, you look." Derrick put an arm around her waist and his other hand on the back of her head and kissed her. Lindsay started to put her arms around him when he let her go and started to say something. Suddenly, he looked past her and took off running deeper into the woods.

Lindsay was puzzled for a second, then ran after him. Ahead, she heard a thrashing in the woods. Derrick had knocked someone down.

"You're not supposed to come around here, you little creep!"

Oh, God, thought Lindsay, not him. He is supposed to be gone. Anxiety churned her stomach. Patrick lay sprawled on the ground rubbing his jaw. A camera had fallen and rolled to the base of a tree. Derrick started for Patrick again, but Lindsay put a hand on his arm.

"Patrick, the sheriff told you not to come around here," she said.

"It's a free country," he mumbled.

"Not everywhere," Derrick said, "and not for you if you don't leave Lindsay alone. Now leave while you still have both your arms."

Patrick scrambled to his feet and started for his camera. Derrick picked it up and threw it hard. It soared through the air and into the river.

"That's my camera. Who do you think you are?" Patrick seemed close to tears.

"Go home, Patrick," Derrick said. Patrick looked defiant for a moment, glanced at Derrick, then ran off toward the river.

"What was he doing in the woods?" Lindsay asked.

"Lurking, I imagine. Trying to get pictures of you." Derrick put an arm around her shoulders. "I've made arrangements for us to go to Atlanta this weekend," he said.

"With all that is happening, Ned in jail and everything, don't you think we should wait—" Lindsay said.

"No. There are things I want to say to you, and I don't want to say them here."

They walked back to the site together, silent, deep in their own thoughts. It would be another hour before it was time to quit the site. Lindsay went to check on the caches of animal bones she had assigned to Sally and Thomas.

• • •

It has been a long day, Lindsay thought. She had promised to meet Sally in the laboratory tent to go over the bones with her. She was tired and wanted to shower and go to bed. She checked the edges of the plastic covering the features she had been excavating to make sure they were sufficiently anchored. As she started toward the laboratory, her path was blocked by Michelle, her hands on her hips, her face red. She clearly was angry.

"Do you enjoy this, or is it so automatic that you don't even know what you are doing?"

"Michelle, what are you talking about?"

"Please, Lindsay, get that sweet and innocent concerned-but-bewildered look off your face."

"I'm sorry I interrupted you today. Is that what you are angry about?" Lindsay started to go around her, but Michelle moved to block her path.

"I don't think you are a bit sorry. But you are so good at what you do, it even took me a while to catch on." Michelle dropped her hands to her sides. Her eyes narrowed.

"What do you mean?" Lindsay's head hurt from the heat, and she was running out of patience with Michelle.

"The way you stay poised between Frank and Derrick. You stand between them, so elegantly undecided." Michelle mimicked graceful arm movements and pitched her voice several notes higher. "Is it Derrick or Frank? Frank or Derrick? Oh, how can I decide?" She stopped for a moment, then spoke in her normal voice. "You make me so sick."

"Michelle, I don't know what you are talking about," Lindsay said. It was the hottest part of the day, and the heat was reflecting off the light, smooth surface of the site. Michelle was already wet from working all afternoon in the heat, and Lindsay could feel the trickle of perspiration down her own face and under her arms. She was having trouble keeping her thoughts straight.

"How do you think Marsha feels?" Michelle asked.

"Marsha?"

"Yes, Marsha," said Michelle. "She deserves more than what she is getting right now, and I think she is being a very good sport about it. Just as soon as she makes some headway with Frank, you come along again with that maybe-it's-you-after-all look, and he goes panting after you again."

"Has she said something to you?" Lindsay asked.

"No, but I can see it on her face."

"Why doesn't she say something?"

"Say what? How can she compete with you? She's a small town girl, and you're the great Lindsay — well-educated, beautiful, self-assured. Hell, you've even got the sheriff panting after you."

Lindsay raised skeptical eyebrows. "Michelle—"

"It's true."

Lindsay's face was hot, although from the sun or from her rising anger she didn't know. "What about you?" she said. "You are well-educated, beautiful, and self-assured. What's your beef?"

"Derrick. It's the same with him. If I try to pursue him, you are always there to turn his head, and you aren't even serious. Like awhile ago. You no sooner turned on your heels in a pout, than he was after you, explaining and apologizing."

"There was no apology. Derrick never apologizes

for anything he is not guilty of. If you knew him better, you would know that. Exactly what do you want, Michelle?"

"Choose. Let one of them go."

"I see, and if I should choose Derrick?"

"At least I'll know. I won't be thinking you've gone on to other pastures only to have you come back. And if you do choose Derrick, I'm giving you fair warning that I like him and intend to fight for him, too."

"Michelle, I suppose it's useless to tell you that you have characterized this all wrong. Whatever Frank and I do, Derrick will always be a good friend. And I will not stand here and play little girl games with you. Sally is waiting for me in the laboratory."

Lindsay brushed past Michelle and hurried to the lab. At first she was angry, but by the time she got to the lab, she was wondering if there wasn't some truth in Michelle's accusation. Come on, she said to herself, Frank and Derrick are adults. They can choose for themselves.

The laboratory was lined with cabinets and boxes for storing artifacts. In the middle were long tables where the crew could sit and sort bags of artifacts separated out during flotation. On rainy days and sometimes after the site shut down at three o'clock, the crew would work in the lab to get a start on cataloging the artifacts before they were taken to the university.

Sally was already working with some animal bones when Lindsay sat down next to her.

"I got Feature 15 out and have divided the bones the way you were telling us today," Sally said. "At least I think I have. I want to learn how to determine minimum number of individuals, and estimate their meat yield, too."

"We'll do that at the university. That requires a lot of weighing and measuring that we are not equipped for here. Let's see what you have." Lindsay looked through the bones. "Not bad. There are several in the category of 'unidentified bones' that can be identified." Lindsay began picking out the bones. "For instance, this is the left maxilla of a fox."

"How can you tell? It's only part of a bone and no teeth!"

Lindsay grinned. "But the sockets where the teeth were are still there."

"Great! Don't all sockets look alike?"

"No. The teeth of different animals have different shapes. Besides, there is enough bone left to identify the animal. I know it's a fox because I know what a fox maxilla looks like. Any time you are identifying animal bones for permanent identification, you use the reference collection and compare this bone with known bones in the collection. I'll show you how when we get back to the university. However, it will save us a lot of time later if we can sort as much as we can now."

"Okay, then it is a fox because it looks like a fox," said Sally. "I'm catching on."

Lindsay smiled and searched around in the boxes. "Okay, here is a good example."

"Another left fox maxilla?" Sally looked at the partial bone that, to her, looked similar to the other one.

"No, look carefully at the shapes of the bones and the number of teeth each had. Count the sockets. Not the spaces for the roots, but the socket for the whole tooth."

Sally took a pencil and pointed to each as she counted, then recounted, each space for a tooth in the maxilla. "The first one has 10 and the second 13, an unlucky number."

"It is. I imagine that is why they have trouble crossing the road."

"What?" asked Sally.

"The second is the left maxilla of an opossum." Lindsay searched around in the box of bones until she found an opossum skull and a fox maxilla with the teeth. Sally leaned in closer to see what Lindsay was pointing out to her. "Different animals have different dental formulas," Lindsay continued. "An opossum is a marsupial. The upper teeth of marsupials have a dental formula of 5 1 3 4, which means on each side of the maxilla they have five incisors, one canine, three premolars, and four molars."

Sally took the bone from Lindsay and ran her finger down the row of teeth.

"The dental formula for the fox's upper teeth is 3 1 4 2," Lindsay said. "Because different teeth also have different shapes, it is fairly easy to identify what kind of tooth came out of an empty socket."

"Clever," Sally said. "It's just like a magician. Once you learn the trick, it's not magic any more. It's easy."

"Great," Lindsay replied. "I have completely destroyed my mystique. And you used to think I was so good."

Sally giggled.

"Let's go through the mammal bones. I'll identify each one by genus and species, and you write it down."

Derrick came in and pulled up a chair beside Lindsay. "You guys want to go eat?"

"Sure. Let us ID this box of mammal bones," Lindsay responded. "It won't take long."

The bones were straightforward, mostly *odocoileus virginianus* (white-tailed deer) and *sciurus carolinensis* (gray squirrel). There were also some *ursus americanus* (black bear), *ondatra zibethicus* (muskrat), *procyon lotor* (raccoon), and, of course, *didelphius marsupialis* (opossum).

Lindsay thoroughly enjoyed herself with the bones.

"Slow down," Sally said. "I've got to write these things down."

"You can put the first letter of the genus along with the species name," Lindsay said.

"Now you tell me."

Lindsay picked up another bone. It had a double row of incisors. "*Sylvilagus floridanus. Sylvilagus floridanus,*" she said again slowly.

"You don't have to go that slow. I got it. *S. floridanus,*" said Sally.

Lindsay looked at Sally so suddenly Sally jumped.

"That's what it is, isn't it?" Sally said.

"What did you say a while ago about a magician?"

Sally wrinkled her brow. "About once you learned their tricks—"

"Derrick, that may be it. I assumed that the rabbit found at the crime scene was *sylvilagus*, but what if it was an *oryctolagus*?"

"Did I miss something?" Sally asked.

Derrick looked thoughtful. "What are you talking about? You think the rabbit at the crime scene is European? How did you get there from here?"

"We have whole theories about how artifacts are lost, saved, and distributed about their site. Those theories are a big part of our analysis, and we failed to apply any of them to the crime scene."

"What do you mean?" Derrick asked.

"Why aren't skeletons of dead animals found all over the woods? The woods are full of thousands of animals."

"That's a good question," Sally agreed. "I've been all over these woods and haven't found any."

"Because they get scattered and carried off by other animals," Derrick explained. "It's part of the process of forest ecology."

"Then why did you find a whole rabbit skeleton at the crime scene?" Lindsay asked.

Derrick's eyes widened. "Because it was buried, and that is how artifacts get saved intact. It wasn't a *sylvilagus*, a wild rabbit that just died there. Its bones would have been scattered. It was an *oryctolagus*, a pet rabbit, that someone buried there."

"Yes," Lindsay added, "the kind a magician might pull out of a hat."

"I'm afraid you're going to have to spell it out for me," Sally said.

"That's what the killer might have used to lure the children. A pet rabbit. The children would know and would not be afraid of a magician who works at school fairs and Fourth-of-July picnics. It fits."

"He wears that big false mustache and has a round face. He could be mistaken for Ned by a small child," Derrick said.

"I guess we'd better see the sheriff," Lindsay said.

• • •

"What? A magician?" the sheriff exclaimed to Lindsay, who sat on the other side of his desk.

"Jacob Tyler," said Lindsay. "Think about it. The mustache Jenna Venable saw. It was a better disguise than he had hoped. She thought it was Ned because Ned's mustache looks particularly large the way it wraps around his face and connects with his sideburns."

"At the same time," Derrick prodded, "most of the kids would recognize the magician they had seen at their school. Parents usually tell their kids not to talk to strangers. He had the same access to the children and the tripod that Mickey had."

"Can't you give me anything more than that?"

"No."

"Then all you have is a guess that because Jenna described a man in mustache and Jacob Tyler sometimes wears a large mustache and sometimes entertains children, that he is the killer. I'm sorry, Lindsay, but that is nothing. Look, people are sleeping more easily now. Many think we have the right man. I don't want to go saying it may be another man without more proof."

"Can we look at the crime scene evidence again?" Lindsay smiled sweetly at the sheriff.

"Why? What have you discovered?"

Derrick grinned at him. "Can we take a look?"

In the evidence room Lindsay spread the rabbit bones from the crime scene out on the table next to the wild rabbit bones she brought from the Indian site. The sheriff and Derrick looked over her shoulder.

"Look how much larger they are," she said. "These are not the bones of an American wild rabbit."

"You mean this could be the rabbit in the picture of Jacob Tyler in his magician's getup?" the sheriff asked.

"Maybe, but I doubt it. I'm sure he has used lots of rabbits."

"I'll admit this is a good clue. But it might be like the dog. The killer grabbed a little girl with her pet rabbit."

"I hadn't thought of that," Lindsay said, a little dismayed. "But the girls' mothers can tell you if any one of them had a pet rabbit. Don't you have enough reason to talk to Jacob Tyler now?"

"I can talk to him, and I will. But he doesn't even need a lawyer to know that what we have is nothing."

"But maybe if he knows he is being watched, he will stop," Lindsay suggested.

"Maybe for a while," the sheriff responded. "What we need are the pictures the killer took at the crime scene. They weren't in Micky Lawson's files or at his house. They've got to be somewhere if they haven't been destroyed. I'm afraid any first-year law student could get either Ned or Mickey off. And both of them are sticking to their innocence."

"The Tyler mansion. That's where the tripod was found. That's where the pictures are," Derrick said. "Can you get a warrant for it?"

"I don't know."

"Then you think this is credible," said Lindsay.

"What you said makes sense. That pet rabbit got itself buried at the crime scene somehow."

Pain wanders through my bones like a lost fire;
What burns me now? Desire, desire, desire.
                                        —Theodore Roethke
                                        The Marrow

Chapter 12

LINDSAY AWOKE EARLY, as usual. The sounds and smells of night were still in the air. After today's digging, Derrick and she would be going to Atlanta, and she was surprised at how much she was looking forward to it. She stretched, then jumped out of bed. It was a cool morning, so she put on jeans and a long-sleeved, white cotton shirt. She could change later when the site started to heat up. No one else seemed to be stirring, so Lindsay decided to take a walk by the river in the cool morning air before the site crew arrived.

The sun was just below the horizon, and the sky was a faint orange. The deer trail she followed through the woods was barely visible. As the silvery glitter of the river came into view, Lindsay caught the smell of something out of place, but vaguely familiar. Suddenly, someone grabbed her and put a rag across her face. It was chloroform, someone was— She tried to scream and almost choked. She couldn't breathe, couldn't move her arms. She tried to kick, but her effort had no effect. The grip tightened around her, and she grew weaker as she struggled to get a breath. She couldn't fight. She couldn't think. Everything went black.

Lindsay awoke sick to her stomach. Her head was pounding, and the taste and smell of chloroform was in her mouth. She was in a moving vehicle, bouncing mercilessly on its ridged floorboard. Her mouth was taped shut, and she tried to move, but her hands were tied behind her back and her feet bound with duct tape. She attempted to raise her aching head but only succeeded in banging it against the hard floor. She managed to roll onto her back and could see the tops of trees rushing by the windows. She was in a Jeep being driven deep into the woods. Each bounce of the Jeep seemed to add tenfold to her misery, and she strained to turn her head to see who was driving. It was Patrick Tyler.

How dare he? she thought. Anger surged through her, partially reviving her, and she struggled at the bindings that held her. Patrick looked back, as if sensing her consciousness, and she saw madness in his eyes and hatred in the twist of his mouth.

"You're awake. I want you to be awake," he snarled before turning around again.

Lindsay continued trying to loosen her bindings, but the tape was too strong and tight. She looked around for something that might cut them. One of the site shovels lay a couple of feet from her. She saw the large black letters of the site number written on the wooden handle. Derrick kept all the site shovels razor-sharp. She tried to scoot toward it, but the ride was too rough.

As the Jeep drove deeper into the woods, Lindsay wondered if anyone had seen what had happened to her. How would anyone possibly know where to look for her? Her aching head and sluggish thoughts prevented her from forming any reasonable escape plan. Suddenly the Jeep stopped, banging her against the front seat.

Patrick came around back, opened the tailgate, and pulled her out. He had a gun tucked in his pants and a knife hanging in a scabbard on his belt.

"How did you like that ride, bitch?" he yelled, pushing her to the ground and kicking her in the side. "Do you know what she did to me because of you? She screamed at me, called me a stupid moron in front of everybody. And she beat me with that cane of hers. Even after what I did for her. They all stood around, watching and grinning. Even Mother stood there with that stupid grin of hers, afraid to do anything to help me."

Lindsay tried to talk, to answer him through the tape covering her mouth. Her nose was running, and she was sick to her stomach. It was hard to breathe. Patrick laughed at her distress.

"Not such a prima donna now, are we, bitch!" He reached his big hand to her face and ripped off the tape.

Lindsay gasped at the pain, and she choked on the fresh air as she inhaled. "What are you talking about?" she protested, coughing and trying to breathe slowly so she would not throw up.

"Don't pretend you don't know. I know you went to the sheriff and gave him the gifts I left for you, showed him the panties. Why did you do that? Those were intimate things between a man and a woman. You had no right to show them to the sheriff."

"You had no right to steal my underwear. What was I supposed to think about you?"

"I just wanted something of yours. I loved you. I would've been nice to you. Now I'm going to treat you like what you are, just another bitch. I'm not going to be nice to you. I'm going to take what I want, then bury you out here in the woods where no one will ever find your body. Then I'm going back and shoot that boyfriend of yours in the head. He shouldn't have done that to me. No, he shouldn't have. Maybe before I kill him, I'll tell him what I did to you. Yeah, I'll do that." Patrick nodded his head up and down, grinning.

Lindsay's fear, along with the lingering effects of the chloroform, were making her sicker. God, she thought, he wants to kill Derrick, too. She had to stop him. Lindsay tried to move, but her side hurt and waves of nausea surged through her continuously. Think, she thought, think. You have to get out of this.

"You have nothing to say, bitch? I'll bet you wish you had been nice to me now. It was me that followed you in the car that night. You almost wrecked turning onto the dirt road." He grinned wickedly. "I came out to the site with the mayor and sheriff when you all first got here, but you didn't notice me, did you, bitch? But I noticed you. Even all covered with mud, I could see you were for me." He scowled. "Say something, bitch!"

"Do you have any water?" she asked.

"Sure." He grinned. "Anything you need. You're going to need all your strength to dig your grave."

He knelt and shoved a canteen at her, and she took a couple of small sips before he pulled it back, but that was all she wanted. Any more than a sip or two would further agitate her queasy stomach.

Patrick reached into the Jeep, brought out the shovel, and stood it against the side of the vehicle. He slid the knife from its scabbard in a slow menacing motion and waved it in front of Lindsay's face before cutting the tape that bound her legs. When he pulled her to a standing position, she staggered and fell against him. He stood there with his arms around her and began to rub his hands all over her.

"I'd wait until the effects of the chloroform wear off, or I'm likely to vomit all over you. I don't think that is what you have in mind."

He pushed her away. "I can wait. Nobody knows you're here. I have all the time in the world. There's a clearing at the end of the trail. That's where I'm going to bury you. A little digging will work the chloroform out of you. You should be good at digging graves." He laughed as if he had said something clever. "Besides, I haven't decided everything I want to do to you yet. I'll tell you what I'm planning while you dig. You ought to enjoy that."

"You don't want to do this." Lindsay tried to think of something persuasive to say, but everything that went through her mind sounded like begging. She didn't think that begging would work.

"You don't know what I want to do. You don't know what I can do. She thinks she's in charge of everything. She doesn't know the things she made me do make me stronger than her. I'll show her. I'll show you. I'll show them all. Then I'll see them stand there, scared shitless of me."

As Lindsay walked along the narrow path, her hands still bound behind her, she only half listened to Patrick's babbling. She concentrated on finding an escape route. A clearing was visible just ahead, and beyond it the woods grew thick. If she could reach the dense undergrowth before he caught or shot her, she might get away.

"I can't wait to see your Derrick's face when I tell him what I did to you."

Lindsay blinked back the tears. Escape, she thought. Concentrate on escape, not fear. Not nausea, not pain. Escape.

They reached the clearing, and he cut the tape that bound her hands, then pushed the shovel at her. "Now dig," he ordered, taking his gun from his pants.

Lindsay didn't even think. She turned and swung the sharpened shovel, hitting him as hard as she could, and ran. She heard gun shots and felt a burning pain in her thigh that knocked her to the ground. She rolled over and managed to get back on her feet. The pain in her leg was intense, but she struggled to run faster. She tripped over a root and fell again.

Risking a backward glance, she saw Patrick running toward her with the gun. His left arm dangled at his side bleeding profusely where the shovel had cut into it. She tried to scramble to her feet as he aimed the gun. He was screaming at her, and his right arm was shaking. She prayed for him to miss.

As if by magic, the point of a spear emerged from Patrick's stomach. He fell to his knees, dropping the gun. Bright, red blood dripped from the shiny obsidian point, but only a little blood seeped around the wooden shaft. Patrick put a hand around the thick shaft protruding from his abdomen and looked at Lindsay, bewildered. She was bewildered, too. Then she saw Derrick running toward them. He was carrying his atlatl.

Derrick reached Lindsay and knelt down beside her.

"He shot me, Derrick." Lindsay's voice was weak and pitiful.

"I know." Derrick cut her jeans with his knife and exposed the wound in her thigh. He tore a strip of cloth from his shirt and placed it over the wound.

"It hurts really bad," Lindsay said, starting to cry.

"I know, baby. I'm going to get you help real soon." He tore another piece from his shirt and placed it around the back of her thigh at the entry wound. Then he tied his bandanna around her leg.

"Is he dead?"

"I don't know."

As if answering, Patrick groaned.

"Why is he still on his knees like that?" she asked.

"I don't know. Don't look at him, sweetheart."

"We should do something."

"I'm going to get you out of here first."

Derrick picked her up and carried her through the woods to his Jeep, just as the sheriff's car came charging up the old roadbed and stopped beside them. The sheriff, a deputy, and Frank jumped out.

"Patrick is down that trail. He shot Lindsay. I have to get her to the hospital."

The sheriff waved them on. "I'll talk to you at the hospital."

"I'll drive," Frank said. "You hold Lindsay in the back." They climbed into Derrick's Jeep, and Frank started the engine and headed out of the woods. "Is it too rough?"

"Just get her to the hospital," Derrick begged. "She's losing a lot of blood." Frank drove faster.

"How did you know where to find me?" Lindsay asked.

"Marsha. She arrived at the site early and saw Patrick's Jeep heading into the woods like a bat out of hell. She thought something was wrong," Derrick answered.

"Marsha," whispered Lindsay. "That woman is everywhere."

"Hush," Derrick said.

"My leg hurts. Would you get me an aspirin?"

"It will be all right. The doctors will give you something when we get to the hospital," he whispered.

Frank arrived at the dirt road, drove a mile, and turned onto the paved road leading to town.

Derrick held her closer. "Hurry," Lindsay heard him say before she lost consciousness.

Lindsay awakened in a hospital room. Her head was throbbing, and her leg ached. When she tried to move, her side hurt. She turned her head and saw Derrick asleep in a chair. He opened his eyes, sensing her movement.

"Welcome back," he said, coming over to her.

"I feel so …"

"They had to do a little repair on your leg, but you'll be fine, dancing in no time," he said, taking her hand.

"Dancing … I'm sorry about this weekend …"

Derrick shook his head. "There'll be plenty of weekends. Try to get some sleep." He stroked her hair.

"What happened to … to … Patrick?" she asked.

"Patrick is in intensive care. He had surgery. I don't know how he is."

"Thank you for rescuing me."

He took her hand and kissed it. He was all out of smart replies, and his eyes misted over.

"I'm all right," Lindsay said.

"I know."

Lindsay tried to sit up

"Try to rest," he told her.

"No, I need to be awake. Please help me."

Derrick helped Lindsay into a sitting position and put extra pillows behind her. "How's that?"

"Better. What did the doctors say?" she asked.

Derrick moved the chair closer, sat, and held her hand. "The bullet went clean through. It didn't hit an artery or bone or anything. You didn't lose as much blood as it looked when I brought you in. You have a slight concussion, and the doctor wants to keep you for a couple of days. You also have some bruised ribs. What happened? How did he get you?"

"I went for a walk by the river before daylight. He caught me from behind and held chloroform over my face. The next thing I knew, I was bound in the back of his jeep, riding through the woods."

"What else? Tell me about it if you can."

"He wanted me to dig my grave, and he wanted to kill you."

"God, Lindsay. I'm sorry I let him hurt you."

"It wasn't your fault."

"I told you I'd keep you safe."

"Aren't we getting rather traditional all of a sudden? I thought that was my job. Everything is all right now. Did you call my parents?"

"Yes. I talked to your father. I told him you were going to be fine."

"What time is it? How long have I been here?"

"It's about 2:00 in the afternoon."

"Have you been here the whole time?"

"Yes, of course."

"Why don't you get Frank and Marsha to take you out to eat, and I'll call my father?"

"All right. I'll be back in about an hour." Derrick kissed her and left.

Lindsay called home, and her father answered the phone. He must have been sitting beside it, she thought.

"Lindsay," he said and hesitated. "How are you? Tell me the truth." Lindsay tried to tell him she was fine, but he interrupted. "Derrick said you'd been shot."

"In the leg. It didn't hit anything. I'm fine. Just a little sore."

"He said you have a concussion."

"Just a slight one."

"Anything else? Tell me exactly what happened, Lindsay. Don't soften it. Your mother and I want to know what happened to you."

"It all happened so fast. I got hold of a shovel, hit him with it, and ran. He shot me in the leg and was about to shoot me again when Derrick caught up with us and stopped him."

"I'm relieved to hear you're all right, Lindsay.

Here, your mother wants to talk to you."

Lindsay talked to her mother. Her practical no-non-sense conversation was comforting. Her mother didn't dwell on what might have happened. She made everything seem normal again.

Lindsay hung up the phone just as Michelle walked into the room with some flowers. She set them on the night stand and sat down in the chair beside Lindsay's bed.

"Thank you." Lindsay eyed her suspiciously.

"Don't worry. They aren't poisonous." Michelle smiled. "Well, Lindsay, you do have a knack for getting everyone's sympathy, including mine. Of all the things I might have wished on you, this sure wasn't one of them."

"Thanks ... I think."

"I understand you were supposed to go with Derrick to Atlanta for the weekend?"

"Just taking your advice."

Michelle gave Lindsay a crooked smile. "Marsha will be happy, I'm sure. I just wanted to tell you, I don't intend to give up. You'll have to work hard to keep Derrick if I have anything to say about it."

"Thanks for the warning."

"Everyone at the site is really upset over this. I think several more of the scouts have left. Boy, we sure gave them a distorted view of archaeology, didn't we?"

Lindsay laughed, and her leg hurt. "I can't imagine what they must be thinking."

"Well, I'll go and let you get some rest. I really am sorry this happened to you."

"Thanks, Michelle."

Derrick returned as Michelle was leaving. "I'm glad you had company," he said, smiling at Lindsay. "Michelle's a doll, isn't she."

"Yep," said Lindsay. "A doll."

Derrick stayed the night and most of the next day in Lindsay's hospital room. The doctors wanted to keep her another night, so she talked Derrick into going back to the site where he could get some rest.

After the lights were out and the nurses had made their rounds, the hospital room was quiet. A light left on in the bathroom supplied the room with faint illumination. Lindsay drifted in and out of sleep and strange dreams. In one dream a shadow, slow and menacing, drifted toward her. A face slowly formed on the shadow, a hideous angry face, its dark arms raised above its ugly head. It was then that Lindsay realized it wasn't a dream. She raised up in bed, threw herself over the side, and screamed. The dark form came around the bed, raising the knife again. Lindsay rolled under the bed and screamed as loud as she could. Something clattered on the floor, and she thought she heard running. A few seconds later the night nurse came hurrying into her room.

The nurse turned on the light and helped Lindsay out from under the bed. "What happened?" she asked.

"Didn't you see him?"

"Who?"

"Someone attacked me."

"You must have been dreaming," the nurse said as she helped Lindsay back into bed.

"I didn't dream that." She pointed to a large knife lying on the floor.

"Oh, dear," the nurse gasped, looking confused.

"Mrs. McGilles was having a rough night, and I was helping her … I didn't see anyone." She started to pick it up.

"Don't touch it. It may have fingerprints."

"Of course. I'll … I'll get the sheriff."

Lindsay stared at the knife while waiting for the sheriff. She brought up the face in her memory and tried to recognize it, but it had been too dark and she had been too drowsy.

"Are you all right?" the sheriff asked when he arrived. Lindsay looked up from the knife to the sheriff coming through her door, followed by the nurse.

"No."

He took out his handkerchief and picked up the knife with it. "Did you get a look at the attacker?" he asked as he took out his phone and called one of his deputies. "Andy, you and Ricky get over to the hospital. Now."

"I just saw an ugly face," Lindsay answered.

"I'm sorry, Lindsay," the sheriff said. "I have a man watching Patrick's door. I didn't think you needed anyone here. I was wrong."

"That's all right, Sheriff," Lindsay said, hugging her arms tightly to herself and shivering.

"I'll post Andy at your door for the rest of the night. Do you want me to call someone from the dig to sit with you?" he asked.

Lindsay shook her head. "Would you take me to the site?"

"Now?"

"Yes."

"You can't leave the hospital," the nurse said.

"Yes, I can. I'm scheduled to be released in the

morning anyway." Lindsay got out of bed and hobbled over to the closet. She began collecting her things. She didn't bother changing clothes. "If you can't take me, I'll call Derrick or Frank."

"I'll take you if you're determined."

The nurse protested again. "You can't do this. This is most irregular."

"It is most irregular to have someone come into my room and try to kill me."

"We are sorry, but …"

"Look, I don't blame you. I mean, who knew? And you have taken good care of me here. But let's face it. You aren't given combat training. I'll come by tomorrow to see the doctor and check out."

"But—" the nurse protested.

"I'm going," Lindsay insisted. The nurse looked at her for a moment, then sighed, shrugged, and gave her some extra strength painkiller.

After the deputies arrived and began making a thorough search of the hospital, the sheriff took her back to the site.

"Did you find the bullet he shot me with?"

"Yes. It was from the same gun that shot Plackert, if that is what you're asking."

"And Burial 23?"

"No, the gun is not old enough," said the sheriff.

Lindsay was disappointed.

"I think Patrick shot Plackert. He said some things." Lindsay rubbed her eyes. "Something about things she made him do. How it changed him. Made him able to do things like kill me. I know that is not a lot, but …"

"I'll investigate it. We think we know where Plackert was killed."

"You do?" Lindsay was surprised.

"Yeah, we took the notion that you really did hear the shot that night and estimated a time frame from what you were able to tell us. We know the flow of the river, so we looked for several places along a stretch of bank that might be a good place to dump a body. It turns out there's an old boathouse up the river. Mostly a shack now, but anyone could dump a body without being seen, just drop it through the floor. There was some blood in it. We're having it analyzed."

"I'm impressed," Lindsay said sincerely.

"I guess you've been wondering what we did before you got here." The sheriff chuckled. "Here we are," he said, driving into the parking lot. "You need any help?"

"No, thanks," she said, getting out. "I'll be fine."

"I'm not sure this is the right thing to do," he said.

"I am."

Lindsay limped over to the living area with the help of a cane the hospital staff had found for her, then hobbled to her tent. She stopped in the doorway. Someone was in her bed. Her first instinct was to run, but as her eyes grew accustomed to the darkness, she saw the form more clearly.

"Derrick," she whispered. He moved in his sleep. "Derrick," she said, a little louder.

"What? Lindsay?" He rose to a sitting position and switched on the battery-powered lamp. "Lindsay, what are you doing here?" He got up and put his hands on her shoulders, guiding her to a chair where she sat down. "You are going back to the hospital right now. What did you do, sneak out? How did you get out here?"

"The sheriff brought me."

"Has he lost his mind?" Derrick looked around for his clothes.

"I'm not going back. What are you doing in my bed?"

"You are going back, and I just wanted to sleep here."

"No, I'm not. I'm not staying in that hospital with Patrick and whatever crazy maniac tried to stab me. No telling who will come after me next."

Derrick stopped, one leg in his pants. "What are you talking about?"

"Someone paid me a visit in my hospital room with a really long knife."

"What?" Derrick stared at her. "Are you hurt? I knew I should have stayed."

"I'm all right. I'm just not going to stay in the hospital."

Derrick looked confused for a moment. "Okay. You were going to be released tomorrow anyway."

"Would you get me something to drink?"

"Sure. Stay here." Derrick slipped on his jeans and went out. He came back with a ginger ale. Lindsay took a couple of painkillers.

"Are you in pain?"

"A little. But I'm all right."

Derrick stripped Lindsay's bed, took the mattress from his tent and put it on top of hers, and made up the bed. He picked Lindsay up and laid her in the bed, then slipped in beside her, putting his arms around her.

"What are you doing?"

"I won't bother you. I just want to make sure you're safe."

"I feel very safe," she said. She closed her eyes and quickly fell asleep. In the morning Derrick took Lindsay back to the hospital where the doctor examined her and pronounced her fit. He admonished her for leaving the hospital but apologized for the incident, as he called it. While Derrick and Lindsay were there, they learned that Patrick had died during the night, shortly before the attack on Lindsay.

Outside on the hospital steps, Lindsay stopped and looked up at Derrick. "Are you all right?"

"Yes. I wouldn't be if something had happened to you."

"I don't think I have ever had a digging season quite like this one," she declared.

"No. And I don't think I want another one like it," he exclaimed.

"Who do you think attacked me last night?"

"One of the Tyler family, I imagine. Let's not think of that right now. It won't happen again. I don't intend to let you out of my sight."

*As Cuvier could correctly describe a whole animal
by the contemplation of a single bone, so the observer
who has thoroughly understood one link in a series
of incidents should be able to accurately state
all the other ones, both before and after.*
— Sir Arthur Conan Doyle
Sherlock Holmes in *Five Orange Pips*

Chapter 13

LINDSAY WORKED IN the lab while her leg healed.
Marsha occasionally worked beside her, sorting and
labeling artifacts with other members of the crew.

"I haven't thanked you for sending Derrick and
the others to rescue me," Lindsay told Marsha.

"I'm awfully glad I did. I really didn't know Patrick had kidnapped you. I just had a bad feeling about
him driving off into the woods like that."

"I'm glad you saw it and followed through on
your feelings."

"Me, too." Marsha returned to her work, which
was painting a small stripe of white-out on artifacts
and writing an identifying number on them.

"You're in danger of becoming a serious archaeologist," Lindsay told her.

"That is what Frank said, too." Marsha smiled
slightly. "He said I should go to college, but I don't
think I would do very well. I was never good in school."

"It gets easier when you're older."

"Is that true? I've always heard the opposite."

"I think it is." It suddenly occurred to Lindsay that Marsha was afraid Frank was trying to make her over into a scholar and that she could not measure up. Michelle's words rang in her ears.

Derrick came in just as Lindsay was about to say something to Marsha. "There is someone here who would like to talk to you," he said.

"Who?" Lindsay asked.

"None other than the queen herself, Isabel Tyler," Derrick said.

Lindsay looked shocked.

"My God!" exclaimed Marsha. "She came here?"

"Limousine and all," Derrick replied. "Lindsay, do you want me to tell her you're resting?"

"Is anyone with her?"

"The sheriff and Frank."

"I'll see her."

Lindsay grabbed her cane, and she, Derrick and Marsha went outside to face the grand lady of Tylerwynd.

Isabel Tyler sat straight-backed on a bench at a picnic table. Her diamond-studded hands rested on the silver knob of her cane. She eyed Lindsay for a moment, looking at her as if she were a lizard that had been turned into a human.

"The sheriff tells me you found a skeleton out here and have identified it as my sister, Augustine."

"It is not a positive identification, but I believe the bones we found are hers. Would you like to see the reconstruction I made of her face?"

"No. I know what she looked like."

"Then you believe that the bones are hers?"

"I fear they might be."

"Do you know what happened to her?" Lindsay asked.

"I have been afraid that my departed husband Edward, God rest his soul, killed her. She was a troublemaker, and she was interfering with our—what do you call it these days—relationship? We were in love, you see, and Augustine was insanely jealous. I have not wanted to believe Edward capable of anything so heinous, but he feared she had gotten herself pregnant and was going to blame it on him and force him to marry her." She hesitated, glancing at the sheriff for a moment, and shifted her austere gaze back to Lindsay. "The sheriff tells me that Augustine was shot."

"Did he?"

"He did. Then I suppose it might have been Edward. He was trying to save us from her wickedness, of course."

"Your husband was a tall man, wasn't he? Over six feet?" Lindsay asked.

"Six foot one. Very tall in those days."

"Then I can put your mind at ease. Augustine was killed by someone her own height."

Isabel was silent. Her blue eyes bore into Lindsay like icy shafts. When she spoke, her voice was as cold as her eyes. "How can you possibly know that?"

"Quite easily. Had her killer been taller, the bullet would have traveled in a downward path. The path it traveled in Augustine's skull was slightly upward."

"I suppose Edward could have been on his knees pleading for her to leave us alone."

"The angle is not that great. No, Mrs. Tyler, they

both were standing. Augustine saw what was coming," Lindsay said, staring back at Mrs. Tyler with equal nerve. "She raised her hand." Lindsay put her left hand in front of her face. "And her killer shot her through the eye. She would have died instantly."

Lindsay saw a crack in the mask that Mrs. Tyler had developed over the years. The sheriff may never be able to prove it, but Lindsay knew Isabel had killed her sister. It was not Lindsay's frankness that made Isabel shudder, but the accurate reenactment of a deeply held secret.

"I see," Isabel said at last. She rose and spoke to the sheriff. "I will go home now." She turned to Lindsay. "Thank you for putting my mind at rest." But she did not look grateful.

Lindsay watched the limousine drive off, followed by the sheriff's car.

"Kind of tough on her, weren't you, Lindsay?" Frank commented.

Lindsay shook her head. "I don't think I have ever seen an individual so devoid of conscience."

"She has always been a strange woman," Marsha said.

"It looked to me," Derrick observed, "that she was trying to pin a murder she committed on her dead husband. I think the sheriff got that impression, too."

After several days of working in the lab, Lindsay told Frank she wanted to be outside.

"All right, but rest when you need to," he said.

"This will be a rest."

While Lindsay was taking up burial goods from a grave, an idea came to her. She stared at the artifacts. The items were important to the person they were buried with. In one way or another they defined their lives. She unconsciously rubbed her sore leg and looked at her watch. It wasn't yet 8:00, but the sheriff would probably be in his office. She walked to Frank's car, limping only slightly, got in, and dialed the sheriff's number.

"Sheriff Duggan," said the voice on the other end of the phone.

"Sheriff, this is Lindsay."

"Lindsay. I hope you haven't found any more bodies."

"No. It was just an idea. It just occurred to me where the photographs of the children might be."

"Really? Where?"

"This is based on the presumption that Jacob Tyler is the murderer, you understand. It seems to me that a magician might think the best place to hide something of value would be in his magician's paraphernalia. You know, in a secret drawer or something like that. You could get someone familiar with magic equipment to help you search his."

There was a long pause before the sheriff spoke. "I talked to Mickey about Jacob. I showed him a picture of Ned and one of Jacob in his magician's costume so he could see how similar they were and how a scared little girl might mistake Ned for Jacob."

"Really," exclaimed Lindsay. "What did he say?"

"Mickey is pretty tired of being the prime suspect in Peggy's murder and is opening up a bit. I think the idea that Jacob might have murdered little Peggy got to him. Mickey said that when Jacob was 17, he was accused of molesting the daughter of one of the maids at the estate. The maid was paid off and dismissed, and nothing came of it. I have yet to find any incidents in Mickey's past, and I've been looking."

"Does that mean you think it might be Jacob and not Ned or Mickey?" Lindsay asked.

"It means I give your theory a lot of credibility. Magician's equipment." He seemed to muse over the idea. "I have seen Jacob perform. He has lots of fancy cabinets. I'll talk to you later." He hung up the phone, and Lindsay walked back to the site.

Derrick was at a picnic table drinking a large glass of water. Lindsay went over to him.

"You've been detecting again," he said when he saw her face.

"Just an idea. I called the sheriff about it."

"Tell me," he said.

Lindsay sat down next to him. "How are Michelle's dancing lessons going?"

"Pretty good. She's very enthusiastic. I think she'll make a good dancer. But not as good as you," he added. "I'd like to plan another trip for us as soon as you are all healed and free of pain."

Lindsay smiled broadly and took a big drink of Derrick's water. "I'm feeling better all the time."

"What is the idea you had for the sheriff?"

"It's not that much." She told Derrick what she had said to the sheriff.

Derrick nodded his head. "That's a good idea. You sure are smart, Lindsay."

"If I were so smart, I wouldn't have gotten in so much trouble this season."

"You have a point there."

"I guess I should get back to my burials," she said.

Derrick and she walked back over to the site together. Derrick went to the structure he was helping Michelle with, and Lindsay went to her burial.

"Quitting time."

Lindsay looked up, shading her eyes from the sun. Derrick stood over her and the cache of bones Sally had uncovered. "Take me to a movie," she said. "I would like to sit in a cool theater."

"Sure." He picked up the black plastic sheet that was used at night to cover the pit Lindsay had been working on. Lindsay helped him anchor it down with large rocks.

Both looked up to see an all-too-familiar sight— the sheriff—striding toward them. This time he seemed to have a look of excitement on his face.

Lindsay glanced beyond the sheriff to the parking lot. Three men and a woman were standing near the sheriff's car. Lindsay recognized two of the men as deputies. The other man and the woman were strangers.

"I have a warrant," said the sheriff, "to search Tylerwynd. It was not easy to get. I thought you might like to come to the mansion as a consultant."

"A consultant?" Lindsay smiled. "Are you expecting to find bones?"

"No, but you never know."

Derrick put an arm around Lindsay's shoulders. "She doesn't step into any spider's web without me."

The sheriff grinned. "I figured as much. We'll just call you a consultant on this case, too."

"We need to clean up a little," Lindsay said.

"Make it real quick."

After Lindsay and Derrick took quick showers, they changed into fresh jeans and shirts and joined the sheriff in the parking lot.

"This is Paul Durant and his daughter Estelle. Mr. Durant owns The Magic Emporium in Atlanta. I called him after I talked to you this morning, and he agreed to come down," the sheriff said.

Paul Durant looked to be in his late fifties. He was tall and lean, with silver hair. He looked cool in his cream-colored suit, and his mannerisms as he took Lindsay's outstretched hand seemed vaguely French, though he had a completely American accent.

"I'm glad to meet you, Lindsay and Derrick." His blue eyes twinkled.

At first Estelle Durant looked to be in her late twenties, but a closer look revealed that she was probably in her late thirties. She had dark hair, a dimpled smile, and the same blue eyes as her father. "We've never done anything like this," she said. "It sounds exciting."

The Durants obviously knew little of the recent history of the Tyler family. Lindsay and Derrick smiled back at them as best they could.

"The Durants can ride with us," the sheriff said. "I thought Derrick and you could follow in your Jeep."

"Sure," Lindsay said.

"Does this strike you as kind of strange?" Derrick asked when they were alone.

"What do you mean?" asked Lindsay.

"I mean, the sheriff taking us over to the Tylers," he said. "Not that I have any love for the Tylers, but it strikes me as a little cruel. After all, I did kill Patrick."

"I see what you mean. Remember the story the

sheriff told us about when he and his friends were caught by Isabel Tyler in her strawberry patch? He made it sound funny at the time, but I wonder if there was more to it. I've seen how the woman can terrorize little kids—like the one in her house looking for a bathroom on the Fourth of July."

"You think maybe the sheriff is getting even after all these years?" Derrick asked.

"Perhaps not consciously. But maybe he is exorcising an old ghost," she replied.

"Maybe so. Or maybe he is helping us exorcise ghosts."

"You may be right. Are you okay about Patrick?" Lindsay asked.

Derrick didn't answer right away. He looked as if he hadn't heard the question and simply stared at the road ahead.

"It's not easy," he finally said. "I'm angry he made me have to do it and live with it. But when I picture the scene in my mind, I see you on the ground, shot, bleeding, and trying to get away from him, and him aiming that gun to shoot you again. Then I think of what he wanted to do to you." Derrick looked over at Lindsay sitting beside him. "I'll cope with it. It won't ruin my life."

"We've never talked about it. I didn't know if I should ask."

"Lindsay, you can always ask me anything."

"Well, I didn't know if you wanted to talk about it."

"When I think about it, I think of saving you, not killing Patrick."

"Me, too."

• • •

When they reached the huge wrought iron gates of Tylerwynd, a deputy was holding them open for Derrick's Jeep. He followed the sheriff's car through and stopped to wait for the deputy to close the gate and walk to the sheriff's car. They drove around the curved drive and stopped in front of the house. They all met on the sidewalk leading to the house.

Estelle Durant sidled up to Lindsay. "They told us on the way over what happened to you. I'm glad to see you're much better."

Lindsay looked into her sincere blue eyes and smiled. "Yes, I'm much better. Thank you."

The sheriff walked up to the door, carrying what looked like a thick briefcase, and knocked. The group followed but hung back when they reached the porch. It was several minutes before the doorbell was answered by a young woman dressed in a black-and-white maid's uniform. The sheriff showed her the warrant and explained that they were coming inside. The woman stared at the paper with a wrinkled brow, then looked behind her, as if searching for someone to tell her which authority to obey.

"I'll have to ask," she said timidly.

"I don't need permission," the sheriff said, not unkindly. "I have a search warrant."

The maid's eyes grew wide, as if she just understood the implications of a search warrant. She opened the door and stood aside.

"Please," she said. "Let me get Mrs. Tyler."

The sheriff nodded and entered the house. Lindsay, Derrick, and the others followed and stood in the foyer.

"This place is a museum," Estelle whispered. "Look at the old furniture."

"What's this about?" The voice came so suddenly and was so full of hostility that they all jumped slightly.

"I have a warrant to search the premises. In particular, the possessions of Jacob Edgar Tyler." The sheriff handed her the search warrant.

Mrs. Tyler made no move to take it from his hand. "I don't care what it says. You are not searching my home."

"I'm afraid you are wrong, ma'am," the sheriff said. "As I explained to the maid, I have all the permission I require. Now, will you show me to Jacob's room? We will begin there."

"What is this about?" came a voice from the stairs. They all looked up to see Jacob standing halfway down the stairs, his hands clutching the polished banister. He looked like an overgrown child coming down to see what the adults were doing. "Winifred just told me the strangest story."

"I'm glad you're here," said the sheriff. "You can show us to your room. I am particularly interested in seeing your magician's equipment."

Jacob looked nonplussed. "Well, I ... why? Mother?"

"Sheriff Duggan. Haven't we been through enough, and why did you bring them here?" She pointed a gnarled hand in the direction of Lindsay and Derrick.

"They are here for their expertise," the sheriff answered. "Now, the sooner we get on with this, the quicker we will leave. Jacob, will you show us to your room?"

Jacob looked at his mother, who nodded her head. He turned and climbed the stairs to the second floor. The sheriff, the deputies, the Durants, Derrick, and Lindsay followed, leaving Isabel Tyler standing at the foot of the stairs staring malevolently at their backs.

Jacob led them down a long, dark hallway that held sepia photographs of dour Tyler ancestors. Their footfalls were muted by the long Persian carpet that had grown bare in spots. The rooms off the hallway were closed. A few doors had open transoms, and Lindsay thought she could hear soft music from one. Suddenly, a door behind them burst open. They all turned to see a madwoman in black advancing toward them.

"Rachel?" Lindsay whispered. No, Rachel rushed out behind the woman and put an arm around her shoulders. Ruth Tyler, thought Lindsay, mother of Patrick.

"You killed my son," she said, glaring at Derrick through red-rimmed eyes.

"I'm sorry," Derrick softly said. "I truly am. I wish things could have ended differently."

She seemed not to hear him, but turned her sorrowful mad gaze to Lindsay. "Couldn't you have just gone to dinner with him? He just wanted ... he just ..." She buried her face in her hands and sobbed.

"It's all right," Rachel soothed, though Lindsay and the others knew nothing would ever be all right for her. "Come back to your room. I'll get Winifred to bring you some hot milk."

Lindsay felt sad for her, sad for them all in this dark mausoleum of a house with its darker secrets. Derrick put his arm around her waist, and they turned around to follow Jacob, who stood watching the whole scene with a pitiless expression on his fleshy, round face. Lindsay felt someone take her hand. She turned her head to see Estelle standing beside her with a friendly smile spread across her face.

"I think we need to stick together in this creepy place," she whispered.

Lindsay smiled back, blinking back the tears that were threatening to spill out onto her cheeks. "I agree."

The first thing that anyone noticed when they entered Jacob Tyler's bedroom were the posters and photographs covering his walls. There were several posters of Harry Houdini advertising a variety of his famous escape tricks. A poster of Howard Thurston and the floating lady hung over the head of the bed. There was a large black-and-white photograph of P.T. Selbit sawing a woman in half, and several posters of Blackstone, Dante, and an autographed photograph of David Copperfield. Lindsay did not see any photographs of Jacob himself. The rest of the bedroom consisted of a four-poster dark mahogany bed covered with a white chenille bedspread, a matching mahogany chest of drawers and nightstand, a bookshelf containing only books and catalogs about magic and magicians' paraphernalia, a stuffed chair, and a threadbare Oriental carpet—all rather bland compared to his wall decorations, but easy to search.

Jacob stood by at stiff attention as the sheriff and the deputies put on rubber gloves, searched the drawers, the nightstand, the books, the backs of the posters, and between the mattress and springs. Jacob's closet held few clothes, all hung precisely four inches apart. His shoes were lined up just as neatly. The single top shelf held two hats, a brown fedora, and a wide-brimmed straw hat. The search turned up nothing, but no one had expected to find anything in his bedroom.

"Now," said the sheriff, "where is your magician's equipment?"

"What do you want it for?" Jacob asked. Lindsay noticed that he did not seem unduly nervous.

"Where is the equipment?"

"In the basement."

They followed Jacob down the main stairway and through a door under the staircase, where he turned on a light switch and took them down another flight of stairs. The room at the bottom was for storage. Stacked so that there was only a narrow passageway through the room, a hundred years of memorabilia filled the large basement room. As she passed, Lindsay noticed old baby furniture, toys, broken tables and chairs, and boxes filled with gilt-framed photographs, probably of all the relatives and marriage partners that had fled Tylerwynd. The room smelled like old dried roses.

Jacob led them through a door at the far end of the room to where he kept his equipment. Here the walls were decorated with pictures of him and his performances. Several cabinets having a vague Oriental look with their red-and-black lacquered finish and numerous drawers stood against one wall. A long, polished wooden box for sawing people in half sat in the middle of the hardwood floor looking like a coffin. Beside it stood a curtained wardrobe. Large metal hoops stood against one wall, and several objects Lindsay didn't recognize hung on hooks. Five trunks covered with travel stickers sat side-by-side against another wall. It was a tidy room, but with so many trunks and cabinets it looked like the search would take a long time.

Lindsay and Derrick stood with the sheriff, and the deputies stood near Jacob. Lindsay watched Jacob as Sheriff Duggan handed the Durants each a pair of rubber gloves. Jacob looked puzzled but did not seem to recognize the Durants. Lindsay wondered why. Surely someone as interested in magic as Jacob would have frequented a magic shop as close as Atlanta, but perhaps they were a mail order place.

They started with the wardrobe and a box in the center of the room. They found nothing, but watching them quickly find hidden places and doors was interesting. Next they went to the cabinets, and Lindsay noticed that Jacob was becoming fidgety.

Paul and Estelle Durant opened the drawers and searched with expert hands for hidden drawers or panels. They found many, but all were empty in the first cabinet. They went to the next, continuing the same methodical search. Estelle slipped out a false bottom to a drawer and whispered something to her father. She reached in and came out with a stack of magazines. Estelle carried them to the sheriff while her father continued the search. Lindsay looked at the top magazine. It contained child pornography. A chill ran up Lindsay's spine, and she felt sick. Derrick grasped her hand and squeezed it.

The sheriff took the magazines, kneeled down, and opened his case. He took out a large plastic bag, sealed the magazines inside, took a magic marker, wrote some information on the outside, and placed the package in the case with the same efficiency that Lindsay bagged and labeled artifacts. The sheriff stood, grim-faced, and watched the search.

Jacob was showing stress. His eyes were wide and his breathing quick and shallow, but he stood calmly enough.

Paul and Estelle came to the third cabinet, which looked to Lindsay much the same as the others, but they approached it differently. They slid it out from the wall. Estelle searched the front as usual, but Paul studied the back. He placed his hands on the back in several places, then the sides. His hands looked like a baseball manager signaling to a pitcher as they moved over the cabinet—almost magical. A drawer suddenly sprung out. Lindsay saw Paul's mouth twitch slightly, as close as he would allow a smile under the circumstances.

He reached in the drawer and took out a shiny black box shaped like a cigar box.

"Oh, no. Oh, no," came breathy exclamations from Jacob. "Mother! Mother," he called, as if she could hear him and would come running.

The deputies walked over to him and grabbed both arms, and he sagged slightly. Paul carried the box to the sheriff, who ignored Jacob as he opened the box and reached a gloved hand inside. Lindsay could see there were pictures, but she turned her head away and did not look.

"Read him his rights," the sheriff said. He was as red-faced and angry as Lindsay had ever seen him as he bagged and labeled the box of photographs.

"I can explain. I can explain," Jacob began babbling over and over as Deputy Andy Littleton droned out the Miranda rights.

The sheriff told Estelle and Paul to search everything, then turned and walked toward Jacob. "Take him upstairs," he told the deputies.

"I can explain. I can explain," Jacob continued as they led him up the stairs.

Lindsay didn't quite know what to do—follow the sheriff or stay with the Durants. Suddenly, she wanted to be outside.

"I need some fresh air," she whispered to Derrick.

"Me, too," he said.

"We're going outside," she told the Durants, and they nodded, continuing their search.

When they reached the first floor, Jacob started calling for his mother again.

"What is this?" Isabel Tyler demanded as she came out of the parlor. "What are you babbling about, Jacob? What are you doing to my son?"

"We're arresting him for the molestation and murder of Marylou Ridley, Amy Hastings, and Peggy Pruitt."

"I thought you had Mickey and that other boy for that," she said. "Can't you make up your mind?"

"We have found evidence," the sheriff said.

"What is he talking about, Jacob?"

"I can explain, Mama. I can explain." His voice was rising to a higher pitch. It sounded as if he were a child trying to avoid a switching.

"He took pictures of the victims," the sheriff replied.

Isabel Tyler was visibly shaken, but it lasted only for a moment. She glared at Jacob, then turned and walked out of the room.

"Don't leave me, Mama. Don't leave me here."

He is in some other place and time, thought Lindsay. Where, she wondered. His room. The basement. A closet? She turned and walked with Derrick out of the house.

They watched the deputies drive Jacob away, sobbing in the back seat. She heard the sheriff tell them to put him under a suicide watch.

"I kind of feel sorry for him," Lindsay said to Derrick.

"I know. He never had a chance in that family."

Lindsay started to respond as her eyes left the sheriff's car and glanced at the house, but she gasped instead.

"What's wrong?" Derrick asked.

"In the window on the second floor. I thought it was Patrick for a second. It must be Jarvis. Remember him at the picnic? Jacob's son."

Derrick looked up at the ghostly figure in the window watching the car with his father winding down the drive.

"He didn't even come downstairs," Derrick whispered. "Let me take you home."

"We may need to take the sheriff and the Durants back, unless the deputies return with the car."

The sheriff came toward them, carrying his case of evidence. "You can go, if you want," he said. "Andy will send a car for us."

"I think we will," Derrick said.

"I know this was hard, Lindsay," the sheriff apologized, "but I thought you might want to see some kind of ending."

"Yes, thank you. I did."

"Smart thinking about his magician's stuff," the sheriff said. "Smart thinking about a lot of things. How do you do it?"

Lindsay shrugged. "I suppose I just understand people and their artifacts. They always fit together."

The sheriff shook his head in amazement and glanced back at Tylerwynd. "Hard old lady, isn't she?" he remarked.

"Certainly cuts her losses," Derrick commented. "Think you can get her for murdering her sister?"

The sheriff shook his head. "There's not a shred of evidence and none to be found after 60 years. We've got Jacob for the child murders, and I believe Patrick killed Plackert. It was Plackert's blood in the boathouse, and Patrick's fingerprints were on the door. But that is all we're going to get. Sometimes you just don't get to know everything."

"Why do you think Patrick killed Plackert?" Derrick asked.

"I think Isabel Tyler didn't want the site dug because she was afraid Augustine's body would be found. She started by hiring locals to try and scare you away. What she didn't know was that you all were so used to pothunters, you didn't think anything about it. Then she directed Seymour Plackert, the family lawyer, to try and get rid of you. I don't imagine Isabel understood anything about recovery laws. She probably thought the power company could just order you off with a little pressure from Plackert. Plackert knew the laws, but he probably got the idea of planting the marijuana to delay you, thinking that would satisfy the old lady. My guess is that when I told him about the body, he went to Isabel and tried to blackmail her, and she got Patrick to kill him and dump him in the river. But as I said, there isn't a shred of evidence."

Peace to her bitter bones ...
—Stanley Kunitz
The Dark and the Fair

Chapter 14

THE BANNER STRETCHED across the picnic area at the site read: Welcome Back Ned. Mylar balloons were tied to the ends of the tables. There was a cake, a keg of beer, and assorted sodas in a large ice-filled barrel. Ned stood looking at the sign. Lindsay thought he was touched by the sentiment, but with Ned it was hard to tell.

"It was nice of you to give this party for Ned," Lindsay told Frank. She had to lean close to his ear for him to hear above the din of the partying crew.

"Well, it can't have been fun in jail. If we want to get this site dug, we need to bury the hatchet, as it were."

Derrick brought Lindsay a drink, sat down beside her, and squeezed her hand under the table. Michelle sat down across from them.

"Well, Lindsay," she said. "There you are between Frank and Derrick." Only this time she smiled. Lindsay smiled back, and Frank and Derrick sipped innocently on their drinks. Marsha drove up, and Frank got up to meet her.

Someone—Ronald probably—had brought a radio and turned it on. Soon the tables were moved apart, and the crew started dancing.

"Come on, Derrick. Let me show off some of my new dancing skills," Michelle said. "You don't mind, do you, Lindsay?"

"No, please, go ahead." Lindsay said, sounding more calm than she felt. She watched them dance together, hoping her complexion wasn't turning green with her envy. She unconsciously rubbed her sore leg.

"Lindsay." Ned sat down beside her. He spoke shyly. "I want to thank you for your faith in my innocence. It meant a lot to me in jail. Derrick and Frank told me what you did to clear me. You're very clever."

"None of us really thought you were guilty."

Ned was not accustomed to thanking people. He was hesitant, as if Lindsay might get up and leave in the middle of his speech, but he continued, a new behavior. Lindsay hoped it would stick, for it would make Ned's life easier in the future.

"I was sorry to hear about what Patrick did to you. I hope you're all right," he said.

"Yes," Lindsay agreed. "I'm fine," which was almost true. She had bad dreams occasionally, and her leg still ached. But she would be fine. She would make herself fine.

The site was quiet. The corners of the anchored black plastic covering the excavation waved faintly in the breeze. Lindsay scanned the sky for the rain clouds that were supposed to have materialized by mid-morning, but only a few small cottony puffs were scattered about the clear blue sky.

They were finished digging the site. All that was left was the clean-up. Lindsay did not go into town very often these days. She did not want to be asked questions about what happened to Augustine Beaufort. Now that the children of Merry Claymoore were safe, this older mystery connected to the tragic Tyler family was far more interesting to the community. Isabel Tyler kept to her mansion, seemingly unfazed by the accusations and rumors against her.

The crew were gathering for lunch. Derrick was already there reading the accounts in the paper. "Tough old lady," he said when Lindsay sat beside him.

"She'll never suffer the consequences for killing her sister, will she?" Jane said.

"I don't know about that," Frank commented. "It seems to me she is probably suffering a lot these days."

Lindsay shook her head. "She's not suffering. She's too skilled at blaming others and cutting her losses."

"After all this time, there is just no proof," Marsha said.

"No," said Frank. "Even though everyone is pretty sure she did it, she'll never be tried. I'm not sure she would be even if there were enough evidence. She is pretty old, and it all happened a long time ago."

"Yeah, but I didn't think there was a statute of limitations on murder," Sally replied. "She may be old, but she is still causing a lot of mischief: siccing that odious Seymour on us, abusing her kids, and sending them to kill people, covering up their wickedness, and then leaving them twisting in the wind when they get caught. I say we all storm the mansion and string her up. I'll get the torches."

"I say we finish the site and go home," Frank replied. "This is the last day. Tonight I'm treating everyone to dinner and dancing."

"I'll go along with that," Derrick said.

"Me, too," Lindsay agreed, standing up and taking her leftovers to the trash. "I'm going to start packing the lab. I'd like to get away before any more bodies are found."

"I hear that," Brian said.

Lindsay and the lab crew were packing up and labeling boxes of artifacts. She still had the bones of Augustine and her reconstruction, which she was packing separately. She must remember to ask the sheriff where they were supposed to be sent.

"I don't know what to do with this."

Lindsay looked up at a field student who was holding out a bag to Lindsay. "It was in the bags for Burial 22. We thought it might be European in origin. Besides the skeleton of the horse, it would be the only European artifact we have found. But I think it may belong to Burial 23."

Lindsay opened the sealed plastic bag and looked at the contents. "Well, Isabel Tyler, I think I've got you," she said aloud. She grinned at the puzzled face of the girl in front of her and opened the bag. Smiling, she took out a broken porcelain rose leaf that would make Isabel's broken pin whole again, as it was in her picture taken 60 years earlier at the Fourth-of-July picnic, the day Augustine disappeared.

From *Questionable Remains*, the second volume in the Lindsay Chamberlain series.

Chapter 1

DR. CHAMBERLAIN." GERALD Dalton, Denny Ferguson's defense attorney, lay a hand on the mahogany witness box. "Dr. Chamberlain." He made a sweeping gesture with his arm, taking in the entire jury, who sat fanning themselves with their notebooks and gazing at Lindsay through skeptical eyes. "You ask these twelve men and women to believe that you can positively identify my client as being the man who shot Ahyoung Kim, even though the perpetrator wore a ski mask ... and you only got a glimpse in his mouth as he was yelling at you to hand over your purse?"

Dalton removed his glasses and pretended to clean them with his handkerchief, shaking his head as he focused his gaze on his task. "My client could go to the electric chair," he said, replacing his glasses on his nose. "Are you willing to have that on your conscience? Weren't you scared? This fellow, whoever he was, had just shot Mr. Kim, and now he fixed his attention on you. You must've been terrified."

"Your Honor." The prosecutor, Max Gilbert, rose to his feet. "Is Mr. Dalton going to cross-examine Dr. Chamberlain, or is he going to testify himself?"

"Get on with it, Mr. Dalton," the judge ordered.

"Dr. Chamberlain, don't most bone experts like yourself use dental records to identify people, or are you able to Zen your identifications?" Dalton gave Lindsay a broad, sarcastic, toothy grin.

"Your client has very distinctive overlapping teeth," Lindsay replied, "as I have described in detail. I saw them clearly and noticed them in spite of my fear because observation is automatic for me. It's my job."

"It's your job," Dalton repeated. "Haven't you told your students on many occasions that you need much more evidence to make a positive identification than to rule out a person?"

"Yes," she answered. The heating system in the old, small-town courthouse was on high, and Lindsay could feel the prickly sensation of perspiration forming on her forehead. I must look guilty, she thought ruefully. She saw Mrs. Kim and her son Albert out in the spectator seats. Mrs. Kim understood little English, but she could read faces; her own was filled with worry. Albert, who had dropped out of the university to help his mother, looked angry. The defendant, Denny Ferguson, sat staring down at his hands. Occasionally he would look up at Lindsay with a half smile on his face.

Dalton's co-counsel sat tapping a pencil silently on her pad of paper. She watched the jury for a moment, then shifted her attention back to Lindsay.

"Well, then," Dalton continued with exaggerated sarcasm, "forgive me if I don't quite understand. It seems to me that all you can say about my client—after your brief look in the perpetrator's mouth—is that you can't rule him out. This is a far cry from saying that Denny Ferguson is positively the man you saw."

"The man who shot Mr. Kim was your client." Lindsay realized she sounded more stubborn than professional.

"Dr. Chamberlain, you require more supporting evidence when you identify skeletal remains. Why are you requiring so little for a man's life?"

"I have described your client's dentition in great detail. I am sure of my identification."

The jury wasn't convinced. Lindsay could see that. Too much rested on her testimony, and they didn't believe she could identify Ferguson by having seen only his teeth. They would not have noticed his teeth in that detail, and they didn't really believe she would either. Denny Ferguson would go free, even though Lindsay knew he was the one who shot and killed Mr. Kim, the neighborhood grocer—simply because Mr. Kim did not have enough money in the cash drawer to satisfy him.

"You like the Kim family, don't you?" The defense attorney's voice was quiet, almost gentle.

"Yes."

"You want to see the murderer caught. We understand your sadness and sympathy for the Kim family." Again he gestured with a sweep of his arm, including the jury as if they were on his side. He shook his head and raised his voice, drawing out his words. "But just how can you convince me, and these twelve very sensible people, that you can say for sure it was my client who shot Mr. Kim and not someone else with bad teeth?"

"Mr. Dalton," said Lindsay, raising her hands to grip the top of the witness box and leaning forward slightly. "You had orthodontic work as an adult. You had four teeth pulled. Two upper second premolars and two lower premolars. You wore your braces quite a long time, and the constant soreness caused you to develop the bad habit of grinding and clinching your teeth at night."

Gerald Dalton gawked at Lindsay, surprise evident on his face. His mouth dropped open, and he was speechless for a moment. It was that moment of surprised hesitation that swayed the jury. Lindsay could see them shift their gazes to one another the way people do when they simultaneously see and understand a truth. In that moment she saw Albert nod his head and turn to whisper something to his mother; she saw the prosecutor smile and the defendant look around as if someone had told a joke he did not understand.

"Okay, how'd you do it?" Gilbert asked Lindsay, handing her a cup of coffee from the cappuccino machine in the corner of his office. He grinned broadly. "Your timing was perfect."

"My timing was from desperation."

Gilbert sat down and propped his feet on his dark oak desk. "But tell me how you did it."

"It wasn't that hard. His theatrics made it possible. The way he tried to intimidate me, leaning over me, drawing out his words with that big voice of his, gave me a good look into his mouth. I saw that he had premolars missing. When he looked down to clean his glasses, I caught a glimpse of a permanent retainer behind his lower incisors. A retainer is used to prevent shifting of teeth."

"And grinding his teeth?"

"His lower incisors were beveled where they ground against his upper incisors."

Gilbert gave a satisfied laugh. "I'll bet there's going to be a great gnashing of teeth in his office when the verdict comes in. With circumstantial evidence and a witness who only saw in the perp's mouth, ol' Dalton thought this was going to be an easy one."

"You think they will find Ferguson guilty, then?" asked Lindsay. She couldn't quite share in Gilbert's confidence.

"I think so. Of course, I've been surprised and even shocked by juries before, but I feel good about this. You're a good witness."

Lindsay took a sip of her coffee. "I can't stay for the verdict. I have to give an exam. Call me when you know something." She set down her cup and rose, offering Gilbert her hand.

He stood up quickly and shook her hand with a firm grip. "Sure. Glad to work with you, Lindsay. We don't usually have this kind of thing going on in our little town. I hate to see this kind of crime come in."

"Me, too," said Lindsay. "I'm going to miss Mr. Kim."

Sally, Lindsay's graduate assistant, was setting up the classroom for the honors course final exam when Lindsay returned to Baldwin Hall, home of the Department of Anthropology and Archaeology. Sally's dark blonde hair was pulled back into a ponytail, one wayward strand falling into her face. She had on

a pair of well-worn jeans and a black T-shirt showing
a white skeleton of a rat on the front along with the
words: *Rattus Rattus*.

"I like your shirt," said Lindsay.

Sally looked down at the picture on her chest.
"Yeah, I do, too. We're selling them to raise money for
the anthropology club." She paused a moment before
she asked. "Is it over?"

"It's with the jury."

"I'm sorry about Mr. Kim, Lindsay."

"So am I." Lindsay tried to fight off the depressing
mood in which the trial had left her. "Did you get
students from the advanced osteology class to help
you with the exam?"

"They'll be here in a few minutes." The graduate
students came in, followed by six honors students
from Lindsay's class. There were the usual moans,
groans, and the predictable question, "Is it hard?"

"I don't think so," said Lindsay, smiling. She gave
each of them a long strip of black fabric.

"What's this?" asked one of the students.

"A blindfold," she answered.

"I knew it," said another. "A firing squad. She's
going to shoot us if we fail."

"We have to get our bones somewhere," offered
Sally.

Lindsay smiled at the group of four male and two
female undergraduate students as they dropped their
backpacks on the floor and sat down. "Okay, everyone
listen up. As you have probably guessed, your test will
be to identify some selected bones by touch alone.
After you've named each bone, the graduate student
assigned to you will write your answer down for you.

You can get extra credit if you can identify the correct side—left or right. Don't try to listen to what the other students are saying because I've put different bones in each of the boxes on the tables. Now, pick a box and begin."

Each student picked a spot next to one of the covered boxes on the laboratory tables and tied their blindfold across their eyes. Lindsay watched as they removed the lids from their boxes, reached in, took a bone, and felt for identifying characteristics. She smiled when their faces lit up as they felt a trochanter or a condyle or when they frowned as they searched with the tips of their fingers for a fossa or muscle attachment. Sometimes they would roll the shaft of a bone in their hands to determine the shape of the cross section. After a while she left the exam in Sally's supervision and went to her office.

Lindsay's office had no windows. The walls beside and behind her desk were lined with bookshelves filled with books and journals. Her walnut desk had belonged to her grandfather, the only other archaeologist in the family. The brown, straight-grained wood surface was marred, and the left front leg still had her father's initials carved into it where he had tried out a new pocketknife on his ninth birthday. Her mother had wanted to have the desk refinished before they gave it to her, but her father had said no. Lindsay was glad because the marks left on artifacts reveal their history in a kind of code that she took pleasure in deciphering. The coffee cup rings told of her grandfather's long nights sipping coffee and working on articles. The cuts and scratches were evidence of the stone tools he laid out on the surface to examine and catalog.

The desk faced the door to the archaeology lab. An oak filing cabinet inherited from the previous occupant stood behind the door. On the other side sat a single stuffed leather chair next to a brass floor lamp. Her grandfather's trowel rested on a bookshelf, and an old photograph hung on the wall behind the chair, showing her grandfather as a young man dressed in a tie and rolled up shirtsleeves, holding a shovel and standing in front of an Indian mound in Macon, Georgia.

There were no artifacts or bones displayed in Lindsay's office. The only artifact she possessed was in an old cigar box inside her desk. It was a treasured possession: the first Indian artifact she had ever found. When Lindsay was five, her grandfather had taken her on the first of their many trips to do surface collecting. She had earnestly examined the freshly plowed ground as she walked beside her grandfather, getting hot, tired, and restless. Then, there it was: the tip of a point partially covered by the moist earth. She had dug it out with her fingers and wiped off the dirt that clung to it. The point was beautiful, and it was huge, longer than her hand and almost as wide, made from black flint.

"It's a Clovis point," her grandfather had told her. "The oldest point there is. It could have killed a woolly mammoth." Lindsay had held on to her find so tightly the edges had cut her hand, but that didn't matter because she had found something wonderful. Since that day she had found many things, but no discovery had ever made her feel as she did that time she found the Clovis with her grandfather. From that day on, Lindsay knew she would be an archaeologist.

Lindsay was reaching for a term paper to grade

when a figure appeared in her doorway. She thought it was a student before she recognized Gerald Dalton's co-counsel. Lindsay hadn't gotten a good look at her in court. Now she saw that she was a small, fine-boned woman, not over five feet, four inches tall. Lindsay guessed she wore a size two. She looked as if she had the hollow bones of a bird, she was so thin and delicate looking. Her short, glossy-black hair was cut in a pageboy, and her skin looked as though it would be translucent if her makeup were washed off. She stood stiffly in the doorway, still in the snug-fitting dark blue suit she wore to the trial.

"Can I help you?" asked Lindsay.

"Have you heard the verdict?" Her voice belied her small frame. It was low and husky.

"No, I had to give an exam ..."

"Yes, I saw your blindfolded students. I suppose that fits ... teaching them that they can make a positive identification without looking." The woman walked into Lindsay's office and stood, putting her palms on the desk and leaning forward.

"Is there a point to your visit?" asked Lindsay.

"I wanted to be the one to tell you that the jury found Dennis Ferguson guilty. I hope that pleases you."

Lindsay frowned. "Nothing about this event pleases me."

"What really gets to me is that you don't have any misgivings about convicting a man on the flimsiest of evidence."

"I was sure."

"How can you possibly not have doubts? Are you that arrogant?" She stopped and looked at Lindsay for a moment, her green eyes clearly showing her anger.

"God, you are, aren't you? You've set yourself up here as some great ... bone ... guru, haven't you? And that performance really topped it."

"Performance?" asked Lindsay.

"The way you pulled the rabbit out of the hat on the stand. It was the drama that convinced the jury, not the facts ... It was the damn show you put on. You are the most arrogant, manipulative woman I have ever met."

Lindsay started to speak when the woman turned on her heel and left.

Sally, who had been standing just outside the doorway, watched after the retreating figure before she came into Lindsay's office. "Well, who peed in her Wheaties?"

"I suppose I did," replied Lindsay. ...

The March winds lingered into April, and it was unseasonably cold as Lindsay showed the students at Barrow Elementary School how much you can learn about people by examining their tombstones. Lindsay and the class of sixteen young students were in the old cemetery beside Baldwin Hall. Campus lore said it was where the university buried deceased students in centuries gone by when it was inconvenient to ship the bodies back home. The story may have been true, but the graveyard was actually the remnants of the old City of Athens Cemetery, encroached on over the years by the expanding university. Most of the residents had been exhumed long ago and moved elsewhere so that only a fraction of an acre of the cemetery remained on the campus. Lindsay had just finished talking about identifying the different kinds of rock the tombstones were carved from and asked if there were any questions.

"Can we dig one up and look at the bones?" asked a nine-year-old dressed in a red and black UGA sweatshirt.

Lindsay was saved from answering by Sally, who had come to tell her she had a phone call from Max Gilbert, the prosecutor of Denny Ferguson. She left the students and their teacher with Sally and hurried to see what he wanted.

"I have some bad news," he told Lindsay when she picked up her office phone. "Denny Ferguson is on the loose."

"There's a call for you." Susan Gitten leaned from the door of Lindsay's cabin, yelling to her. "Do you want me to tell them you've gone?"

Lindsay turned from stroking her horse's neck and glanced at her Land Rover, packed and ready to go. "Yes ... no, I'll take it." She rested her cheek on Mandrake's velvet-soft nose, gave his neck another pat, and walked to the cabin.

"Lindsay Chamberlain," she said.

"Dr. Chamberlain, this is Sheriff Howard, over in Cordwain. We met last year at that cemetery flooding thing."

"I remember. What can I do for you?"

"A farmer up here's found a skeleton in a field he's plowing. I wonder if you'd come take a look. I got a deputy guarding it right now." Lindsay looked at her watch. She had planned to be on the road by now, but then, she had also vowed to have a leisurely trip and a flexible schedule. "We don't have anybody here who can tell us what to do with it," he added as he gave her directions to the farm.

"I'll leave right now. It should take about forty minutes."

"Thanks. I sure do appreciate this. It's probably an Indian burial ground he's stumbled on, then again ..."

BEVERLY CONNOR weaves her professional experiences as an archaeologist and her knowledge of Southern culture into interlinked stories of the past and present in her Lindsay Chamberlain mystery series. Originally from Oak Ridge, Tennessee, Connor now lives in Oglethorpe County, Georgia, with her husband, her dogs, her horse, and her cats. *A Rumor of Bones* is the first volume in the Lindsay Chamberlain archaeological murder mystery series.